Witl...

Rog...

To Anne,

I hope you enjoy

Copyright © Roger A. Price 2024.

The right of Roger A. Price to be identified as the author of this work has been asserted by him in accordance with the Copyright, Designs and Patents Act, 1988.

First published in 2024 by Sharpe Books.

For my sister, Chris.

WITH PREJUDICE

Prologue

Ballygawley, Northern Ireland, Summer 1985.
Constable Ian Dune left the police station and barracks to begin his routine patrol at six o'clock. It was a beautiful evening with clear skies and birdsong all around. He noticed a battered old grey Ford Fiesta drive away as he left the compound. It had two men on board and his sixth sense was shouting trouble. He didn't catch the registration plate number, but put a warning over the radio with what little description his momentary glance had given him. He was wary of raising tensions unnecessarily, but the car drove off with purpose. And that jarred with him.

Constable Dune was twenty years old and hadn't been long out of basic training. He was still a probationary constable and if he'd been in a mainland force, he'd still be working in company with a more senior PC. But over here they didn't always have the luxury to follow the manual of police training. Plus, his sergeant had praised him thus far and said he was capable of solo patrol. A feather in his cap.

Ballygawley is a small but pretty hamlet in County Tyrone not far from the southern border with the Irish Republic. Dune was grateful he had not been posted to Belfast, he felt much safer in rural Tyrone.

Two hours later, as the light was shifting to dusk, on a quiet country road south of Ballygawley, Constable Dune could see a car apparently broken down a couple of hundred yards ahead. It was grey in colour. There was no other traffic on the road, and he was answering a nuisance call regarding some local youths. As he neared the car with its bonnet up, he received a call over his radio cancelling the pest call: the youths had moved off. He considered stopping to see if he could offer the stricken motorist any assistance. Then as he neared further, he realised that the car up ahead with its bonnet up was the same make, model, colour, and condition as the tatty Ford he'd seen earlier when commencing his duty. There appeared to be only one person with it now, and they were partially covered by the upright bonnet. They seemed to be examining the engine bay. Dune could not see anyone in the vehicle.

Constable Dune called it in as he slowed, and Sergeant Jameson responded immediately telling Dune to pull over and observe only until he joined him. He'd be five minutes away, at most. Dune did as he was instructed and noticed that the figure hidden by the bonnet, who was now no more than twenty yards ahead, kept peering around the bonnet. He didn't try and summon the constable for help, he just kept glancing at him. The hairs on the back of Dune's neck stood up as he slowly released the safety strap from his sidearm's holster. He pulled the weapon out and laid it on his lap, keeping hold of it. It was a Smith and Weston revolver containing six .38 rounds. His heart rate was shooting up as he kept his eyes on the car in front. He released his seat belt as he kept his gaze forward. Everything else was out of focus as the car became even clearer as he stared intently at it.

The man stood at the front of the car would soon realise something was up, surely. Sergeant Jameson came over the radio asking for an update, and stated that he was only one minute away. Dune was about to answer when movement in his peripheral vision drew his attention to the hedge at the nearside of the road close to his patrol car.

A balaclava wearing youth burst out from the privet into the road merely feet in front of the police car. He was carrying a handgun, and pointing it at Dune as he traversed the front of the vehicle. Dune realised that he was a sitting duck, so burst out of the driver's side onto the asphalt as incoming rounds smashed through the windscreen hitting the seat he had just vacated. He was glad that he had his revolver in his hand ready as he turned to face his attacker whilst lying with his back on the tarmac. A microsecond saved can spare your life, one of his police firearms trainers had often said. He fired and then jumped to his feet, and continued firing until the chamber was empty. Dune then paused in the eerie silence as time slowed and he inhaled the cordite. He started to take in the scene.

He wasn't sure how many rounds had found its target, but his assailant was lying on his back as blood pooled from under his head. Time restarted and Dune holstered his weapon as he went to check his assailant. He heard two revving car engines; one, was the battered Ford fleeing the scene, and the second was the arrival of Sergeant Jameson.

Jameson told Dune not to approach the gunman for fear of cross-contamination. Dune watched as the sergeant removed the bloodied balaclava to reveal the striking blonde and red hair of his attacker. He was clearly dead as the exit wounds from Dune's bullets had removed most of the rear of the gunman's skull. He could see a black entry hole in the forehead which left the rest of the terrorist's face still recognisable.

'You've done well here, lad. Very well. But do you recognise your attacker?' the sergeant asked.

He did. His mugshot was all over the police station's notice boards. It was Paddy Ryan's nineteen-year-old nephew, Brian Ryan. Constable Dune started to shake as he realised who he'd killed.

Chapter One

Geoff McDonald was thirty-five years old, married with two young children, but officially listed as single with no kids. Of average height and build, he had joined the Royal Ulster Constabulary (RUC) as a fresh-faced twenty-year-old. That had been fifteen years ago. He had risen through the ranks to become a detective inspector after just ten years' service. Almost unprecedented. The flip side of his early promotion to DI was that he was doing a job nobody wanted. Many had turned it down, even after being told that a rejection was uncivil and the individuals would be backtracked with no guarantee that they would be offered a DI's post in the future.

But McDonald was keen and ambitious. That had been five years ago. He was hoping to pass a promotion board to DCI soon, so his life could return to some kind of normality. After five years doing the job shunned by many, he felt he had more than done his bit. The last inquiry he had done, only two days ago, had particularly troubled him. He rarely got home to spend time with his family, sometimes it was only for a couple of days every three or four weeks, such was his considered vulnerability. He spent most of the time working from, and sleeping in police barracks in Lisburn, south of Belfast, where he was officially listed as single with no dependents, and no living relatives. The price he had to endure for his family's safety.

In 1985 the Troubles were as hot as they had ever been. McDonald held the unique position of being personally hated by the Republican and Loyalist terrorists in nearly equal measure. In particular, the Provisional Irish Republican Army (PIRA) detested him with a passion.

After a rare couple of days off, he had started his early morning journey from home on the outskirts of Antrim towards the barracks in Lisburn. It was getting harder and harder to switch his head back into work mode after a visit home. He'd done all the usual security checks, such as checking under his car, and examining it for signs

WITH PREJUDICE

of disturbance around the doors, bonnet, and boot, before leaving. Always a sobering experience.

McDonald's job, which his wife Sarah didn't actually know the details of, was to visit the scene of all killings of terrorists by the security services. Whether shot by a uniformed RUC officer - as in his last job two days ago - or whether by Special Branch (SB), CID or an Army patrol, it made no difference. His exclusive role was to be the first investigative officer on the scene, and he had to adjudge whether the killing was to be considered a possible 'Justifiable Homicide' or not. And if not, then it would have to be investigated by CID as potential murder. Although technically he came under the CID command, he operated independently. Though the terrorists thought differently.

McDonald's initial assessment was final. If he considered the killing to be potentially a 'Justifiable Homicide' he would refer the death to the Her Majesty's Coroner. And thereafter work for the coroner as a link between those called to do the legwork - the taking of witness statements, forensics, etc - and the coroner themselves. Eventually, the coroner would hold an inquest, sometimes with a jury, sometimes without, and judge whether the homicide was legally justifiable, or not. This final arbitration was solely the coroner's court decision. But the fact that McDonald had sent the investigation along that route from the start was heavily influential. As it would be should he call in the on-duty homicide Senior Investigating Officer (SIO) if he decided that the killing was potentially unlawful - as in murder or manslaughter.

It was extremely rare that the latter was the case. And that was not because he was biased as the terrorists thought, but it was just the way it was. If a person intent on committing a terrorist act is interrupted by the security services - either by design, or fluke, and ends up dead - there would be little appetite to suggest that such a slaying was other than justified.

What McDonald had noticed during the last five years, was that most, if not all killings by the good guys were of Republican terrorists. And usually the Provisional IRA. Whenever the killing had been a Loyalist terrorist, it was exclusively a random intervention by an RUC or Army patrol. All the pre-planned operations seemed to be against the Republicans and in particular the Provisional IRA. The sheer numbers involved in PIRA membership, and therefore terrorist acts, seemed to dictate this. Plus, McDonald knew that the larger membership of the whole IRA afforded wider opportunities for intelligence gathering, this would drive these pre-planned operations.

But the IRA didn't see it that way, and the Ulster Defence Association (UDA) didn't either. Though the UDA were more easily persuaded that killings by the security services were of random intervention, as opposed to targeted operations by the police or Army.

So, although hated by both sides of the sectarian divide, PIRA really despised him. In fact, he had twice before been the target of failed assassination attempts. The first one involved a gunman wearing a balaclava who jumped out in front of his car on the Falls Road, Belfast and aimed a handgun at him. That had been a tactical error on their part. In the millisecond McDonald had to process the threat, he wondered why the gunman didn't have an Armalite, or such-like. McDonald therefore assumed his role was purely as a distraction. It was intended to make him stop and reverse away from the apparent threat. Thank God he had been correct. A common PIRA method of operation was to direct a target away from an apparent threat, into the face of a far greater one.

On this occasion, the terrorists had taken over two residential addresses, facing each other a hundred yards behind him. This would be done by force, though on the Falls Road, the occupants would no doubt be serving the terrorists tea and biscuits. McDonald was supposed to reverse into what would have become a crossfire killing zone, and would have stood no chance. In the millisecond he had had to assess the initial threat from the lone gunman in the road, it was the handgun that didn't fit. McDonald crouched down as much as he could and hit the accelerator pedal flat in second gear. His car raced at the gunman, who didn't even get a shot off, but panicked and legged it down an alleyway into an estate. It was clear that McDonald's actions had surprised the gunman. An hour later, two families behind where McDonald had been, reported that they had had their homes taken over by the

WITH PREJUDICE

Provisionals, but that no shots had been fired. This happened five years ago, not long after McDonald had taken up his promotion. A welcome to his new role by the Provisional IRA.

Then two and a half years later, PIRA had another go. He was again in a Catholic area of Belfast when a lone balaclava wearing terrorist jumped out in the road a hundred yards in front of him. But instead of pointing a handgun, or even a rifle, on this occasion it was far worse. The would-be assassin had confidence his predecessor lacked. He stood squarely in the road, his feet apart, and on his shoulder was a handheld rocket propelled grenade launcher (RPG).

This was a far more serious weapon and, in the millisecond that McDonald had to assess things, it was clearly the major threat. They could have had a crossfire killing zone behind him as a belt and braces approach, but McDonald considered that as this tactic had already failed on him, it was likely that they hadn't. Probably thought they didn't need it. And they'd be right. Whether McDonald sought to drive forwards or backwards, it wouldn't reduce the threat of a shoulder fired RPG at close range. These were military grade weapons designed to attack armoured vehicles, not Ford Cortinas. The effect would be devastating.

In the next millisecond McDonald had, he decided to reverse in order to make himself a smaller target, and to weave from side to side as he did so. He'd screeched to a halt on first seeing the terrorist, who at this moment hadn't fully raised his weapon. McDonald rammed the car into reverse and floored the loud pedal as he swung the steering wheel from left to right. The car seemed to swerve more dramatically being in reverse, which was some solace. Time was short, and all McDonald could do was to make himself a smaller and erratic target for the gunman. He just hoped that he wasn't entering a crossfire killing zone. At his last glance forward before he concentrated on his reversing skills, he saw that his would-be killer was taking aim. He looked backwards as he tried to accentuate his steering wheel movements, conscious of not overdoing it and spinning to a stop.

Then he heard a sound that turned his blood to ice. The whoosh of the weapon being fired. He instinctively looked forward once more and was transfixed as he watched the grenade eat up the yards towards him. In this last millisecond, he knew he could do nothing more to evade it. He asked God to protect his wife and children as the grenade landed on the bonnet of his car. It skimmed like a stone on water and crashed through the windscreen and fell onto the rear seat.

But no explosion. McDonald slammed on the brakes, bringing to car to a stop moments later, as the airborne bomb whizzed, fizzed, and crackled. McDonald's heart nearly stopped as he heard the grenade bang from the rear seat into the rear footwell as his heavy braking brought the car to a stop. In his rush to react he had forgotten about the laws of physics, and expected an almighty explosion an instant after he heard the bump on the floor pan.

But again, nothing. He flung the driver's door open and ran for his life. Zola Budd would have struggled to catch him. There was no sign of the rocket man, and McDonald could see the discarded launcher lying in the road. Obviously, a single use unit.

McDonald had no idea why the grenade had failed to explode, he just thanked God that it had. This second attack had wobbled him immensely and he came close to quitting the RUC altogether. But after he'd calmed down a steely resolve replaced the fear. He'd carry on. He'd do his job as fairly as he could, and make sure that in his small part he'd give those murderers payback.

Then a thought drifted in as he left Antrim and headed for the A26. An attack every two and a half years. At five years, was he now due a third? He shuddered at the thought.

WITH PREJUDICE

Chapter Two

McDonald loved living in Antrim, the scene of a famous British victory in 1798 against the Irish forces. Its name translated into Lone Ridge. It remained mainly a Protestant community, with roughly a two-thirds split, to one-third Catholic. Antrim was the capital town of County Antrim and sited a few miles away from Lough Neagh, which was the largest fresh water lake on the island of Ireland. Nineteen miles long and nine miles wide covering 151 square miles. McDonald loved spending time with his family at its shores.

The sun was breaking the horizon and the night dew was burning back into a rising mist. McDonald glanced across the fields and distant hills as he drove along the A26 towards the A30. This would complete his thirty-five-mile journey to Lisburn. Having recalled the two previous attacks on his life, for merely doing his duty, he cast his mind back to the job he'd done two days earlier. The one which had bothered him and interrupted his two precious days off.

He'd been called to an attack near the police station and barracks in Ballygawley in County Tyrone. The East Tyrone Brigade of the PIRA, had in recent weeks been sighted in and around the area. A nasty individual named Paddy Ryan had recently taken over the East Tyrone Brigade of PIRA, and activity seemed to suggest that he was planning something. There was no intelligence to confirm this, but together with sightings, there was apparent air of anticipation in the area.

When McDonald arrived at the scene of the shooting on a quiet lane on the outskirts of Ballygawley, the young Constable, named Ian Dune, was still shaking. Before he started with the usual post-shooting protocols and scene protection actions, he reassured the young officer that he had done everything correct. That was his initial assessment based on what he had been told en route, and what he had seen on arrival. He wanted to calm the young policeman before he took a more considered evaluation. But his reassurances bounced off deaf ears as the constable kept muttering that he'd killed a man, and that the deceased was Paddy Ryan's nephew. It was the look of sheer horror on the young constable's face which had etched its way into McDonald's memory. He'd seen similar natural reactions on officers' faces before, but as Constable Dune had killed - although apparently justly - the East Tyrone Brigade's leader's nephew, he was clearly terrified.

Plus, the trauma every officer feels when they take their first life. Taking any life, even morally so, robbed the taker of a part of their soul. It left a stain that they would have to learn to live with. And none more so that the first one. And at such young age, too. Though, the terrorists never seemed to suffer in a similar way. Perhaps, they were all psychopaths who used their twisted logic to bury their conscience. McDonald doubted Dune would ever be the same again. He'd be surprised if he didn't hang up his handcuffs.

He then shook these vivid memories from his mind, for now. He'd call Dune's sergeant when he arrived at work to enquire into the officer's wellbeing. But for now, he would relax into the journey and take in the breathtaking scenery as he turned right onto the A30 Lisburn Road. There was no traffic in either direction as he headed along the arrow-straight road, which would take him past the villages of Glenavy and Ballynadolly before finally arriving at Lisburn.

WITH PREJUDICE

Chapter Three

A year ago, the Provisional IRA had come mighty close to killing Margret Thatcher and members of her cabinet when a bomb had torn through the Brighton hotel they were staying at. It was on the south coast of England during the Conservative Party's annual conference. It was thereafter that PIRA coined the phrase, 'We only have to be lucky once. You have to be lucky all the time.' But this sort of propaganda didn't hold any sway with Thatcher. The sheer audacity of the attack had served to only sharpen her laser-focused determination to stamp out the IRA, and all its splinter groups, once and for all. They were trying to fight an enemy during a very debatable, but technical 'peacetime'. Playing by Queensbury Rules whilst the enemy did what they liked. The scoundrels didn't even adhere to normally accepted rules of war, they hid behind the pretence of being 'Freedom-Fighters'.

Half the cabinet tried to persuade her for restraint while the dust settled. The other half were right behind her. She'd apparently been overheard by a senior civil servant muttering about a reshuffle that would involve fifty percent of her current ministers. But for now, restraint was the last thing on her mind. In the wake of the attack in Brighton she held several meetings with the Defence Secretary, the Secretary of State for Northern Ireland, the General Officer Commanding the Army in Ulster (GOC), and his Commander Land Forces (CLF), as well as the Chief Constable of the RUC. And in an unprecedented move, she included the director generals of MI5 and MI6. It was clear that she wanted to take the fight to the terrorists be they Republican or Loyalist, and she wanted to do so in a myriad number of unorthodox ways. Some say this is when the phrase 'Thinking outside the box' started.

What she apparently wanted, demanded, was a new type of rapid fighting force, drawn from the Special Forces regiments, none of whom were to wear gloves. The military had tried to placate her by stating that several SAS units were already stationed in the province. But that was not enough. Her private secretary was later heard quoting her as saying, 'If we can learn something from these murderers, then we must, irrespective of how unpalatable it may seem. And once we have done so, we must build on that template in new and inventive ways.'

No one at this particular meeting had a clue what she was saying, but it soon became apparent. She begrudgingly admired the cellular fashion with which the IRA now operated its Active Service Units. No one could infiltrate them, and if they ever did it would lead to poor intel as the members were kept in the dark about any specific target details until the last possible minute. On the proactive front, she demanded that the Army emulate this template. The attending Lieutenant General and Major General nearly fainted. She also demanded that instead of the Security Service (MI5) disseminating intelligence for the military and police to use, she wanted this new fighting force to be led by a member of the Security Service who would be attached to the unit fulltime.

More swoons followed, including the director general of MI5. She apparently rounded on him, not only to inform him that debate was useless, but also to demand that their intelligence gathering together with the police Special Branch's intel collection, be dramatically improved. She told the Chief Constable and the DG of MI5 that she expected to see a strategic plan in a month's time.

The DG of the Secret Intelligence Service (MI6) was caught grinning at the latter, but soon had the smile removed when she ordered him to come up with a similar plan to cut off the supply of arms from Libia and the outrageous finances flooding in from America. She told her Private Secretary to arrange a phone conference with the US president as a priority. Ronald Reagan was in for an ear bashing.

Then she even suggested to the military as to whom should lead the unit on the operational side. This caused near anaphylactic shock for the GOC and CLF. Apparently, she had met a certain Lieutenant Vernon Jackson from 22 SAS at an operational debrief a couple of years ago. She had been impressed by his direct and uncompromising style. Lieutenant Jackson was still serving with the SAS, and had been promoted to Captain in an attempt to calm him down, and make him toe the line better. His CO - at the time

WITH PREJUDICE

- had argued that fulfilling a more managerial role would widen his thinking, strategically. It would bring him more into the middle managerial rational that the Army prided itself on. They had been wrong, and his CO soon found himself transferred elsewhere. As for Captain Vernon Jackson, he currently ran the training section at SAS Headquarters at Hereford.

Three months later, Romeo Troop of 22 SAS was created.

Three weeks after this, Captain Jackson had his handpicked team of three troopers, drilled, and ready for action.

The Army's headquarters in Northern Ireland was at Lisburn. And based from there, was the Field Research Unit - which handled informants - together with 14 Intelligence Company, and some SAS units, which carried out their own surveillance and undercover operations. Jackson's Romeo Troop was housed in a separate area not connected with anywhere else. Only the Commander Land Forces, and the General Officer Commanding even knew they existed. They had recently been joined by Bertram Hastings, who in his mid-forties was a career intelligence officer at MI5. It had taken some time for Hastings and Jackson to come to terms with their unique situation and agree the chain of command. Hastings was in overall command and in charge of intelligence. Jackson was in charge of tactics, and once deployed, he was in overall command on the ground.

Chapter Four

Captain Vernon Jackson had decided to give himself a roving position, which unbeknown to him would prove crucial later. He'd been in the SAS for fifteen years and couldn't imagine serving in any other regiment. Though he kept doing a 'Boris Johnson' according to his sergeant, Dave 'Geordie' Crompton; himself a ten-year veteran of the regiment. When Jackson had asked Crompton what he meant. He'd replied, 'Like Boris, you're a charismatic leader, a maverick, but you keep shooting yourself in the foot: metaphorically speaking.'

Jackson was glad he'd added the last bit as he prided himself on his weapons handling, they all did. Jackson had answered, 'Fine, but if I ever hear you calling me Boris, I'll slot you.'

'Only if the round ricochets through your foot.'

They were all wearing the latest Racal Cougar surveillance radios. The best kit on the market. Body transceivers were worn in a similar holder to a sidearm shoulder holster, but on the opposite side. It's operating code, which had to be inputted individually, meant that the whole team were effectively on their own secure channel. And the code was changed regularly. If a body kit or handheld set was ever lost or stolen, then a new code was issued and imputed to the induvial sets via what was termed as a 'Fill Gun'. The handheld set was also used to operate in a car set housing. It was the first time they had radios the terrorists couldn't intercept.

Using the call sign One Alpha, Jackson did a comms check with the rest of the team. Two Alpha was Sergeant Crompton, Three Alpha was Trooper Mark 'Tone Deaf' Harris, and Four Alpha was Trooper Ian 'Tickets Please' King. Bertram Hastings was monitoring their office base set as Zero Alpha.

'One Alpha to the team, acknowledge when on plot,' Jackson said.

All deployed units did so. It was still dark but forecast to be a lovely Summer's morning, so visibility should be good. They were headed out in covert vehicles and civvie clothes into the countryside west of Lisburn. Hastings's intelligence had been extremely detailed. The attack by a PIRA Active Service Unit (ASC) was to be at a T junction on a country road as it met a wider thoroughfare, between Glenavy and Ballynadolly. In the middle of nowhere, and extremely specific. Jackson was intrigued where Hastings had received his intelligence from, but knew better than to ask.

Twenty minutes after leaving their secret base within a base, they reached the coordinates. Two Alpha - Sergeant Crompton took up a position hidden behind a hedge on the major of the two roads facing the junction. Three Alpha - Trooper Mark Harris, took up a forward position on the main road on its west side of the junction, and Four Alpha - Ian King was on the opposing east side. Jackson kept in his vehicle and at distance on the east side of the plot, able to support quickly at short notice.

Dawn broke and it looked as if the forecast would be correct, which made a pleasant change. As Sergeant Crompton had the junction in his sights he was designated as 'The Visual', and every so often came over the radio to announce that there was no change to his view. Then forty minutes after sun up, Jackson's earpiece burst into life.

'The Visual to all units, a farm tractor driven by a male in dark clothing is on the minor road stationary at the junction. There is no other traffic. Stand by, stand by, stand by.'

Seconds later, Three Alpha - Mark Harris - announced an incoming vehicle, a Ford Orion heading along the main road from the west. Zero Alpha acknowledged. This looked like the start of it. The intelligence brief Hastings had given them mentioned a tractor and a saloon car. The Visual - Sergeant Crompton - took up the commentary. As the Ford Orion neared the junction it slowed to a crawl, and then flashed its lights as if it were allowing the tractor out of the side road. But the tractor didn't turn, it drove straight ahead blocking the throughfare. Then it got weird. The Orion accelerated and purposefully crashed into the side of tractor. Both drivers got out and went to the other side of the farm vehicle.

The Orion driver, a male also in dark clothing, suddenly produced a MAC 10 compact machine pistol and took up a firing position across the rear of the tractor's cab. A wholly inaccurate weapon, Jackson knew, but devasting at close range.

Then the tractor driver reached into the cab and produced a surprise. A Rocket Propelled Grenade Launcher with one armament fixed in place. This was certainly not in the intelligence brief. It looked like they wanted to ensure they had both the near and far distances covered. This changed things dramatically. They would have to adapt their tactics. But it was what they were good at.

Then Harris announced a second vehicle inbound. It was the friendly, and it was travelling fast. The road was straight and the fact that the Tangos had a Rocket Launcher added to the tension. Detective Inspector Geoff McDonald would be in range sooner than they had initially planned for. Harris said he would use his vehicle to block McDonald's approach, but warned that they could still be in range for the RPG.

Due to this added risk, Jackson called the strike immediately, and set off inbound from the other direction at speed. He quickly collected Ian King who jumped out of the hedge in front of him.

Sergeant Crompton opened fire through the hedge just as Jackson threw his vehicle into a sideways skid to a halt, fifteen yards from the junction. He and King bailed out and took up firing positions across the boot and bonnet of the vehicle. Harris reported that he'd scooped up the policeman and was extracting him to a safe distance, whereafter he'd rejoin the party as quickly as he could.

The Tango with the RPG had swung around and fired towards Sergeant Crompton's position in a response to his initial burst of gunfire. Excellent, Jackson thought, as he knew his sergeant would have moved as soon as he had let fly with his first salvo. The Tango had just unwittingly made the RPG weapon safe. An explosion could be heard in the distance in the adjoining field seconds later.

Then the second Tango swung around to Jackson's position, alerted by their car's noisy arrival, and fired his 'hit and hope' MAC10 weapon, wildly. It was his last act of terrorism. Jackson and King returned fire simultaneously and neither missed their mark. Jackson had also spat a quick update into his radio set for the benefit of Hastings. A momentary lull descended and Hastings replied shouting for them to take the RPG Tango alive. He could prove a valuable source of intel. Jackson acknowledged, but as he did so the idiot produced a handgun, which at this distance was even less effective than his mate's MAC10. Then their training took over. No one could afford to take a chance and King cut him down with a short burst from his Heckler and Koch MP5 machine pistol, a far superior weapon to the terrorist's.

The whole thing was over in little over a minute. Harris arrived with a shell-shocked looking Geoff McDonald, who couldn't thank them enough. The irony of the situation was not lost on Jackson as he commented, 'Well, I suppose Detective Inspector, this is one 'Justifiable Homicide' scenario you are unable to adjudicate on?'

Sergeant Crompton appeared from the opposite hedge through the whole the RPG grenade had made, and added, 'Absolutely, I'm sure the IRA will be pleased.'

Then Jackson's earpiece went mental again as Hastings screamed new intel through it.

Chapter Five

Brendan Lynch was an ex-member of the Provisional IRA's ruling Army Council, only removed by the ever-growing number of wimps on it. The breakaway Provisional wing was supposed to be the true armed resistance, but more and more he heard voices similar to the original IRA's standpoint. And as much as this annoyed him, it did feel liberating to be in charge of an Active Service Unit, once more. A forty-four-year-old veteran, he was a hardliner, married to Erin - a beautiful name as it was Irish for Ireland.

He'd been brought in at short notice to head up the East Tyrone Brigade who were doing a job initially planned by the East Antrim Brigade. They were at a late stage of the final operational planning when the head of East Tyrone's nephew, Brian Ryan, had met an untimely death in Ballygawley whilst on active service. Today was his funeral, so Paddy Ryan had asked Lynch to cover the job for him. It was all planned and practiced, all he had to do was babysit it.

As they knew where Geoff McDonald lived, Lynch had suggested they hit him at home. It would be more impactive than at a T junction in the middle of nowhere. He'd already had some preliminary action taken the day before, based on his initial brief from Paddy Ryan, just in case they ended up there. But he had been overruled, again. The wife and children were apparently, not the target. McDonald was, and all the arrangements were in place. Lynch understood.

It was just that he personally hated McDonald, not just because of his corrupt protection of the murdering occupying security forces. But years ago, Lynch had fired an RPG at the swine which had failed to explode. This failing made it very personal. He had later discovered that the ordnance had been stored in a leaking barn, and even though he was unsure whether that had actually contributed to its failure, he deemed it so and beat the living crap out of the man responsible for the hide.

WITH PREJUDICE

But, if he was angry back then, he was enraged off the scale now. The Brits had compromised the new attack. God only knew how. But that was a question for another day. He rang Sean Delany, the Northern Commander of PIRA. He got on with Sean most of the time, he had to, as he was his wife's eldest brother. But when he suggested that they immediately strike back, he baulked at the idea.

'Think about, it's the last thing the Brits will expect.'

'I understand you're upset; we all are. We've lost two fine volunteers today. But jumping in unplanned is dangerous.'

You've been sat behind a desk on the Army Council, too long, Lynch wanted to say, but instead said, 'I know what I'm doing. I've done similar before.'

'I know how experienced you are Brendan, but I'm not sure. What did you have in mind?'

Lynch told him.

'Are you off your head! But of course, you are, you always have been.'

'Is that a yes?'

'No, it's a definite no. Just get yourself out of the area. No debate,' Sean said, and then ended the call.

'So, that's a yes, then,' Lynch said as he put the phone down. 'I'll show them,' he added out loud as he left the lonely phone box in the middle of nowhere and got back in his car.

Fifteen minutes later, Lynch slowed the car as he entered the start of the built-up area. He didn't want to draw attention to himself. The car engine tinkled its own unique musical note, as the metal cooled slightly now reduced to a more sedate speed. He drove cautiously through town as he headed to the outskirts. As soon as the buildings started to thin out, he found a quite lane to turn into and stop. He opened the boot of his saloon car, put on a pair of gloves, and collected a the Armalite semi-automatic rifle from a sports holdall. It was a newer iteration of the AR15 designated M16 by the US military. This 1980 model had the added function of 3-round bursts, which Lynch liked. And as the name suggested, it was lightweight. Ideal for urban close-range combat. He checked the action and loaded a full magazine, and also put two spare mags in his coat pocket, before returning to the driver's seat.

He placed the weapon across his lap, did a three-point turn, and rejoined the main road out of the town continuing into the sticks. He knew where he was headed, the address was one of three in a quiet cul-de-sac. Of course, he had no way of knowing if *his* target would be in, but it was still relatively early, so he hoped for the best. It was a speculative attack, he knew, so would just have to give it one attempt and then flee.

He turned off the A6 before Milltown and pulled over. The road entrance was up ahead on the left. He checked all around and saw no one, so quickly put on his balaclava. He then drove past the junction, and started to reverse into the cul-de-sac. It would make for a quicker getaway, and if anyone did see him, it would just look like he was turning around. The seats and rear of the car would also hide the sight of a driver at the wheel with a balaclava on, to some degree, at least.

He kept his gaze rigidly fixed on his rear-view mirror as the house at the end of the dead end grew in his view. He was now only fifteen yards away, when his luck went through the roof. The woman, his target, Mrs Geoff McDonald was walking down her driveway to a parked car, with a kid on each hand in tow.

Three for the price of one. DI McDonald may have survived their earlier assault, but for the rest of his life he would live in abstract torment. Maybe this way was more fitting. More painful. Lynch stated to grin under his mask.

He stopped his car before he became too close and aroused the woman's suspicion. Thankfully, it looked as if the kids were keeping her attention fully engaged; nice one, brats.

Lynch opened his driver's door, and was about to swing into action when his good luck changed dramatically. A car screeched across the entrance to the cul-de-sac and a man in civvies jumped out and levelled an automatic rifle of some kind across the car roof while he shouted something. British accent. A last glance in his rear-view mirrors confirmed what he suspected he'd heard. A warning aimed at his mark. The McDonald woman and her brats dived behind their own car. It was game over.

WITH PREJUDICE

Lynch released a controlled burst of fire over his driver's door before jumping in behind the wheel. He sped towards the car blocking the road as he took in his options. The corner house to his right was fronted by a lawn with no perimeter wall.

He fired through his own windscreen directly at the Brit as incoming rounds peppered throughout his motor, one narrowly missing his neck. He actually felt the heat from the round as it passed by. Then as it seemed that he was on a collision course for the blocking motor, he swerved to his right and drove across the lawn of the corner house. He managed to get a final burst of gunfire off to his left as he passed the back of the blockading vehicle, and just hoped he'd hit the tyres.

Lynch nearly lost control of his vehicle as he struggled to steer it one-handed around the right-hand curve back onto Castle Road. He threw his weapon onto the front passenger seat and used both hands to control his motor.

A final glance before he hit the A6 showed no change to the rear. The car was still where it had been and he could see no sign of the Brit who had attacked him.

Damn, he'd been so close, too. He guessed that the Brits who intervened in their attack against Geoff McDonald, had sent someone to check on the missus. Perhaps, he was a little bit too impetuous at times, as he was often accused of being.

But he'd been lucky; the open plan garden had saved him. It was obvious the lone Brit who attacked him was no ordinary squaddie or SB man. He was SAS, he was sure of it.

Five minutes later, he was driving a hijacked car with its previous driver in the boot. His shot-up motor was well ablaze as he drove away. He always carried a gallon of petrol in the boot of operational vehicles for such a purpose. He was soon on the M2 towards Belfast where he would abandon the new motor and slink off through the estates.

He was sure someone would soon hear the old codger banging from inside the boot. He was also sure that Sean Delany would try and chew his arse as soon as he found out what had happened. Whatever.

Chapter Six

Back in the briefing room at Romeo Troop's base within Lisburn barracks, the mood was one of euphoria after the successful operation. But Captain Jackson's mood was tempered with several concerns he had yet to voice. His irritation was also hardened by the stinging flesh wound to his right calf giving him a pronounced limp, as pain stabbed through him when he put any weight on it.

'Come along hop-a-long,' Hastings said. as he took a seat around their planning table.

'You been taking lessons from these idiots, 'Jackson replied, as he took a seat, sighing in relief as he did so. Sergeant Crompton was already there, as was Trooper Mark Harris. Trooper Ian King soon joined them, with a tray of coffees and a bottle of Irish whiskey to add to the beverage, as was their norm at a debrief.

'What did the medic say, boss?' King asked, as he passed a mug to Jackson.

'The round took half an inch, so I guess I'm lucky, should be alright in a few days. In fact, I'll be alright when the painkillers and that whiskey kick in.'

Jackson noticed Crompton grinning, so asked what was amusing him.

'Just thinking that it's as well that it wasn't Kingy who got shot. Half an inch to him would seem like a lot.'

Jackson smiled and Harris laughed. Tropper Ian King was built like the proverbial brick outhouse, an ex-Para and former Army heavyweight boxer. He stood up and puffed his chest out, and said, 'Come on then, Dave,' aiming his remarks at Crompton, his tormentor. 'Get yours out and let's compare.'

'Sit down "Tickets Please", I've not eaten yet, so keep stumpy safely tucked away.'

More giggles.

Ian King had been a British Transport policeman before he joined the Parachute Regiment, which is where he gained the nickname 'Tickets Please' and it had stuck.

WITH PREJUDICE

King took his seat still keeping a fixed gaze on Sergeant Crompton. Jackson didn't mind inane banter, especially after an operation where they had actively engaged in a contact with the enemy. It helped settle nerves as the adrenalin eased back to normal levels. But he only allowed it for so long before it was time to call the men to order, which he now did.

Firstly, Hastings went through the operational log which he'd kept whilst monitoring things from the base station. They all listened and threw in any amendments that were necessary until everyone was happy with its content. Then they all signed it. It would prove to be a contemporaneous note and team 'pocket book' that they could all rely on in any subsequent court proceedings. Such as giving evidence before a coroner's court, if necessary. It was a tip passed to them by their police colleagues in Special Branch, hence the phrase, 'pocket book'. It was good tradecraft, and gave their testimony a greater air of authenticity in these suspicious times.

Then they talked trough the tactics they had employed, and everyone seemed happy with how they had worked, including their reaction to the presence of a Grenade Launcher.

Hastings then went through the original intelligence in order to confirm its accuracy, and identify any gaps. This always jarred with Jackson. He respected the fact that the team doing the business need not, and should not, have access to the giver of the intelligence; be it from a technical source - such as a telephone intercept - or a live one, such as an informant; or agent, as the MI5 man termed them. But he would love to know more, just out of interest, but Hastings wouldn't even confirm whether he had a live agent, or not.

But that may have to change. 'I have to say, Bert, your intel update at the end which saw me tear-arse over to McDonald's home address came in the nick of time. Seconds later, and I'd have been too late.'

'Tell me about it. You did exceptionally well there,' Hastings replied.

'Only wish I could have slotted him. But his firing control under pressure was impressive. He could even be ex-military, God forbid.'

'Can you talk us through what happened, and we'll make some notes up afterwards, even though no one was hurt,' Hastings said.

'Apart from me of course.'

'You know what I mean.'

Jackson did, and then ran through the events. After which, Jackson commented again on the timeliness of Hastings's update.

Hastings answered the unasked question, 'You know I can't comment. It could have come from a live conversation that GCHQ intercepted. I'm only glad we got it in time.'

Jackson moved on to the other thing that had been concerning him. 'Why plan to attack McDonald on his way to work instead of hitting him at home. They obviously knew where he lived?'

Trooper Mark Harris spoke adding to Jackson's comment, 'Yeah, that's been bugging all of us.'

'Normally, I would suggest that the Provos only wanted to attack McDonald. They must have deemed that his family were not targets,' Hastings said.

'But then they were,' Harris added. 'So, if they were, why do the T junction attack at all?'

'You know what I think?' Crompton said to the room.

'Go on,' Jackson said.

'One question first, boss. How would you describe the attack on the home address?'

'How do you mean?'

'Pre-planned?'

Jackson sat back and replayed the incident again through his mind, and then shook his head.

'And we had just taken out two of their own in a failed attack on McDonald. So, it must have been a knee-jerk attack on the officer's family. There must have been a third terrorist there unseen,' Crompton finished with.

'You know, if that third terrorist had been successful in taking out the wife and, God forbid, children as well. It would have had a massive blow back,' Trooper Ian King added.

'How do you mean?' Crompton asked.

'I'm sure a lot of Catholics, albeit almost all are Republicans, would have thought that an act of terror too far. They are all family people themselves.'

Everyone nodded agreement.

'Which can only mean one thing?' Jackson said, and added, 'It means we have a nutter, a maverick hardliner on the loose.'

'A cheery thought,' Harris added.

'That, or it's personal. Very personal,' Hastings added.

'Any idea from the intel who it was?' Jackson asked. He'd already told them all that he'd only got a glimpse of the man.

'Unfortunately, not,' Hastings answered.

Jackson wasn't sure Hastings was telling them the truth. Something about the way he answered the question jarred with him.

'We need to rule the latter, in or out, first,' Crompton said, interrupting Jackson's thoughts; and they all agreed.

Hastings said that he'd ask Special Branch to do a fuller debrief of McDonald with that in mind.

'What do we know about the two we slotted?' Jackson asked.

'Both East Tyrone Brigade, according to SB. But no idea who the lone attacker you engaged was,' Hastings answered, again quite quickly.

Jackson decided to leave it for now.

Chapter Seven

Brendan Lynch borrowed a car from a contact who lived off the Falls Road in Belfast, and headed to South Armagh. Known as 'Bandit Country' the area is a stanch Republican stronghold. And none more nationalist than the small village of Crossmaglen near to the border with the rest of Ireland. It is populated by well over 90% of Catholics, and Lynch lived in a remote farmhouse on the outskirts of town set back from the road by an old farm track, with a couple of outbuildings. Quite isolated, and very private. His heart sank as he pulled up on the gravel parking area in front of the house as he recognised the other car already there. It was his brother-in-law's. Sean Delany, the Northern Commander of the Provisional IRA.

He let himself in and could hear Sean talking to his wife Erin in the front room. Before he reached the doorway, the chatter stopped and Erin met him in the hall.

'Our Sean is here to see you, he's not been here long, and I don't know what's got into him, but he doesn't seem happy.'

'When does he ever?' Lynch said, as he gave Erin a peck on the cheek.

'Just warning you.'

'Thanks, love.'

'I'll leave you to it. I'll be in the back if you need me,' Erin finished with, before disappearing down the hall towards the large dinning kitchen situated at the back of the house.

Lynch took a deep breath, and decided to surprise Sean by taking a conciliatory approach. He walked into the lounge as Sean stood to his feet from the armchair by the main bay window. Lynch put both arms in the air and said, 'I know, Sean, I know.'

The approach seemed to have some effect, as Sean paused. Lynch sat in an armchair as far away from Sean's as the furniture set up would allow.

'I specifically told you to leave it, Brendan,' Sean said, remaining stood.

'You did, so you did, true enough.'

'But being the hot-headed tosser you are, you didn't.'
'Look, Sean, no harm done.'
'It's just as well that the Sass *were* there.'
'And what the hell does that mean?' Lynch said, feeling his temper restraint slipping.
'It means you weren't able to kill a woman and two children, that's what it means. The Army Council were going to parade you on until I convinced them to leave it with me to talk to you.'
'Why should they, or you, care less about McDonald's family?'
'Because, you eejit, the bad press would have hurt our image and our core supporters. They may vehemently be opposed to the Loyalist scum on the other side, politically, but they are all family folk. They have that much in common. You knew McDonald's family were not the targets, that's why we went to so much trouble to plan the attack on his way to work.'
Lynch fell silent for a moment; he knew in his heart that Sean was right. But he just kept feeling that the slide of attitudes on the Army Council was becoming more and more image-obsessed than they should be. They were at war after all. But he was grateful for Sean getting them to agree to leave it with him, and said so.
'God knows what you would have said to them, with your temper, at least here it is only us, and it stays here.'
Lynch nodded and was keen to move things along, he'd had his bollocking, or as much as he was prepared to put up with. It was time to get back to business. 'I know I was only a stand in, but have we any idea what the hell went wrong?'
It was Sean's turn to fall silent as he re-took his armchair.
Lynch thought they had purged themselves of most, if not all of the black-hearted touts over the last couple of years. Things at one time got so bad, that the PIRA Army Council had set up its own Security Dept. - something he had been canvassing after for a long time. And in the last two years, they had identified, tortured, and killed eight traitors. They thought they had cleaned house.
'Is it another rat?' Lynch asked.
'It must be. The East Tyrone Brigade were drilled hard in the use of, or lack of, telephones. And they have been issued with devices to check their homes and cars for bugs,' Sean replied.

'And it was Paddy Ryan's outfit, and he's no mug.'

'No, he's not.'

'You know, if the Council had taken up my idea to put our own touts inside the enemy we may have got wind. Or at least been able to task them in the aftermath, pick up the chatter.'

'This is no time to grand slam; you know that policy will take careful thinking and planning. They are not against it, but there are many potential pitfalls to work through.'

We are becoming an organisation of planners and not doers, Lynch managed not to say. So instead said, 'So what next?'

'We'll task the Security Dept. to do a thorough search again, if there is a new super rat, they'll find it.'

'I'd be happy to help with that, if you wish?'

'Thanks, but I've got something else in mind, for you.'

'Go on.'

'This one is ultra-secret, especially after the compromise we have just suffered, so it has to stay between us two, and no one else.'

Lynch liked the sound of this and said, 'Of course,' just feeling glad to being trusted again.

'Follow me,' Sean said as he rose from his armchair and headed out the front room.

Lynch followed Sean out the front door, who paused to shout his farewell to Erin, who then rushed in to give him a goodbye hug. Once outside, instead of going to his car, Sean diverted to one of Lynch's outbuildings. Once inside, he pulled a handheld scanner from his jacket and quickly checked the small barn-like space. Satisfied, he turned it off and turned to face Lynch.

'I want you to go to England, and you are to tell no one.'

Lynch didn't respond right away; he didn't like the sound of this. It was as if they wanted him out of the way while they cleaned house. Almost as if they didn't trust him. Or at least didn't trust what he might do if a rat was uncovered. He dug deep and kept his mouth shut.

Sean filled the temporary void. 'There is an ASU in London and their commander has been arrested on non-related issues. And as you know, the protocol in such circumstances is for the ASU to go quiet and end all operations or reconnaissance and cut all contacts until the situation is clear. They are to remain in abeyance and incommunicado until told otherwise.'

'I know the protocol, Sean, I devised it before I was chucked off the Army Council.'

'I know you did, and you had yourself thrown off the Council, but let's not argue over semantics.'

Lynch nodded.

'Everyone, including the Brits will expect the ASU to go dark. I want you lead them into the light.'

Lynch liked the sound of this. Sean went on to explain that the ASU had prepared an attack plan for three possible targets. All were ready to go when their leader had been arrested. He wanted Lynch to run the team in their leader's absence, much like he had done today. He was to pick whichever one of the three targets he thought most suitable. And just do it. Hit the Brits on home soil when they were least expecting it. They may well have trumped up charges against the ASU leader just to ensure the Provos' 'Cease and Desist' protocol was enacted. A disruption tactic by them.

'They probably don't realise that we know that they are aware of the protocol. Making it an ideal opportunity,' Sean said.

Lynch was grinning wildly now. 'But why me?' he asked, suddenly aware at the faith being put in him.

'You are the obvious choice; experienced and currently a minister without portfolio. Though I won't lie, your little escapade earlier nearly put paid to it.'

'I'm sorry. I know I act a little rashly sometimes,' Lynch said, and he was. This seemed to surprise Sean as he stood back and raised both his eyebrows.

'I wasn't expecting that. But thank you,' Sean said.

'What are the three potential targets?'

'No idea. Only the Chief of Staff and the ASU in London know that. But suffice to say that all three targets have been agreed.'

Lynch probably could have guessed this, but thought he'd ask just on the off chance. Sean set off to leave and Lynch followed him. Half-way between the barn and his car, Sean spun around and Lynch stopped and faced him.

'One caveat though. And this must be agreed and adhered to. No exceptions, no matter what.'

'Go ahead.'

'Agree?'

'Agreed.'

'You can choose any of the three targets, but only one of the three. No other action will be tolerated, or receive post action authorisation.'

'I understand,' Lynch said, and he did. He knew he had been lucky today, in many ways.

'Any breach will be deemed an offence compatible to that of a rat.'

It was Lynch's turn to raise his eyebrows.

'That's how serious they are taking it. Today's little detour by you nearly cost you this chance, and I've backed you. So don't let me down.'

'Fair enough, and understood,' Lynch replied. He was grateful to Sean for protecting him, and for trusting and backing him. 'I appreciate what you've done, and are doing.'

Sean just nodded and turned and headed to his car. Lynch stood and waved as his brother-in-law drove off. He took in the evening air as the tail lights vanished down the track. 'This time, I'll really not let you down, Sean. I owe you that,' he said, aiming his words at the disappearing car.

Then he heard Erin's voice from behind him, and turned to see her stood in the front doorway.

'I've been calling you, so I have,' she said.

'Just chatting with your brother before he left.'

'I hope he left in a better mood than when he arrived?'

'All good, so no need to worry.'

'Ah, that's good, then. Fancy a beer?'

'I do, lass, I do' Lynch replied and headed back into the house.

WITH PREJUDICE

Chapter Eight

The cordoned off area within Lisburn barracks for the exclusive use of Romeo Troop was split into four sections: the sleeping barracks, the briefing room, kitchen, and lounge area. It was the following morning after the operation, and Sergeant 'Geordie' Crompton was apparently fleecing Ian 'Tickets Please' King and Mark 'Tone Deaf' Harris at poker. The day after a live op was always a 'chill out' day if circumstances allowed. Jackson knew how important it was to reset oneself after an op which had included a live contact with the enemy. His aching calf continued to remind him of this. The swearing and the banter drifted through to the briefing room where he and Hastings were. The MI5 man was on a secure landline to London.

Harris got his nickname because he played the guitar - badly. Though, he always insisted it was the others who were tone deaf. Currently, he was threatening to play his guitar if Crompton didn't stop winning, and the banter flowed back at him. Crompton threatened to 'put the guitar where the sun doesn't shine' if he did. Fortunately for all of them, Harris played the sniper rifle much better than his musical instrument, a decorated shot who had excelled during the Falklands Conflict.

Hastings put the secure Brent phone back in its cradle and turned to face, Jackson. He looked a little strained.

'There is always an unspoken edge with some of my senior officers,' Hastings started with.

Jackson didn't know what he meant so let him carry on.

'Just because I didn't come through the university route, even now after nearly twenty years' service, I can sense it.'

Now Jackson understood. He suffered a similar bias in the Army, always had, it was probably that which gave him his purposeful edge. He had as many haters as he had supporters.

'It's undoubtedly why they sent me over here - no offence,' Hastings added.

'None taken, and ditto.'

Hastings nodded and the tension on his face seemed to ease. Jackson liked him more and more, there was a shared empathy building, notwithstanding the secrets he kept to himself. 'Just remember; those who despise us usually do so because we achieve what those bedwetters can only dream of.'

Hastings laughed out loud and the tension lifted further. He then went on to explain what his bosses at Thames House had said. It started with the bleeding obvious, in that, after their success of yesterday, PIRA would be looking to find out how they were compromised. And their first, obvious thought would be that an informant was involved.

Jackson took his opportunity to ask, 'Is there a live informant embedded deep in their ranks?'

Hastings rolled his eyes and grinned before answering, 'As you know Vernon, the intel could have come from a myriad of intelligence gathering techniques.' He then quickly moved it on, 'London are worried how the Provos found out where McDonald lived, and how they knew where he would be at the specific time. Apparently, he only gets home every two, three or sometimes four weeks at a time for a couple of days off. It's never the same, but they knew.'

'Having got the address, PIRA could have been watching it for some time?' Jackson suggested. And then added, 'Anyone in Antrim could have bubbled him. It would just take one sympathiser to recognise him.'

'I guess. Special Branch are following up on it. But London is worried they have a source among the police.'

'A cheery though, as Harris might say.'

'Which is another reason for us to keep well and truly off the radar.'

'Agreed,' Jackson said, and then added, 'Have your lot ever considered giving the Provos what they want?'

'What do you mean?'

'Give them the inside person they crave. One of ours working undercover as a sympathiser. They could say that they are scared of being discovered working for the security services. We all know what can happen to Catholics discovered working in police canteens etc.'

Hastings laughed out loud, again, and said, 'We'll make an intelligence officer of you yet. And as cover stories, go, that has a good basis to work from.'

Hastings then elaborated how they had discussed with SB many times of doing so, but they all knew how dangerous such a deployment would be, and the risks involved. It would need careful planning. But the priority was to firstly ensure that there were no PIRA sources amongst them. Especially, if they ever did try to do as Jackson had suggested. A leak there would mean sending the undercover double agent to a certain death. This had come down from the chief constable of the RUC, John Chambers, who still had primacy over all operations in Ulster. And as much as they agreed with Chambers on this issue, it sometimes irked both the Security Service and the Army, that they didn't have total operational freedom.

'But until we are needed again, and while the SB complete a "house search" and their enquires in general, we are to be recalled to the mainland to reduce any exposure risks. Not that we interact with anyone else. All my enquires with SB go through an intermediary, but I guess it's good tradecraft. You are apparently going to receive a call from Hereford shortly to confirm this.'

'No problems, it makes sense, and it'll give the lads chance for a bit of R & R followed by some extra training just to piss them off.'

The conversation was coming towards a close, and Jackson realised Hastings still hadn't explained what had riled him during his call from Thames House. He'd skilfully avoided it. But Jackson knew the rules: 'Need to Know', didn't mean 'Nice to Know'.

***

The following morning Jackson and Romeo Troop packed their bergans ready for the off. They'd previously decided to always travel in two or three vehicles when not on an operation to reduce risks and add to security. Hastings had his own motor and Jackson was to travel with Ian King. Sergeant Crompton said he'd go with

Mark Harris as long as he promised not to sing along to the radio. Crompton reckoned his singing was as bad as his guitar playing.

They were to RV at RAF Aldergrove, which was not far to the south of Antrim with Lough Neagh close by to its west. They left Lisburn barracks ten minutes apart. Once at Aldergrove, there was a Chinnock helicopter waiting to fly them back to Hereford. It was taking other military personnel, too, including a Lieutenant Colonel, so Jackson had been advised not to be late by his Major in Hereford.

Jackson and King left first, with King driving. Jackson knew that the air base was only about six miles south of McDonald's house, and something had been bugging him. He told King to swing past the address en route. They were ten minutes ahead of Crompton and Harris, and in any event, they had plenty of time before the Chinnock was due to take off.

Jackson had spent the previous evening mulling over his conversation with Hastings, and the thought that McDonald had been set up by a leak from within. He knew the sensitivity of what McDonald did, knew he lived in barracks most of the time, knew that he was officially single with no dependents, so if there was a leak within, it would have to be at an extremely high level. This wasn't something picked up by a sympathiser who worked in a police canteen. The thought that the Provos had a source embedded to such a degree within the security services was very troubling. He had also reflected on the events at the home address and his intervention which had thankfully come in time, albeit with only seconds to spare.

They still didn't know the identity of the attacker, and Jackson hadn't been much help on that front, not least as things unfolded so quickly, but also because the gunman had been wearing a balaclava. He'd also been busily involved in a firefight which tends to focus one's attention on other things. But these musings had identified the itch which had been bugging him. How the shooter had managed to flee. Luck? Or was it?

He instructed Kingy to turn off the A6 before Milltown onto Castle Road. They did a quick recce of the area to ensure no SB were not about on their follow-up enquires. He knew that the

WITH PREJUDICE

McDonald address itself was now empty as the family had immediately been relocated. The RUC would buy and then sell the house, but first pay McDonald its market value straight away so they could find somewhere else. The force would also cover all removal expenses and provide safe temporary accommodation for as long as was required. They even had a department set up for such contingencies. Having to relocate serving officers was unfortunately, not an uncommon event.

Content that they would not be stepping on any toes, Jackson instructed Kingy to pull over further down Castle Road with a long-distance view of the cul-de-sac and any approach from the A6 end.

'I'll be two minutes, max,' he told Kingy as he alighted from the vehicle. At the boot, he quickly selected a hoodie from the props back and put it on. He also selected a dog lead. Each of their cars had a props bag in the boot containing all sorts of clothing, hard hats, clip boards, high viz jackets and many other things that could aid a foot surveillance operative. 14 Intelligence Company were the surveillance experts, and Jackson had learned a lot from them during his attachments with them years' earlier.

He pulled the hoodie up as far as it would go and leaned forward as he walked with purpose, carrying the leash in one hand. He was particularly interested in one of the houses that formed the corner with the cul-de-sac and Castle Road. One had a brick perimeter wall around its front garden, and the opposite one - on the A6 side - had no structure of any kind at its border. It's how the gunman managed his escape.

Jackson kept swivelling his head from side to side, while shouting, 'Here boy,' in the best Northern Ireland accent he could. He wouldn't be here long. Outside the house was parked a Morris Marina saloon, but what caught his eye was the Southern Irish registration plates on it. Keeping the vehicle in his peripheral vision he looked at the front garden as he passed. The tyre gouges in the lawn were still very evident. But what he had wanted to check was plain to see. Where the grass bordered the pavement, he could clearly see a muddy hole every few feet throughout its length. There had obviously been a fence of some description here very recently. The rain-filled holes where the fence's uprights had been looked very fresh. Very fresh. Someone hadn't done their homework properly on checking McDonald's neighbours. The good news might mean that there was no breach in security from within, but a preventable error if the occupant of the house with no fence turned out to be a Republican sympathiser. He'd seen all he needed to; he'd get Hastings to action urgent enquires by SB. He turned around and headed back the way he had come.

WITH PREJUDICE

Chapter Nine

As Jackson walked past the end house and towards the road, his peripheral vision caught movement from the front of the fenceless house toward the Morris Marina. He risked a glance as the driver was getting in behind the wheel. A bell rang in his subconscious. He was forced to stop at the kerb as the Marina approached the junction and clearly had no intention of allowing a pedestrian to cross. Which was fine by Jackson as it allowed him to have a front on glimpse at the driver as he turned right into Castle Road and sped off towards the T junction with the A6.

Then the second bell in his head went off. He quickly turned to try and confirm what he thought he saw, but all he could see was the brake lights of the Marina as the vehicle slowed at the junction with the A6. And by the position of the car, it was clear that it intended to turn left towards Antrim town. He sprinted back to their car and jumped in, and said, 'Did you see that brown Marina?'

'Yeah, why?'

'After it - pronto - I'll explain in a minute.'

Kingy didn't question him further, he just reacted. Jackson could tell by his demeanour that he had switched back into operational mode, as had he. All down to training. You did so without thinking. Jackson opened the glove box and ripped the false back from its position to reveal the locked box which all their plain vehicles carried in case of emergencies. He quickly entered the keycode and revealed two Walther P5 pistols together with four magazines of 9 mm parabellum ammunition. Primarily intended to be used as a back-up, defensively, but it was all the armament they had.

Jackson had to steady himself with one hand on the dashboard as Kingy braked heavily for the junction. He glanced right and shouted 'clear' to assist Kingy. He could then swing the car onto the A6 without having to stop. Crucial seconds saved. Kingy then accelerated hard before having to brake stiffly again as he came up behind a white van. It provided good cover, but the blocked view worked both ways. Jackson wound down the door window and stuck his head out to grab a view past the van. He pulled himself back inside and as he wound the window back up, said, 'Target vehicle three down on the van.'

Kingy just nodded as he concentrated on his driving, and was clearly looking for an overtaking opportunity. Jackson loaded both handguns and put one and a spare magazine between Kingy's legs. They both then stuck their respective guns in their rear waistbands and the spare mag in their coat pockets. 'I'm going to have to lose the van's cover, he's getting too far in front,' Kingy said, as he pulled out and manoeuvred the overtake. Two cars must have pulled off the A6 as they found themselves one down from the Marina. They were about to enter the built-up area of Antrim town and traffic speed eased considerably.

As they relaxed into the follow, Kingy asked, 'Who's in the Marina?'

Jackson quickly outlined his disquiet at how the gunman had easily escaped the previous day across the corner house's lawn and how his suspicions had been confirmed during the walk past.

'That's pretty inspired thinking, boss, if you don't mind me saying.'

'Thanks, but you know how sometimes, on reflection after the heat of the moment has passed, things can start to prick you?'

Kingy nodded.

'We've all had them. Anyway, I'd better get on the bugle and get some help.'

'So, who's in the Marina? Kingy asked a second time.

'Sorry, I'm not 100 percent sure, but it looked a lot like a PIRA terrorist called Paddy Ryan. He runs the East Tyrone Brigade, though he didn't look like the guy I engaged with, too tall.'

Kingy nodded.

'But interestingly, it was Ryan's nephew that the RUC constable shot a couple of days ago. The last "Justifiable Homicide" case that Geoff McDonald adjudicated on.'

'Ah, his presence here is very curious, if it is him,' Kingy said.

'That's what I thought.'

Jackson then reached for the multi-channel radio handpiece from

WITH PREJUDICE

the glove box as Kingy managed to stay one vehicle behind the Marina as it wended its way through Antrim Town and then followed the A6 as it turned left and headed towards Belfast.

Jackson had second thoughts and replaced the radio handset, it had been instinctive to grab it, but he knew how important it was for them to stay under the radar. He told Kingy to abandon the follow at the first sign that whoever was in the Marina started to show undue attention to his rear view. Kingy then backed off and they carried on with what was often termed a 'boot lid' surveillance. It was when you were not in possession of a full team, or at worst, on your own as they were. The idea was to be so far behind the target vehicle that you just clocked its boot lid as it disappeared around bends in the road. One would then accelerate hard to the next bend, regain a visual on the boot lid and then back off again. The hope being that you are never actually in the rear view of the target, or for a limited time, at least. It was a difficult skill in itself, aside from the art of surveillance in general; which was challenging enough. But Kingy was doing an admirable job as Jackson utilised the handheld radio to try and reach Hastings.

They were still on the A6 near Dunadry, but would soon be on the A57 which led to the M2 motorway, where things would get more difficult for an intervention. The impetuous side of Jackson's nature was weighing up doing a cut off, if no help was to hand before the Marina joined the motorway. Irrespective of the fall out. The thought of stopping a ruthless PIRA brigade commander such as Paddy Ryan was very enticing. If indeed, it was him in the Marina. Then his radio burst into life, Hastings coming back to him. 'That was quick.'

'Thank you. What's up?'

Jackson quickly brought Hastings up to speed, whereafter he actually ordered Jackson not to intervene. He'd have to consider that one if help wasn't close by. Hastings disappeared for a short time and then came back on the line.

'I've spoken to my SB intermediary and you are in luck, two fully armed RUC vehicles are on the M2 out of Belfast nearing the junction with the A57. One is going to remain there while the second one is towards you. As soon as they take control, stand down and head to RAF Aldergrove. I'll see you there.'

The radio went dead.

'I'm starting to feel exposed, notwithstanding our stand-off position,' Kingy said.

Jackson explained what Hastings had said, then added, 'But if he does freak and bolt, we *are* taking him out, got it?'

'Got it.'

The next five minutes were increasing tense as they followed the Marina from as far away as they dare onto the A57 towards the motorway. The roads converged courtesy of a roundabout, and Kingy had to close up to ensure they didn't miss which exit the Marina actually took. This put them directly in the Marina's rear view and the feeling of exposure was almost intolerable. The driver would surely see them again and be spooked. The only thing in their favour was that the route they were both on, including turnings, was a general route to the motorway. But if the driver did start to suspect, then he would either do a sudden turn off the main road, or floor the accelerator straight ahead. Either way, it would be covert follow over and overt strike on.

Just as Jackson was going through various attack scenarios in his mind a livered RUC car flew past them from the opposite direction. Jackson looked over his shoulder to see the police car do a U-turn in the road. The cavalry had arrived.

Seconds later it flew past them again, and pulled in behind the Marina, then from up ahead the second RUC patrol came into view. It lit up its blues and twos and slew across the road, blocking their side of it. The patrol car behind the target now edged to the Marina's driver's side effectively cutting off any chance of escaping onto the wrong side of the road. It too activated it emergency equipment.

The Marina came to a halt, and Kingy edged out onto the other side of the road and slid past as four cops poured out of their vehicles, weapons drawn, and put the driver under an armed challenge. Jackson could see that the driver was staring straight ahead with both his hands on top of the steering wheel. He was being compliant.

'Fun time over, we'd better get to Aldergrove, sharpish, we've got a Lieutenant Colonel waiting for us,' Jackson said.

WITH PREJUDICE

Chapter Ten

Hastings was in an office at RAF Aldergrove and let out a huge sigh of relief as he put the phone back in its cradle. The Marina had been subjected to a hard stop and the RUC were jubilant to discover that its driver was none other than Paddy Ryan, the hardline leader of the East Tyrone Brigade.

Among many other atrocities, he was suspected of recently shooting a Catholic woman in the face in front of her children, for the crime of working as a cleaner at a police station. His arrest was an excellent coup. Jackson had done well. SB were over the moon. Ryan would be grilled over several days in custody at Castlereagh interrogation centre in east Belfast. The thought of that alone warmed Hastings's heart. He didn't know whether Special Branch had much in the way of hard evidence against the Provo but that was their job now.

They'd said that the house with no fence had been rented out by the previous owner, which is how it had not been picked up. The renter was indeed a Republican sympathiser, who would shortly be losing his front door, and his liberty, to go along with the missing fence. Hastings's SB intermediary reckoned that the renter would not have been an active member of PIRA, but more likely a clean skin sympathiser, and as such would not be a hardened terrorist and would hopefully be falling over him or herself to cooperate once their options were fully explained. It still didn't explain, however, how the Provos knew where the McDonald family lived. Maybe the renter would know. He hoped so.

He was then aware of an RAF Flight Officer waiting to speak to him. 'Can I help you?'

'Yes sir, well it's just that Lieutenant Colonel De Souza is demanding that the Chinook takes off, he says he's not prepared to wait any longer.'

'The other passengers will be here any minute, I'll have a word if you like.'

The Flight Officer thanked him, and looked relived. Hastings glanced out of the window and could see that the Lieutenant Colonel had now disembarked and was walking up and down the side of the aircraft. He didn't look happy.

Two minutes later, Hastings approached and saw the Colonel come to halt as he took in the approaching Hastings dressed in casual clothes.

'Who the hell are you?' the Colonel opened up with as Hastings came to a stop in front of him.

'Sorry, Lieutenant Colonel De Souza for your delay, but the remaining two passengers will be here any minute.'

'And you are, again?'

'Sorry, sir, that's classified.'

'Well, you don't look very military, I can always tell, so you're a spook then?'

But before Hastings could answer he heard a car approaching fast with tyres screeching as it came to a halt. He rushed over to it to have a quick word with Jackson and King as they got out and grabbed their bergens from the boot. After a quick exchange, Jackson fist pumped the air on hearing the news that it was indeed Paddy Ryan driving the car.

'We'll chat later when you can, should know more by then anyhow, but suffice to say the SB and others will be having a party later, thanks to you two. You'd better get going there is a Lieutenant Colonel over there with his knickers in a right twist.'

Jackson nodded, and Hastings walked with him and King as they approached the front open door of the helicopter. De Souza was stood by it and his chin dropped as they approached.

'You?' De Souza shouted. 'I might have known I was being held up by you, of all people.'

'Sorry about that, Colonel,' Jackson said and they reached the doorway.

'I should have guessed that it would be an impertinent soldier such as you, causing all the trouble.'

'It was an urgent operational matter that couldn't be avoided.'

'Brief me, now Jackson.'

'Sorry sir, its classified.'

WITH PREJUDICE

'I am a Lieutenant Colonel.'

'Sorry, sir, its Top Secret.'

'And what the hell are you doing in Northern Ireland?'

'Just leaving, sir.'

'OK, clever arse, what where you doing in Northern Ireland?'

'Classified, too, I'm afraid.'

'I've just been for an interview for a position within the office of the Commander Land Forces for this province. And if I'm successful, I look forward to parading you on and asking you again.'

'I'd be only too glad to brief you, should you be successful, Colonel. As long as the Commander Land Forces clears you,' Jackson finished with before climbing on board the aircraft. Hastings reckoned that last bit would enrage De Souza, who appeared to be a pompous self-entitled swine. He hadn't realised the CLF's office had a role for a junior field officer. And he saw the look of dread on Jackson's face when he first saw De Souza. He'd have to ask him about that later. There was certainly history between the two.

But his mind was now concentrating on his next task. He was expected back in London tomorrow so he wouldn't have long. But first he headed to an MI5 secure site that even Captain Jackson didn't know existed, right in the centre of Belfast. It was below a newsagent's shop staffed by one of their own.

Forty minutes later Hastings wandered into the shop and perused the paperback stand while Derek - a forty-year-old native of Ulster - served a customer. As soon as the shopper left, Derek nodded at Hastings and they had a brief exchange before they headed through a curtain into the back of the shop. He pulled a rug back to expose wooden floorboards. A second later he heard an electronic buzzer, which he knew Derek was operating from behind the shop counter. A moment after that and a yard square area of the flooring opened up to reveal a stairwell leading down into a cellar. Lights came on as he climbed down and the floor entrance closed behind him.

Below was a large room with several tables, Brent phones, computer desktop terminals and an armoury. It was bombproof, bug proof and with a huge Faraday cage build in around what was once just a cellar. It was impenetrable by any kind of electronic device. He checked his watch, he had thirty minutes to wait, then he could head to the airport. He logged onto one of the computers which looked like a portable television. He mused over the events of the last few days and his chats with Jackson as he waited. He hated not being able to give Jackson the fuller intelligence picture; the more he worked with him, the more he liked him. The unusual pairing they made might work out as London had hoped, after all. He'd expected to face more resentment and resistance from Romeo Troop, but the opposite had proven to be the case.

At one of his chats with Jackson, he had suggested leaking some disinformation within police and Army circles with a specific geographical location as part of it. Jackson had said that his men could monitor it and if the Provos turned up they would know that they had a problem. He liked the idea. Jackson thought like a spook and acted like a soldier. An unusual mix. He'd let the SB finish their 'housecleaning' search first, it may tell them all they needed to know, but if in any doubt, they could revisit Jackson's proposal.

He made himself a quick brew and had just sat back down at his terminal when the screen lit up. He quickly put a headset on and waited.

WITH PREJUDICE

Chapter Eleven

Lynch was given a new Irish passport in the name Mathew West, and travelled from Dublin by ferry to Liverpool with just his backpack as luggage. He then caught a train from Liverpool Lime Street which joined the main West Coast line, and two and a half hours later he arrived at Euston Station, London. The safe house was a fifteen-minute walk from the station. Time enough to make sure that he wasn't being followed. He'd been looking for a tail since he left Ireland, but the stroll on London's busy streets would enable him to lose any tail, if he'd missed one.

The address he was headed to was an old Georgian town house situated on a side street off Tottenham Court Road, in the Fitzrovia district. It was a corner house where the flats covering the first two levels shared a communal door, whereas the converted attic flat, had its entrance on the gable end in the next street. Nice and private. The clean skin who had rented the premises had chosen well. There were two schools of thought: one, locate in the outer suburbs far away from the action, or two, hole up close by. Lynch always preferred the latter option, sooner off the street, quicker one was out of sight. Outer bases did have their own benefits, but you had to make it there safely to enjoy them. By the time Lynch had passed Warren Street tube station he was content he was alone; albeit surrounded by hundreds of people.

He was looking forward to seeing Harry Murphy and Stuart Kelly again. Both very experienced Active Service Unit members, whom he had worked with before. They could crack open the bottle of Bushmills he had brought with him, tonight, as they briefed him fully. All he knew was what his brother-in-law had told him. He didn't even know if the three approved targets were actually in London, though he suspected that they were.

Pleasantries over, he first asked about their estranged leader, John Cairns. Lynch had never met him but his brother-in-law, Sean spoke highly of him.

They were sat around a coffee table in easy chairs in the lounge, and Murphy, a six-foot, thirty-year-old with shocking red hair and a prison complexion answered, 'He's estranged from his wife, as you know.'

Lynch didn't, but nodded.

'And has run up a few debts on the old maintenance front.'

'But that's no reason to remand him in custody. Are you sure they are not on to him?' Lynch asked, suddenly wondering if Counter Terrorism were watching them as they sat here.

'Absolutely,' Kelly jumped in with. Quite forcibly, Lynch noted. Obviously, very loyal towards their leader. Which could be a good or a bad thing.

'He's just let things slide too long, that's all,' Kelly said, and was on his feet as he spoke. He was of similar age to Murphy but with a normal build, and only five foot seven at most. An excitable short arse, Lynch remembered. Kelly pulled his hands through his jet-black stock of thick Irish hair as he explained. Murphy just sat back in his chair and let his partner take over.

Apparently, as Cairns's missus had re-located to the UK mainland from Dublin, he had thought that he could ignore the letters. Different jurisdiction. This, Lynch knew was true. But the unpaid child maintenance had become huge, and the debts had then become fines, and the fines had become non-payment of fine arrest warrants. Still, not normally a problem as Cairns - an Irish national lived in Donegal in southern Ireland, close to the border with Ulster. But before being deployed to London the eejit should have declared his debts to his next in line in PIRA. Lynch knew why he hadn't, he'd have lost the command of the ASU. Which, incidentally, was his first. And probably his last now.

The inevitable had happened. He got stopped for speeding and the cop giving him a ticket checked his details and this flagged him up as wanted. The local magistrates probably realised any punitive sentence or payment order wouldn't be effective on a foreign national, so they wrote his debts off in exchange for a nice cell for the next six weeks. Not only could their operation not wait six weeks, but Cairns was marked now.

'Why didn't he use his fake identity?' he asked them both.

'What you mean these?' Murphy said, scooping up a passport and driving licence from the coffee table, with obvious sarcasm in his voice.

WITH PREJUDICE

'He no doubt left them on purpose, keeping a safe passage out protected,' Kelly jumped in with, again very defensively. Lynch decided not to criticise Cairns, who had clearly made an error of judgement. Protect yourself now and worry about later, later would have been his way. But he needed to keep them both on board. They had a job to do. Cairns would be out in three or four weeks with good behaviour, plenty of time to consider what excuses he could come up with before the Army Council in due course. Though if he were Cairns, he'd kick off inside and make sure he did the full six weeks. More chance of the Army Council calming down by then. 'And we are sure that his real status is unknown?'

'Absolutely,' Kelly said, though Lynch didn't know how he could be certain. He started to feel exposed and instinctively walked to the window, where the thin translucent curtains were pulled to. He peeped through the gap, but couldn't see any vans or temporary workman's huts or suchlike outside.

As if reading his mind, Murphy said, 'No worries, Brendan, we binned the safe house straight away as a precaution. Bleached everywhere and took the binbags with us. This is our back-up place. We've only been here since yesterday. Booked into a hotel first and spent a day watching this place to make sure it was sound.'

Lynch smiled and nodded. He liked Murphy, he was the switched on one of the two of them. Moving things along, he asked, 'Tell me what the three approved targets are, I've been dying to know since Sean sent me over here.'

'Probably easier if we show you. Stuart, do you want to get the van?'

'Aye, give me five,' Kelly said, and headed towards the staircase.

Lynch had no preconceived ideas whether the three targets were actually suitable or not, he'd reserve judgement. He knew that Murphy was an excellent bombmaker with a chemistry degree. He knew that they had a lock-up in East London which a clean skin had slowly filled with Ammonium Nitrate fertilizer over a period of time. Bought at farm suppliers and other rural wholesalers; but always done a bit at a time in amounts small enough so as not to attract attention. They had plenty of diesel and oxidizing agents together with blasting caps and fuse wires. They could make a substantial car bomb. He'd also been briefed that they had a hide in Epping Forest in Essex with semi-automatic weapons. It was his job to weigh up the targets, pick one and then decide the most effective way to attack it with the resources they had to hand.

He trusted Murphy implicitly; he'd worked with him in the preparation of the Brighton bombing the year before which so nearly cut the head off the UK's snake leader. *They had to be lucky all the time, PIRA had only to be lucky once.* And although neither ended up on the actual deployment, he'd rated Murphy then, and rated him more so now. As for Kelly, he was a good lad, keen, loyal but with limitations.

The van drew up with Kelly at the wheel, Murphy and Lynch climbed in the back via a side sliding door. The sides of the van had blacked out windows, but they could see clearly out from the inside.

The first target was the BT Tower on Cleveland Street W1. Murphy said that Cairns had suggested a car bomb with a an apparently broken-down car with two flat tyres. They didn't expect to be able to bring the tower itself down, but it was glass fronted so would be extensively damaged. Lynch didn't comment.

The second target was the British Museum on Great Russell Street. It had a huge spread of classically designed buildings with gothic architecture and huge entrances with tall white columns. Plenty of scope to attack with a car bomb crashing into something, and then they could remote detonate as the police arrived. It was clear to Lynch that Murphy liked this one due to the detail he went into, and that the tactical suggestions were obviously his. Lynch quite liked this one, too; it would be a real stab at the heart of the Brits. And with lots of scope for various approaches to attack from.

The third target really appealed to Lynch, in principle. It would be an attack at the heart of the British Government itself. He knew that the Palace of Westminster would be nigh on impossible to attack, due to the high security, made even more so after the Brighton bombing. This was why they had chosen The Grand

WITH PREJUDICE

Hotel in Brighton in the first place. If they couldn't attack Thatcher in her ivory tower, then an attack during their conference season was a far safer bet. He just wished they'd had their conference last year at Blackpool. He couldn't stand Blackpool and would have loved to have the opportunity to blow up the Imperial Hotel there with Thatcher and her Cabinet in it.

But Cairns's choice had been thought out on a similar line of thinking. Forget Westminster, House of Common, House of Lords, go for where they go afterwards. There was a bar close to the Westminster Parliament called Black Rod's Rest, where all the la-de-da underlings and many MPs with their secretary mistresses would go to drink wine and talk shite. The boys had done many recces of the place, and reckoned that two of them with automatic machine pistols could cause absolute carnage in sixty seconds, and then out and away. A car idling outside wouldn't be approached in such a short time period. Apparently, the place was stuffed to the rafters on Friday afternoons. The House of Commons rises at 2.30 p.m., whereafter they all went drinking and shagging before returning to their constituencies the following day. Four p.m. would be an ideal time. And all three locations were close to their safehouse.

Lynch had to admit, even though he was in favour of bombs, not least due to their dramatic headline grabbing nature, and not to mention the anticipated casualty rate. He thought the bar close to Westminster was an excellent idea, with an even greater casualty rate potential.

'I've got to say, I'm not a fan of the first but like the second and absolutely love the third target,' Lynch said to Murphy as they headed back, but loud enough so that Kelly behind the wheel could hear him, too.

'That's pretty much in line with what we were thinking,' Murphy said.

'The bar has always been my favourite; up close and personal,' Kelly shouted above the van's revving engine.

'Are we going for the third option, Brendan?' Murphy asked.

Lynch was dying to say yes, but instead said, 'I'd love to, but I've actually got something else in mind. I'll run it past you both back at the flat. See what you think?'

Murphy nodded, but Lynch could see disappointment on his face. He quickly added, 'Just an idea I want to explore with you both, nothing is definite until it's talked through properly and decided fully.' This seemed to placate Murphy. Lynch was glad, he needed to keep him in particular on board. But he also knew his ideas were fairly fixed, he was never one for too much debate.

WITH PREJUDICE

Chapter Twelve

Jackson hadn't expected to be back in Ulster after just 24 hours, especially given the target. But he was grateful to Hastings, and it also proved that Hastings knew a lot more about their background than he would ever know of Hastings's. Geordie Crompton had volunteered to come with him, which was good of him, but given that he had a rare 24-hour pass to visit his home in Newcastle, Jackson declined. In fact, the other two had also put their names forward, and he had gratefully accepted Mark Harris. He may be tone deaf - according to the others - but Jackson had never seen anyone play a sniper rifle like Harris. He was only in his mid-twenties, but as good a shot as any Canadian: and they were the experts. Not that the US Army would agree with that, but they were. Often smaller military countries within NATO would pick a specialism to excel in to make up for their lack of size, and the Canadians certainly did that. But Harris was as good, if not better. He was young and athletically built in a Bruce Lee sort of way, and although he didn't do Kung Fu, he was a black belt in Judo. He'd also been decorated for his long-range kills during the Falklands Conflict a couple of years' earlier.

They were both sat in the back of a Chinnock, on their own this time, as they headed towards RAF Aldergrove. Jackson thanked Harris for giving up his time off. He also asked him when he'd last managed to get any range practice in with his preferred rifle of choice. Jackson knew this was a NATO Winchester .308 bolt action.

'Spookily, only yesterday. I thought I would take the opportunity to get my sharpness back with this bad boy,' Harris answered as he patted the long nylon bag at his feet.

'Excellent.'

'Who's the target?'

Even though it was very noisy in the back, Jackson nodded in the direction of the flight crew, and Harris nodded back his understanding. In truth, they probably couldn't hear them, but he wanted to delay any further discussions until they were sat down with Hastings.

An hour later they were in the briefing room at their barracks within the barracks at Lisburn. Hastings was waiting for them and seemed in a lighter mood than when they'd last seen him. Perhaps, his quick visit to Thames House had gone well. 'You seem happy?' Jackson opened with as they took their seats at the ops table.

'Always happy to get away from London,' Hastings replied.

Jackson wasn't entirely sure what his answer meant.

'Glad you've brought Mark with you, an excellent choice.'

Harris just smiled a reply at Hastings.

'In fact, had London had their way, they'd have left you at Hereford for this one,' Hastings said, aiming his remark at Jackson.

'I don't doubt it, and for this opportunity, I thank you deeply,' Jackson replied. He could see the look of surprise on Harris's face, it was time to give him the backstory before Hastings briefed them on the current situation. But from his earlier phone conversation with Hastings, it was obvious he knew all about it, so he faced Harris.

Jackson leaned back and started. Five years' earlier in 1980, before Harris had joined the regiment, Jackson had been a sergeant deployed into Ulster. Initially, they were there to work with 14 Intelligence Company to do surveillance and gather intel on known IRA targets. He was part of a four-man team who were all CROPs trained. The acronym stood for Covert Rural Observation Post. He had been part of a two-man OP dug into fields surrounding a farmhouse on the outskirts of Londonderry. They'd been doing twelve-hour shifts with the other two from their unit. It just so happened that Jackson's sidekick was also his best mate. Trooper Steve Constantine, who was also a ten-year veteran of the regiment. In fact, they had come through Selection together, which was where they had first met.

The intel told them that an occupant at the farm was an active PIRA member from the Southern Command, brought north of the border to complete making an IED. The bombmaker was called

WITH PREJUDICE

Michael Raffety and he had yet to appear. Members of 14 Intel had already done a Covert Method of Entry in a large barn at the rear of the premises and confirmed the presence of a large amount of Ammonium Nitrate in the form of commercial fertilizer together with fuel and oxidizing agents. Only missing were the detonators.

The brief was that as soon as Raffety arrived and entered the barn, they were to attack. They didn't want to give Raffety time to put the constituent parts together. They had enough to move in and arrest him. He was to be taken alive unless he forced the issue. The potential intel he would have would be significant. Jackson and Constantine had not long taken over the OP from the other two who had done the night watch when it all went to rat shit. Raffety was seen *leaving* the premises in an unmentioned vehicle on Southern Irish plates. No one had put him inside the premises. He must have arrived during the night. It would later prove highly embarrassing for their two mates, and a very unusual cock-up, but Jackson knew how tricky an OP in pitch darkness can be to maintain. Even with night vision goggles, which in turn came with their own limitations, such as a narrow field of view.

A surveillance team which had been plotted up with them throughout, scrambled to follow Raffety, everyone believing that this could be game on. And as they had no intel as to who or what the actual target was, it was imperative to stay on Rafferty. However, he drove straight down the A5 to Strabane and crossed over the border back into Southern Ireland. They arranged a pull by the Gardai but he was clean and let go. No one knew what was going on. Then a Land Rover left the premises, Jackson and Constantine had to scramble from their OP to their vehicle, to try and get on the motor while other surveillance cars were being scrambled to join them. It was 6 a.m., and only just coming light. They never saw the Land Rover again.

Thirty minutes after the vehicle left the farm an alarm went off at a car dealership on the outskirts of Londonderry. A few minutes later, a coded call was received by the RUC warning that a bomb had been placed at the dealership as it was 'guilty' of supplying vehicles for use by the RUC.

53

'Me and Six-Seven headed there with all speed,' Jackson said. 'Something was seriously amiss.'

'Who is Six-Seven?' Harris asked.

Jackson apologised and explained. Constantine when training in the Killing House at Hereford, always got a perfect score. There would be seven potential targets; six Tangos and one hostage. All mixed up each time. Steve, without exception, always slotted the six terrorist pop-ups and never shot the hostage one. Infuriated, the Directing Staff tried and tried, but never beat him. They eventually, changed the numbers involved, but by then his nickname had stuck. 6.7, as in six out of seven, correctly, every time.

Harris nodded his understanding and then asked, 'But why the warning on this occasion? You'd have thought they would have let the alarm bring the cops into a booby trap. Either with a timer or a long command wire out the back of the premises.'

'That's exactly what Steve and I thought. We shouted for the RUC to put a containment on it until bomb disposal arrived.'

'And did they?'

'They did, but it still didn't explain the warning,' Jackson answered before carrying on his tale.

They arrived at the scene and were joined shortly thereafter by a Royal Logistics Corps unit, which quickly discovered a holdall left in the foyer of the premises. It had a small, but viable device therein. They quickly made it safe but commented that it would probably have only taken out the reception area at most. This just added to the enigma of it all. Jackson and Constantine stopped the RUC going in to search for clues, they wanted a quick look first. Nothing added up.

'Maybe the whole thing was a distraction for something else that for whatever reason didn't happen?' Harris offered.

'You are right and wrong,' Jackson answered before continuing. He explained that they took the keyholder with them for a cautious recce before the cops came in with their size tens. Past the reception area was a kitchen which then linked to the main car garage and workshop. Everything seemed in order. The keyholder left and Jackson and Constantine followed. As they walked through the canteen area, Jackson led his mate, and was suddenly aware that Steve was no longer behind him as he reached the reception area.

Jackson turned to see what was holding his mate up and looked along the short corridor which connected the reception to the kitchenette. He could see Steve stood by one of the three tables, looking down at something.

"What is it?" Jackson recalled shouting.

"This, check this out," Constantine had replied smiling as he picked up a magazine from the table top.

In that horrible instant, it all made sense. Jackson could see by the front cover that the magazine was a men's girlie mag.

"Wonder what the centrefold is like?" Constantine had said.

Jackson screamed "NO," but never got the chance to add DON'T OPEN IT, as his mate did just that, and in so doing connected the circuit. The 'letter bomb' blew his mate's hands off and took most of his face with them. The blast knocked Jackson off his feet, but he was otherwise unhurt. Those dirty Provos bastards had got what they wanted. They must have reckoned the attending RUC would have trodden very carefully on arrival. Doing it this way ensured their arrival en masse followed by the murder of a security force member rather than just blowing up a few cars.

Tears welled up in Jackson's eyes as the vivid memories flooded back. It took his mate three agonising days to die.

'Did you ever get them?' Harris asked.

'Raffety the bombmaker was south of the border and running free. Intel suggested that the PIRA man from the farm was the driver of the Land Rover and probably planted the devices.'

'Did SB get him?' Harris asked.

'Yes, but the oxidizers from the farm must have left with Raffety. Probably well hidden inside his vehicle along with the detonators, too.'

'The Gardai?' Harris asked.

'You never know. But if nothing was obvious, they probably felt that they did not have "probable cause" to rip his motor apart.'

'What about the other guy? Harris asked.

'It's not illegal to have fertilizer and fuel on a farm. And with no other evidence against the Land Rover man, he was eventually released no charge. But apparently, he just grinned at the detectives throughout the many interviews and kept repeating "what a shame only one was killed."'

Harris shook his head in disbelief.

'They couldn't prove that he was an IRA member, so couldn't even charge him with that. He said he was a sympathiser and that Raffety was just an old friend.'

'And that is what brings us here today, gentlemen,' Hastings added. 'It's payback time.'

Chapter Thirteen

Hastings then took over to bring them up to date. The Land Rover man, in the following five years had been suspected of committing many terrorist atrocities. The planting of at least two further devices killing thirty-one and injuring many more. He was also suspected of at least fifteen shootings, killing a further eleven. Never caught by the RUC or SB, and with extraordinarily little intelligence on him.

'Why is that?' Harris asked.

'A good question. He has been extremely well protected by the Provos and is well liked among the Republican communities at large. I'm not sure why,' Hastings replied.

'What has changed?' Jackson asked.

'Yesterday, a Protestant mother of two was shot and killed in front of her seven-year-old twin boys on her way home from church in Omagh, County Tyrone.'

'My God, that's awful. I've not seen the news,' Harris said.

'Nor me, and it's a new low by anyone's standards,' Jackson added.

'There has been a news blackout for 24-hours due to intel, but it's starting to leak out. You can't keep a story this terrible quiet for long. And it gets worse.'

'Go on,' Harris said.

'The shooter was overheard saying as the young mother lay dying, "That's the last Proddy dog bairn you'll have".'

Jackson knew this bit from his earlier brief on the phone from Hastings but hearing it out loud again made it even harder to stomach. A moment of quiet descended before Hastings continued.

'So shocked are both sides of the sectarian divide that the RUC hotline has been ringing off the hook. Most of it conjecture and naming anyone and everyone as being responsible. However, we at Five have received more credible intel.'

It was this bit that Jackson didn't know; he was all ears.

'Apparently, the assassination was not authorised by the Northern Command or the Army Council of the PIRA. And the intel we have received is two-fold: one, naming the gunman, and two, that PIRA would not retaliate against any security force action against the induvial.'

'They don't want tarnishing with it,' Harris said.

'Exactly,' Hastings answered.

Intrigued where Hastings had received his information from, Jackson asked, 'Has this come from PIRA itself? Get us to do their dirty work against a hitherto well-liked Provo?'

Hastings paused before answering, 'I don't believe so.'

Jackson wasn't convinced, but didn't want to rile Hastings, not as he'd let Jackson in on this op, and given the personal nature of it, he probably shouldn't have done so. Instead, he asked, 'OK, so what's the update?'

The shooter is set to start attacking RUC uniform patrol officers and his first mark is personal.

'Who is it?' Harris asked.

'Constable Ian Dune. The one who was attacked recently in Ballygawley.'

'The one who shot Brian Ryan; the nephew of the guy we followed and had arrested?' Jackson asked.

'The very same. This guy is Paddy Ryan's brother and has temporarily taken over East Tyrone Brigade since Paddy's arrest.'

'So, he's Brian Ryan's father?' Harris said.

'The very same and the Land Rover driver. He is Billy Ryan, and the intel is that he is after revenge for the slaying of his son.'

***

Several hours later, Jackson and Harris were plotted up on the outskirts of Ballygawley. It was approaching 10 p.m. and Constable Ian Dune was about to start his nightshift, which was his first since the shooting. He had apparently chosen to come back to work sooner than advised as he had told his superiors "If I don't come straight back, I may never do." Jackson had debated with Hastings whether they should warn the RUC of the threat. But after much consideration, they decided that if they did, the RUC would move the constable and Billy Ryan, even if he showed, would be guilty of nothing. According to Hastings's intermediary at SB, they may well know it was Billy Ryan who had slain that poor woman in Omagh, but they were yet to find a shred of evidence. All the witnesses had failed to pick out Billy Ryan's mugshot. Eyewitnesses were a rare commodity in Ulster. Jackson could only sympathise with the police difficulty in ever bringing prosecutions. But if they caught the monster in the process of committing a further act, then things would become vastly different.

Hastings was back at the barracks manning the base station. Jackson and Harris were about to split into two vehicles and were going to follow Constable Dune as he went about his duties. The original intel was that Ryan would attempt a shot from distance, which was why Jackson had chosen Harris to accompany him. But they had spent the last hour covertly searching the field opposite the police station and there was no sign of Ryan or a hide. His chance for a long-range attack would only be as Dune arrived in his own car before commencing his tour of duty, and that ship had just sailed.

At 10.15 p.m. Dune drove out of the police station in his armoured Land Rover. He would be safe whilst in the vehicle. Hastings was monitoring the police frequencies so that they would know in advance when Dune was called to a job. This allowed Jackson and Harris to follow from a discrete distance. Harris had voiced their joint concerns about an RPG attack but Hastings said the intel had ruled that out. He was to be shot. Again, Jackson wondered how Hastings could have such specific intel and have so much faith in its accuracy. But nevertheless, they went along with it.

They were conducting a rare and difficult form of surveillance. They were neither in front nor behind Dune, but parallel. Jackson always on Dune's east side, and Harris on the west. This way, the Provos would not know they were there. But they would have to move in as soon as Dune prepared to leave the vehicle, which Hastings could tip them off about, as Dune went about his duties. There were vulnerabilities to the plan, which after the Constable's first stop they sought to reduce. Harris quickly slapped a tracker on the police car. Every time it stopped, whether attending a job or not, Jackson and Harris would close in.

The first hour passed without event. The constable attended three calls from the public all verified prior to his deployment. All were minor events and passed off without incident. Dune then drove around the town a few times, clearly checking that everything looked as it should, and once satisfied, he parked up by a Farm Cottage holiday let, on Dungannon Road. A quite country route surrounded by fields.

Then Hastings came in with an Intel update: this was not just an assassination attempt, but a kidnap, too. Ryan wanted to torture Dune at his leisure before killing him. If Jackson had been in any doubt that Hastings had a 'live' source, all such suspicions were now long gone.

WITH PREJUDICE

Chapter Fourteen

The next update was even more specific: Billy Ryan and one other were on their way. This had to be coming from PIRA itself. They were being used, but Jackson didn't mind if he gave him the chance to avenge in part the slaughter of Steve Constantine, he'd take it all day long. And he would be eternally grateful to Hastings for letting him in on it. Hastings also told them that he had SB on stand-by, to be used as and when required. They were formulating a plan, but firstly needed to keep Dune static and safely in his armoured vehicle. Hastings had reaffirmed that no heavy armament was to be used in the attack. The added news about SB gave Jackson an idea.

As requested, Hastings got onto his SB go-between, and Dune was firstly asked to confirm his location and then told to stay there as SB were about in the area and wanted a word with him about the previous attack. They were on their way to him. This was fed into Dune's sergeant via SB.

Harris set himself up, covering all eventualities in the field opposite where the police Land Rover was parked. Jackson plotted up behind the holiday let cottage, which looked unoccupied. It was probably why Dune had chosen to park there. Jackson had a visual of the rear of the police car and a limited view to the east and west along Dungannon Road. Now that this was to be a kidnap attempt, Jackson was beginning to wish he had Geordie Crompton and 'Tickets Please' King with him. But the ability to adapt and face increased odds were the SAS's bread and butter.

Long minutes passed and no further updates were forthcoming from Hastings. The ASU were on their way so Jackson didn't expect anything further now. They would be reliant on their own observations and instinct.

Then Harris using the call sign Three Alpha shouted in Jackson's ear. An incoming vehicle from the west. It was quickly confirmed to be a taxi. Could be a clever approach so as not to put Dune ill at ease. Jackson checked his weapon and was on full alert now. Then Harris reported that the taxi was slowing down. Jackson quietly alighted from his vehicle and crept closer towards the rear of the idling police car.

'The car is coming to a halt in front of the friendly's vehicle, and the front passenger door is opening,' Harris said in Jackson's ear.

This was it.

'A youth in his twenties has got out, no weapons apparent,' Harris added.

Jackson took up a position at the rear corner of the cottage and could see the youth coming into view as he walked up the drive towards the police car.

'He's approaching the driver's side and is putting his right hand inside his coat pocket. I have him clear in my sights, stand-by,' Harris said.

'Yes, yes. I have his legs in my sights,' Jackson whispered into his radio transceiver. He knew that the first sign of a weapon being drawn would be their tacit order to engage.

'WAIT,' Harris said.

Jackson acknowledged and eased the pressure on his sidearm's trigger as he did so.

'The youth has just passed a note to Dune…wait further,' Harris added. A short pause, and then, 'The youth is back towards the taxi and is in, in, in to the front passenger seat, and the vehicle is pulling away from the kerb, continuing straight on. Instructions?'

'Leave it, record details, we can follow it up later. Stay on the friendly,' Jackson replied as he tried to make sense of what was happening. He ran back to his vehicle and threw his kit on the back seat. It was parked down a side track just to the north of the cottage. He was glad he did so, as seconds later, Harris announced movement on the police car. He was driving off, north, and at speed. Moments later, Jackson saw the car pass the end of his track. As he arrived at its junction with Dungannon Road, he could see the police car's tail lights in the distance, and in his rear view he could see Harris fast approaching on foot. 'Come on, come on,' he said out loud as Harris neared. Moments later Harris dived in through the open rear door across the back seats together with his kit and Jackson floored the accelerator. He shot off so fast that

WITH PREJUDICE

momentum closed the rear door for him and Harris climbed over the central divide to join him in the front.

'The sneaky bastards,' Harris said.

'The kid probably didn't even know what the note said,' Jackson replied, and then quickly brought Hastings up to date over the radio, who said he'd get SB to go straight to the local taxi office and follow it up. But what was worrying Jackson, was what was in the note. Whatever it said, it had prompted and immediate reaction by Dune. He asked Hastings to find out where Dune lived and if he had any family living in the area. He then concentrated on his driving. Dungannon Road soon became Ballygawley road which soon reached the A4 from where Dune could go anywhere. They hadn't caught him up, he was clearly driving fast. Then he remembered the tracker that Harris had manged to put on the vehicle, thank God for that. Harris took the receiving device from his kit and worked the dials.

As they reached the A4, Jackson shouted, 'Which way?'

'Got it, go east, towards Dungannon, but put your foot down, I'm losing the signal.'

'What do you think I'm doing,' Jackson answered as he powered up the slip road to join the A4 eastbound. They were doing eighty as they reached the main carriageway.

Hastings came back on to say that Dune's widowed mother lived on her own in Dungannon. Harris confirmed that Dune's vehicle had just left the A4 at Granville and was now on the A45 towards Dungannon. Hastings gave them the address and advised that SB were five minutes away.

Four minutes later the address came into view. A suburban semi-detached with a long-raised drive. Parked on it was the police Land Rover. Empty. Parked across the bottom of the drive was a Ford Cortina saloon. At first, Jackson wondered if it was SB, but a second later it sped away from the kerb. A driver with two men in the rear; one wearing a police uniform. Jackson picked up the follow and advised Hastings, who said he get SB to check on the mother. But the house was in darkness, so Dune probably hadn't got as far as the front door. Hopefully, they hadn't harmed her, just used her existence as bait to ensure Dune's attendance.

The Cortina sped through the outskirts of Dungannon and headed south on the A29 towards Armagh - bandit country. Jackson tried to keep at a distance that didn't give the game away too early. It would be safer and easier to initiate a contact once away from the built-up area. And as soon as they were, it became obvious that the follow had now turned into a pursuit.

As they headed towards a town called Moy, Jackson saw the rear seat person next to Dune lean out of the window and point a MAC10 machine pistol at them. 'Incoming,' he warned Harris, but knew he would have seen it too. He also knew how pointless such a weapon would be aimed at a fast-moving target at fifty plus yards behind. But as the gunman opened fire his body jolted, sending the salvo wildly towards the side of the road. Dune had pushed him. Brave man. Jackson could see what looked like the butt of the weapon, or perhaps an elbow then ram into the side of Dune's head for his trouble.

But more importantly, he could see that Harris was ready, as he wound down the passenger window and leaned out. He shouted back at Jackson, 'Bit nearer if you can.'

Jackson accelerated to within fifteen yards of the rear of the Cortina, which was starting to lose traction on some of the bends, as Harris made ready with his second weapon of choice, a Heckler and Koch MP5 sub machine gun. The road straightened out and street lights appeared as they headed towards a built-up area once more. It was now or never.

As he thought this, he heard Harris let rip. He'd aimed at the rear tyres and had managed to shred both of them. The car went into a dancing weave from left to right before the driver lost total control and the motor spun violently around on itself until it came to an abrupt halt in the road, facing back towards them. Jackson stamped on the brakes and they came to a halt ten yards away.

Jackson and Harris both alighted in a flash, the many hours of drilled-in training paying off as both took up a firing position behind their open car doors as close to the inner hinges as they could. Using the car's body and wings for added protection.

The unknown gunman in the rear dragged Dune out of their car as the driver also stumbled out. Their haphazard egress compared to Jackson and Harris's practiced vehicle exit bought them the vital few moments they needed.

As the rear seat gunman started to orientate himself and point his weapon at Dune's head, Jackson fired two rounds in quick succession from his Walther P5 semi-automatic pistol and dropped the gunman. Both rounds tore through his side torso which he had left exposed.

The driver stood facing them, momentarily stunned, but then he grabbed Dune by the arm. A near-by street light clearly illuminated him. It was Billy Ryan. Without doubt. Jackson's long-time nemesis. As Ryan steadied himself and pointed a pistol at Dune's head, Jackson was aware that Harris had disappeared around the blind side of their car, on its nearside.

'I'm going to walk away backwards now with this copper as my hostage. If you make any move towards me, I'll take his head off and run at you and to hell with it.'

Jackson didn't answer. But was well aware that with every retreating step, Ryan was becoming out of pistol range. Plus, the target was getting smaller. Ryan was better practiced than his gunman mate had been as he kept himself perfectly in line behind the constable.

'Lower your weapon or I'll do him now and take my chances with you soldier boy.'

Jackson knew he had to buy time, and quickly, as the distance between them extended. He slowly lowered his gun, appearing to be compliant, but kept hold of it.

'And you can tell your mate, wherever he is, to do the s—' Ryan started to say.

But the terrorist was interrupted by the loud crack of a Winchester .308. In the melee, Harris had taken up a prone position on the grass verge to their left. Initially, out of sight by virtue of the terrorist's car, but as Ryan slowly walked Dune backwards, he would have come into view. A clever tactic as Ryan's total attention had been straight ahead of him by virtue of Jackson.

Harris was effectively at a 45-degree angle to Ryan and as Jackson heard the discharge, he saw Ryan's head explode into a pink mist. He dropped to the floor before he had chance to pull his own trigger. Poor old Constable Dune fainted, but was unhurt.

Jackson walked over to the terrorist's headless cadaver, looked down and said, 'That's for Steve.'

He was then joined by Harris and they helped Dune back to his feet.

WITH PREJUDICE

Chapter Fifteen

Back at the safe house in Fitzrovia, it was obvious to Lynch that both Murphy and Kelly favoured the third option. The Black Rod's Rest pub. And he had to admit, but for his ulterior motive, he would have willingly agreed with them. But he knew he would have to be careful now, he couldn't share all his reasons just yet. He needed them to agree to his suggestion, it was critical to his wider plan. He praised both of them for all their hard work, and the selection of three excellent targets. This seemed to please them, especially, Kelly who reminded Lynch of a loyal puppy who adored his master's praise. He could use that to his advantage, especially, if Murphy proved more reluctant as Lynch surmised what he wanted to do. Murphy was the cleverer of the two. The thinker, the expert bombmaker.

'OK, lads, here's what I suggest to you as an alternative,' Lynch said, and then gave just the headlines at this stage.

He explained that the US Foreign Secretary Mitchell Wilson Jr. was doing a flying visit to London in a couple of days' time. It was a 24-hour stopover en route to a meeting of European Foreign Secretaries in Paris. He was to attend a reception at the US Embassy in Grosvenor Square, Mayfair, followed by a breakfast meeting at 10 Downing Street the following day before heading across the Channel. A timely opportunity.

'But for this popping up, I would have definitely gone with the pub target,' Lynch added.

'We'll never get anywhere near, security will be massive, and anyway, the Americans are our allies. Well, the forty or so million of them who claim Irish descent, are,' Murphy said.

'And are you forgetting the hundreds of thousands of dollars that those would-be Irish Americans donate to The Cause every year,' Kelly added.

'The US Foreign Secretary isn't the actual target. And you are correct, we would get nowhere near to his vehicle, which is armour plated in any event,' Lynch said.

Both Murphy and Kelly looked at him nonplussed.

'But we can take out some of the UK cops on motorbikes escorting.'

'I'm not sure, how and I'm not sure, why?' if I'm being honest,' Kelly said.

'In fact, why don't we hit the pub in Westminster as the American arrives; it'll give us massive coverage with US film crews here,' Murphy suggested.

Lynch had to smile, but for his real reasons Murphy's suggestion would have been excellent. 'I'll deal with the why in a bit. But the how is easier than you might think. The cortege surrounding Wilson Jr. will be long. It will involve outriders going ahead to close off junctions to allow the convoy to pass uninterrupted,' Lynch said.

'So the advance outriders will be an easier target?' Murphy said.

'Exactly, we will be nowhere near Wilson himself, but any attack on the convoy as a whole will appear as an attack on the Foreign Secretary himself.'

'Still not sure as to why? But I'm getting the attack possibilities on the forward police motorcyclists' bit,' Murphy said.

He was warming to the idea Lynch thought. He then explained the how fully. They knew that as soon as the US politician had landed, he would be escorted direct to their Embassy in London. So, they knew the where, and roughly the when. Opposite the Embassy was the Grosvenor Square park. Lynch was an accomplished motorcyclist himself, which is where he'd first got the outrider idea. The park would be policed, but he could ride across the park quickly as the convoy neared, with Murphy on the back, they could attack a couple of cops on bikes who would be static, to allow free vehicle access to the Embassy. Then they could scramble back across the park to Kelly waiting in a motor, and away.

Murphy and Kelly went quiet as they considered what Lynch had just outlined to them. He took the opportunity to break the atmosphere and went into the kitchen and returned with a bottle of Bushmills whiskey and three mugs. He put the items down on the coffee table and poured three healthy shots. He sat back down and took a sip of his as the silent deliberation continued.

WITH PREJUDICE

Murphy was the first to speak, 'OK, it's feasible. We can shoot a couple of cops anywhere, but I can see by being linked to this particular convoy it will massively multiply the publicity effect. But why the American convoy? It could backfire on us if - as you suggest - if the US assumes that their man was the target.'

Kelly added, 'Too risky, and in any event the Army Council will never agree it.'

Now it would become tricky, Lynch knew. He took a gulp of his drink and paused to choose his next words. 'The Army Council are not aware of the plan.'

'What?' Murphy and Kelly managed to say in unison.

'Nor will they ever know.'

'And how do think that will happen? Plus, you haven't told us the why, yet?' Murphy said.

Lynch could tell by the body language on display that they were becoming increasingly agitated. He didn't answer the last question but pushed on with his own, aimed directly at Murphy. 'Can you make a pipe bomb?'

Murphy rocked back in his chair with a pained expression. Lynch knew the answer. He knew that Murphy's skills were far greater than a simple pipe bomb. He also knew that PIRA had long ago moved on to the far more effective, and sophisticated devices they now used.

'I don't get it,' Murphy eventually said. Adding, 'Pipe bombs are low yield, low effect and mainly used by those Loyalist scumbags who occasionally irritate us.'

'But could you knock one up to throw at the bike cops?' Lynch pushed on with.

'Well, yes, piece of piss, but a MAC10 machine pistol would be far easier to use. And we have two, as to know.'

It was time for Lynch to explain part of his rationale, but he'd leave the deeper strategy until much later. 'So, if we tossed a pipe bomb at the outriders, who are part of the convoy escorting the US Secretary of State for Foreign Affairs whilst in London; what would the police initially suspect?'

A further pause ensured, so Lynch topped up their three mugs. Kelly looked like he would never get it, but Lynch saw Murphy's eyes open wide in realisation.

'It would look like a Loyalist terror attack on the yanks using their crude, limited explosives.'

'Exactly, and in so doing, no US citizens are harmed. Further US outrage across the pond will only add to the coffers aimed at us, and our Army Council will also think it is the Loyalist UDA's so-called Ulster Freedom Fighters or the Ulster Volunteer Force who are responsible.'

'I know you are holding back more,' Murphy said.

'I am, but I promise I will fully level with you both once you are fully behind me.'

'I must admit, I do like the thought of killing cops and blaming the Proddy dogs,' Murphy added.

'And what of our planned operation?' Kelly asked.

'We can just say we have shelved it for now due the heightened security following the *'Loyalist'* attack on the US.'

Kelly nodded, and Lynch could see Murphy was grinning now. He was sure that once Murphy had signed up, Kelly would follow.

Then Kelly surprised Lynch with the depth of his next question. 'But Loyalists would never kill Brit cops.'

Murphy, turned to face Kelly, and stared to nod.

'That's true. So, what if we made it look like a misfired, botched attempt on the politician's vehicle,' Lynch replied. Noting that he should not underestimate Kelly.

'Aye, and we can even shout something like, "Stop funding the IRA," or suchlike,' Murphy added.

Lynch nodded his agreement and smiled. He had them onside.

WITH PREJUDICE

Chapter Sixteen

Jackson and Harris decided to stay at the barracks due to the lateness of the hour and hitch a lift back to Hereford the following day. Jackson couldn't wait to visit Steve's widow and give her the good news. But he decided on a phone call first instead once he was back on the mainland. He was aware that she had remarried and he didn't want to cause her any problems just turning up at the door.

Hastings said he wanted a catch up with him before they departed the following day, now was not the time as they cracked a few beers. He said he'd see him before they left for RAF Aldergrove.

They'd probably sunk more ale than they should have, as Jackson was struggling to clear his head the following morning. He'd been up an hour and the paracetamols he'd taken had only taken the edge off. Harris was still in his pit when Hastings walked in. They both pulled up a chair at the ops table.

'I keep forgetting to ask you how your calf is?' Hastings said.

'Healing nicely, thanks, though it's feeling a bit tight and is throbbing a bit this morning.'

'Didn't slow you down last night?'

'Na, it's amazing what adrenalin can do. It's just the day after when the aches and pains kick in. But that's normal after any combat, with or without an injury.'

Hastings made the coffees and then they caught up properly, firstly going through the events of the previous evening, though they had quickly done the Surveillance Log last night before the lager flowed.

'Pity we couldn't have taken Ryan alive,' Hastings said, and narrowed his eyes slightly as did so.

'I know what you are probably thinking, Bert, but he really gave us no choice. And in any event, it was Harris who slotted him.'

'Fair, enough, and I don't suppose he would have been flowing with intel for us.'

'How are SB getting on with his brother, Paddy?'

'They've charged him with being a member of a proscribed organisation which is enough to remand him in custody while they try and get enough evidence together to prove some of his historical atrocities.'

'I don't envy their job,' Jackson said, and he didn't. 'Anyway, who is doing DI McDonald's job since the attack on him? We keep piling up cases for them.'

'The RUC have decided, for now, to have the local CID DI do what McDonald used to. That way a different, geographically placed detective does the initial assessment rather than one induvial that the terrorists can blame, or target.'

'I'm guessing then, we have two DI's queuing up to interview us?'

'You do, and it will need doing at some time over the next few days, but I'm bothered about Romeo Troop having it's faces shown to too many.'

'That's a fair point, what do you suggest?'

'The SB intermediary I link in with, is a detective superintendent named John Field. He is head of SB for Belfast and third in charge for the whole of SB across the RUC. He will collate the induvial DIs questions on behalf of the coroner and sit down with you all when I can arrange it. I'll be present to ensure nothing is asked that could compromise you. You will all need to be in green army battledress, and use your old regiments identities from before you joined the SAS to add to your cover. It's the best we can do.'

Jackson nodded. It was at least a firewall to some degree.

Hastings added he would create cover stories to explain why they were at any given point. Jackson knew that BS was his forte and trusted him. He used the previous night's fun as an example.

'We can say that after the initial attack on Constable Dune, we chose to covertly provide security for him in the short term, and then Billy Ryan turned up.'

'Sounds OK. I'll make sure Harris is properly briefed.' Moving the conversation on, Jackson added, 'Any idea how the Provos found out about McDonald's movements and where he lived?'

'Nothing concrete yet, unfortunately. But they are concentrating on the sympathiser who rented the house with no fence.'

WITH PREJUDICE

'Yeah, but they knew where to rent in the first place.'

'They did. The previous owner was approached and they threatened his family if he didn't move out and rent it to them. He's too frightened to make a written statement saying so.'

'I'm guessing we are no nearer to identifying the gunman who was about to attack the wife and kids?'

'I'm afraid not, but we are working on it, Vernon.'

Hastings then went on to congratulate Jackson, not that he needed him to, but it was nice, nonetheless. With the removal of the East Tyrone Brigade's leader, brother, nephew and three operatives, the whole ASU was pretty much destroyed; for now.

Hastings told Jackson that PIRA's Army Council had wasted no time in releasing a public statement an hour earlier, thirty minutes after the RUC released details of last night's exchange. They had apparently firmly stated that Billy Ryan had not been operating under PIRA's instructions. That although, his unauthorised attack on a constable from Ballygawley was on a legitimate target, it had not been sanctioned by them. Nor had his attack on the woman in front of her twins. Had the security forces not 'murdered him' last night, he would have faced Courts Martial and subsequent punishment.

'They've not wasted anytime in cleaning house, have they?' Jackson said.

'No, and not all of their number will agree with the statement, either.'

'I notice they couldn't help throwing in the "murder" word.'

Hastings nodded.

'How is Constable Dune doing?' Jackson asked.

'He'll be OK. He sends his heartfelt thanks. The RUC are relocating him and his mother, and I suspect he'll now be moved to the mainland. There is an opening in the Lancashire Constabulary if he wants it. It's the nearest force.'

Jackson was glad to hear that Dune was safely out of it, properly this time. And the speed with which the IRA had released their statement only served to confirm to Jackson, that on this occasion at least, the intel must have come to Hastings from within PIRA. But he knew better than to ask.

Harris then joined them, and offered to top up their mugs which Jackson gratefully accepted but Hastings politely refused.

'You not travelling back with us?' Jackson asked.

'No, I've got some stuff to sort out first. I'll speak to you tomorrow when I'm back in London. But there is something else I want to discuss before we all shoot off.'

'Go ahead,' Jackson said.

Hastings then went on to brief them about the US Foreign Secretary's forthcoming visit to London on his way to Paris. All the usual security protocols were in place, and there was no intel as to any threat. However, announcement of his forthcoming visit has caused a lot of bemoaning chatter from the Loyalists about the American's Irish community financial support of the IRA.

'Can't say I blame them,' Harris said as he joined them at the table.

'Yeah, we need to cut off Noraid's support,' Jackson added.

'I'm reliably informed that MI6 and the CIA are very active in that area,' Hastings said.

'They need to try harder,' Jackson said. 'They must know enough to dismantle it.'

'They do, but they don't want a replacement to just pop up. Our American cousins are working hard to dispel all the false beliefs and propaganda that these misguided idiots are being fed. They are looking for a permanent solution.'

'We could give them a permanent solution,' Jackson added.

Hastings moved it on. The Prime Minister was overjoyed with the results Romeo Troop were obtaining so far. She's been awoken in the night with the last result as she had instructed her Private Secretary to so do.

'She's really taking a personal interest in us,' Jackson said.

'She is, as it was her idea. And don't forget, she suggested you by name to lead the unit on the ground.'

'I only met her once. We'd done a job and she turned up at the debrief to congratulate us personally. Which, I have to say went down well.'

'I remember that job, I was there. You don't lose it, you old schmoozer,' Harris added.

WITH PREJUDICE

Jackson just raised his eyebrows at Harris.

'Well, you certainly made an impression,' Hastings said, and then moved the conversation forward. The PM is keen that Romeo Troop - to those in the know - do not just appear to be targeting Republican terrorists. Although, by sheer numbers, the majority of our work will always be aimed that way.

'She wants you to appear as balanced as possible,' Hastings said. He then explained that they were to deploy during the US Foreign Secretary's whistlestop visit to London.

'Why?' Harris asked.

'There is no intel about anything planned, but apparently, back home the Foreign Secretary, Mitchell Wilson Jr. has made some stupid comments in the past, not supporting Irish Americans who fund the IRA, but stating that he could "understand it".'

'Nob head,' Jackson said.

'I think unwise, would be a better phrase. But yep, granted. With this mind, the Met and SB over there are anticipating some demonstrations as he arrives at their Embassy in Grosvenor Square. If you can just hang about in the area, the PM can tell Wilson when she sees him at number 10, that her most special of special forces have his back.'

'Sounds like nothing more than political BS, to me,' Harris said.

'Granted, again. I'll leave you lads to work the details. I've got to shoot now,' Hastings finished with.

They bade farewell, and Jackson said he'd give him specifics once they were back in Hereford. Hastings nodded and rushed off. Jackson would love to know where his next urgent appointment was. He trusted Hastings, and was enjoying their ever-closer relationship, but he could see that the MI5 man kept a lot of stuff close to his chest. But then that was just the way with spooks, he guessed.

Chapter Seventeen

An hour after his meeting with Jackson, Hastings was on foot towards the central Belfast newsagent's shop which was MI5's secure site. Fortunately, there were no customers inside, so Hastings just had to nod twice at Derek behind the counter before heading through to the back. He was soon in the underground comms room free of unwanted intrusion from the outside world. He logged on to one of the terminals and first contacted Thames House, in London. They had no intel updates for him; be that from telephone intercepts, listening devices or from any other of their technical intelligence gathering techniques. He confirmed that he would call into Box in person the following day. The Post Office address for MI5's Thames House headquarters was Box 500, which is where the nickname came from.

He checked his watch as he pulled on his headphones and made himself comfortable. He had fifteen minutes to wait for the next opportunity to receive a call. There were different protocols in place should urgent contact be needed - either way - but as neither of these had been initiated, he was relaxed. This was merely a normal contact/welfare check.

Exactly fifteen minutes later, the screen lit up to signify an incoming call. He answered it appropriately by saying, 'Lovely, day, so it is,' in his best Ulster accent, which was poor.

'No, it's not, my son, it's bucketing it down,' came the brusque response in a strained yet believable mockney accent.

There were three different verbal keys Hastings could use and each had its own response. Lessons learned during the current Cold War with the Soviets were still on-going and prudent. Most signals could be intercepted, and if they couldn't, the user could be. Hastings knew all was well, and returned to his usual voice for the rest of the conversation, as did the person on the other end of the line. Had either of them used the correct narrative, but without the daft accents, then the other would have known that a compromise had taken place.

'Look, I haven't got long,' the caller said.

'Understood. Have you got anything for me?'

'Nothing you haven't seen on the telly. They are relieved and worried in equal measures.'

'And you are sure our house is clean?'

'You keep asking me this, and it's the same answer. Yes, I'm as sure as I can be, but that doesn't mean it is.'

'I know, I know.'

'You're as paranoid as they are, look, got to go.'

'Before you do, any update on Pídàn?'

'No idea. No one knows anything, really go to go now,' then the line went dead.

Hastings sat back in his chair and replayed the short conversation in his head. It didn't get any more informative. Was the source holding back? Or just in a position of limited access? Had he touched a nerve mentioning Pídàn? He'd have to give it some thought. He could also initiate a test if he was concerned. He knew his bosses loved periodic tests just for the sake of them. Considered them good tradecraft. He did, too, but not unnecessarily so. If a source sussed out you were sending them on a test, then the fallout could be catastrophic, and usually meant an end to the relationship. As with all agent handling, it was built on trust which had its foundations in mistrust. All very flimsy and easily brought crashing down.

He knew that a lot of his disquiet crept in at times because he hadn't worked out the source's motivation. If he knew that, then he would feel a lot better and even be able to structure things accordingly. He'd never openly asked the source why? He'd always shied away from it. It could seem confrontational and if they didn't want to tell you, they'd make the answer up anyway. On reflection, he'd park that conversation for a while longer yet.

What he had learnt from the brief chat was that there had been no initial kick back, no obvious problems, and nothing planned on the front foot. One often learnt more from the unsaid than the said.

Hastings then put a further call into Thames House, and his immediate supervisor, Jeremy Schofield answered. It wasn't that they didn't get on, they just came from different worlds. Jeremy was the typical 'been tapped on the shoulder' recruit from

Oxbridge, whereas Hastings had not. He'd started off as an analyst and had initially been approached because he'd shown certain aptitudes, and also as he'd been learning Chinese at night school as a hobby. This, he later realised, was the real reason, but ironically had since dropped his studies, it was getting too technical for him. But by then, he was firmly on board. He also suspected that Jeremy resented this, even if he appeared to actually like Hastings.

'OK, old chap, any whispers of note?' Jeremy answered the call with.

'Nothing at all, unfortunately, but of course that means nothing bad, either.'

'Time for a test?'

'Not yet, but I'll keep that in mind.'

'Be sure you do. Any update on Pídàn?'

'Negative.'

'Have you briefed, Romeo re the US visit?'

'Yes, and they will be deployed as requested.'

'That will please the PM. See you tomorrow,' Jeremy said before ending the call.

Hastings reckoned he had gone to the same school of telephone etiquette as the source.

WITH PREJUDICE

Chapter Eighteen

'OK you lot, get your stuff together, you've had a couple of days off, which is more than me and Harris,' Jackson said as he entered the briefing room at Stirling Lines Garrison, at Credenhill, near Hereford. The home of the SAS. He'd addressed Dave Crompton and Ian King.

King groaned and said, 'Are we sure there is no intel, Boss?'

'Hastings said not as such.'

'I hate these political things,' King added.

'If it keeps the PM happy, then we stay in favour, don't forget that.'

'I guess.'

Then his sergeant Dave Crompton added, 'You said, "not as such," Boss.'

'Yeah, well, there is apparently a group of Loyalist sympathisers planning a "scream and shout" as the Foreign Secretary arrives at his Embassy.'

'Nothing more sinister among them?'

'Apparently, not. It'll be an easy couple of hours for us.'

'A walk in the park,' King added, and they all laughed.

Romeo Troop left Stirling Lines in two black Range Rovers for the 150-mile journey to Central London. It took three and a half hours to reach Wellington Barracks, from where they would base themselves. It was a sunny afternoon and dry, which Jackson knew was a shame. The police often referred to the rain as the best demonstration police officer there was. Gob shites never hang around long when it's pissing down.

They kitted up with sidearms hidden among their civilian casual clothing. Mark Harris had a long nylon backpack with a Heckler and Koch MP5 machine-gun in it, just in case. All four of them also had a green army beret with the insignia of their parent regiment on the badges should they need to go overt.

It was a short drive to a pre-arranged spot close to Grosvenor Square, which was a small park which had the Italian Embassy at one end and the US Embassy at the opposing end. The park, including the road around it, of the same name, was not actually a square. It was a stadium shaped rectangle. Two flat sides, and two rounded ends where the Embassies were located. The road around it was one-way. The park was open to the public and was lined with established trees with a glade in its centre. It also featured a couple of monuments and statues.

Jackson and Harris covered the flat south side, near Upper Grosvenor Square, and Crompton and King covered the opposing Upper Brook Street side. The rounded ends were called Grosvenor Square. It was 1 p.m. and everything appeared normal. There was a gathering of about fifty to a hundred protestors on Upper Grosvenor Square, opposite where the road swung onto Grosvenor Square leading to the front of the US Embassy. They had banners with 'Down with Noraid' and other such phrases written on them. They were small in number and hemmed into a corner by a continuous line of uniformed police. Hastings had confirmed that they were just a 'shout and scream' mob, but that they had a couple of their own among them to pick up any chatter, so Jackson should quickly know if anything changed. It was not expected to.

Dave Crompton called up on the radio to state that he had been chatting to some local in the park to ask what was going on, and was told that the new American president Ronald Regan was due to visit the Embassy. This was obviously a Chinese whisper but it better explained the demo. Jackson realised that the crowd could grow quickly if the rumour spread. The thought heightened his awareness, not that he or any of the troop would be off guard.

Having satisfied themselves of no obvious threat in or around the area, Crompton and King took up a position close to the Italian Embassy where they could give advanced warning of the convoy's approach. Jackson and Harris were near to the Eagle Squadron memorial, which was close to the Upper Grosvenor Square side, near to where the convoy would veer right towards the front of the Embassy. There was a rear access according to Hastings but Mitchell Wilson Jr. always insisted on entering via the front door.

As they whiled away the minutes, Jackson studied the monument. It had inscriptions on four sides but the main engraving read;

WITH PREJUDICE

"EAGLE SQUADRONS.
THIS MEMORIAL IS TO THE MEMORY OF THE 244 AMERICAN AND 16 BRITISH FIGHTER PILOTS AND OTHER PERSONNEL WHO SERVED IN THE THREE ROYAL AIR FORCE EAGLE SQUADRONS PRIOR TO THE PARTICIPATION OF THE UNITED STATES OF AMERICA IN THE SECOND WORLD WAR. THEY SERVED WITH VALOR. FOUNDED BY CHARLES F. SWEENY, JUNE 1940. ERECTED THROUGH THE GENEROSITY OF THE HEARST CORPORATION OF AMERICA IN THE NAME OF WILLIAM RANDOLPH HEARST, PUBLISHER."

Jackson considered what he had read, those brave US citizens had volunteered to join the RAF and fight the Nazis before America had officially joined the war. What heroes. He glanced around to make sure no one was watching, and then threw a quick salute to the fallen. Harris clocked him, and after reading the inscription, did the same.

'I never knew this,' Harris said.

'Me neither,' Jackson replied. 'Makes you think, doesn't it.'

Harris nodded.

They then wandered down the path that cut right through the entire centre of the park, to the pavement. Where the road split and Grosvenor Square branched off Upper Grosvenor Street, the access was currently blocked by two Norton Commando police bikes.

Then Jackson's earpiece burst into life; it was Sergeant Crompton: *'Two Alpha to the team, standby, standby, standby, convoy approaching.'*

Jackson and Harris acknowledged, and then Crompton went on to describe the approaching entourage. Police outriders at each side. Two bikes had raced ahead to ensure Brook Street and the following side road were blocked to traffic. This would allow the cortege an unobstructed access around the park to the entrance to the Embassy itself. Harris commented that the two bikes blocking the link road access near them, had now moved out the way.

The small crowd opposite must also have seen this as they suddenly became more vocal. Jackson nodded at Harris as Crompton further described the vehicle procession. There were five black vehicles in all. The first and last would have Special Branch officers on board, the inner vehicle was the amour-plated Embassy vehicle with Wilson Jr. inside. The vehicles immediately in front and behind the Foreign Secretary's motor were black Ranger Rovers, and Jackson knew they would be carrying US Secret Service personnel. It was as Hastings had described.

King commented as the caravan of vehicles passed the Italian Embassy and started to turn right onto Upper Grosvenor Square. Jackson could see the lead vehicle start to emerge.

Then Jackson's earpiece was filled again with King's voice, but Jackson could tell that he was running as he spoke; *'Scrambler bike has just appeared from nowhere, two up, and over the pavement into the park from our position. Towards you One Alpha and Three. Pillion is pulling something from a backpack. Consider hostile. I'm making ground.'*

Both Jackson and Harris acknowledged as Crompton shouted, *'Two Alpha making ground.'*

Jackson glanced down Upper Grosvenor Square and could see all five cars in the motorcade in a line and indicating to turn right into the link road. Harris had drawn his weapon and put on his green beret and had taken up a defensive position facing into the park, Jackson did the same from the opposite side of the path. He heard the revving motorcycle moments before he saw it. It whizzed past the Eagle Squadron memorial, and Jackson could see that the pillion had a cylindrical object in his hand. Time seemed to slow as Jackson's awareness lifted to combat reality.

Knowing how hard it is to hit a moving target at speed with just handguns, nearly impossible, he knew that he had to put himself in front of the bike's trajectory and between the convoy, which was almost upon them and totally oblivious to the threat.

Jackson could hear screaming from park walkers on sighting their weapons, and he steadied himself as he took up a firing position. All this had happened in a couple of seconds. Then he heard Harris shouting in his earpiece, *'Pipe bomb: repeat, pipe bomb.'*

Jackson opened fire from the front in the same instant that Harris opened fire from the side, they both missed, and Jackson had to dive and roll to his side to avoid being run over. He let loose two more rounds as he rolled, a practiced but difficult art. He heard a metallic response, so must have hit the bike somewhere. He only hoped he had incapacitated it as he jumped to his feet.

The bike slew to its side, as the lead vehicle passed. One of them on the bike shouted, 'Stop funding the IRA.' This was immediately picked up by the crowd opposite which repeated the mantra, but amplified a hundred times. This added to the overall confusion.

In the moment of disruption which followed, the pillion passenger threw his pipe bomb. Jackson could see a short-lit fuse at one end. It bounced off the roof of the centre vehicle and then smashed into the windscreen of the vehicle immediately behind. A millisecond later this was followed by a huge explosion within the vehicle sending glass and metal shrapnel flying everywhere. The vehicle failed to make the turn and crashed to a halt into the two stationary police bikes. The crowd went silent. Then everyone all around started to scream. The cacophony which ensued gave the whole grim occurrence a surrealness. Time then caught up, momentarily, before it slowed to a crawl once more as Jackson took it all in and reacted.

He knew there was probably nothing that could be done for the poor souls inside the vehicle. He had to force his attention back towards the bike as it started to skid back the way it had come. He was back in combat mode after the brief hiatus and time accelerated. Up ahead in its path were King and Crompton, both had separated to create a vector, and were each on one knee, both in a firing position with weapons drawn.

As Jackson hurried to bring up the rear, he could see Harris ripping open his backpack.

Crompton and King opened fire, forcing the bike to slide sideways to a halt as it attempted to turn right away from them, but the soft grass it was tearing up impeded it. This caused the bike to effectively stop, albeit only for a second.

That was all the time Harris needed, as he let fly with his Heckler and Koch. The pillion passenger who had thrown the bomb flew off the machine in the direction of Crompton and King as the rounds tore through him. The bike wheelied in response as it shot off, even quicker than before. All four of Romeo Troop chased rounds after it, but Jackson knew it was pointless at this distance.

Crompton took off on foot across the park in an effort to head the bike off, but as valiant as his effort was, it was a one-way race. The bike disappeared through the trees in the far corner, and moments later Crompton's breathless voice came over the radio to say that at least he'd been able to put the rider to a waiting vehicle, which shot off down Brook Street. He didn't see the plates, but commented that the driver had one of the rear doors open ready, and the bike rider dived into the back seat in a well-drilled and practiced manner, before the vehicle took off. The same technique was used on mobile surveillance when the rearmost car had to quickly pick up a foot team once a target has suddenly left in a vehicle. A practiced art, indeed, Jackson thought.

He'd managed a good side-on glimpse of the rider, but he was wearing a full-face helmet, making any future ID impossible. But the way he conducted himself was definitely memorable.

Then his musings were interrupted as armed police swarmed around him, and Harris and King, who had joined him. 'Armed police, drop your weapons or you will be shot,' one of them shouted.

WITH PREJUDICE

Chapter Nineteen

Hastings had been patiently waiting outside his boss's office in Thames House, for fifteen minutes. It wasn't unlike Jeremy Schofield to be late, but Hastings reckoned he was doing it on purpose. He then heard the pompous overweight forty-something-year-old approach as he talked excessively loudly to anyone he passed. He beckoned with his head for Hastings to join him in his office. Once inside the Oxbridge graduate took a seat behind his desk in full headteacher-mode and Hastings took one of the two chairs facing it.

'As you can image, the Americans are going nuts. The PM has chewed both director generals of Six and us, and I've just come from the DG's office; my kicking has been postponed an hour, so for God's sake Bertram, you better have some answers for me,' Schofield started with.

Hastings knew shit rolled downhill, and could tell that Schofield was eager to dodge his own dirt snowball and let it land on him. Typical. And he'd used Hasting's Sunday name. Only his mother called him Bertram and not Bert. 'The fact that we had no intel to suggest a Loyalist attack is not my fault, with respect.'

'Not, just your fault, granted. But if we knew about the small demo, we must have missed something.'

'I've been over and over the original intel, which came in from the Met, and there was nothing. It was just a few Paddies from the local Irish pub, who support the Union and wanted to let off steam. It was Romeo Troop who picked up the intel that a rumour had spread that Reagan could have been there.'

'I'll come on to your Romeo Troop in a minute, that's a whole new can of worms, now.'

Hastings didn't like the sound of this, but at least Schofield had unwittingly given him a few minutes warning.

'What are we hearing in the aftermath?'

Before he answered, Hastings asked how the American Secret Service agent was doing? He that knew three in the car had died but that one had gone to hospital with serious injuries.

'Serious, but stable. He is expected to survive but only God knows how? The current hypothesis is that he noticed the threat and was reaching down into his nylon arms bag when the bomb hit the windscreen. He would have been bent down behind the driver's seat at the time.'

'Well, that's something.'

'It is a small mercy, but as you know pipe bombs work from condensed and expanded pressure. The poor man will never hear again; there's nothing left of his inner ears.'

Hastings took a second, he couldn't imagine surviving critical injuries only to realise you were now deaf to the world forever.

Returning to Schofield's question, he told him what he must already know, that the UDA has said it was nothing to do with the Ulster Freedom Fighters or the Ulster Volunteer Force. But as far as we can tell from the chatter we have picked up from the Provos and the INLA, they believe it to be a Loyalist hit.

'So why aren't the Loyalists singing from the rooftops about it? Milking it for all it's worth?'

It was a question Hastings had wrestled with. He conceded that the attack was against the US, for its citizens who are pervaded by propaganda into funding the IRA. And that all the casualties were American. But they may not have been. Any number of the UK escort personnel could have been hurt. It was a risky strategy to say the least. One that could still backfire against the terrorists if their Protestant Unionist support were dismayed by what could have been. He explained his thoughts to Schofield, and added, 'Imagine if any Loyalist attack killed British policemen, for example?'

'I can see that. But as we had no intel at all, the DG is panicking about another scenario in play here,' Schofield said.

Hastings had no idea what he meant so stayed silent.

'He is concerned that there is a new breakaway, hitherto unknown, Loyalist terror group in play.'

'Christ, I hope not.'

'You and me, too. What about your source?'

'I thought I'd leave it 24 hours until the next scheduled contact, to give them time to pick up any talk.'

Schofield nodded his understanding, and added, 'Keep me informed.'

'Of course.'

'Moving it on, that just leaves Romeo Troop, for now.'

Hastings was ready and opened his mouth to respond when Schofield waved his hand to silence him.

'The PM is extremely embarrassed. She is the one who waxed lyrical to Reagan about Romeo Troop being deployed.'

'I know, but there were only there as—'

'And they failed to stop the attack,' Schofield interrupted with.

Hastings knew it was scapegoat time and he was having none of it. 'That is profoundly unfair.'

Schofield looked as if he were about to speak, so Hastings waved his own hand to silence him, and pushed on. 'But for their intervention, the attackers would have had time to better aim their bomb and it could have hit the windscreen of the Foreign Secretary's vehicle.'

'Which is bomb-proof,' Schofield quickly threw in.

'But is the windscreen? I know it's about two inches thick and bullet-proof, but would you want to test it against a pipe bomb? And furthermore, their spontaneous reaction manged to eliminate the bomber. It's only a matter of time before we get the rider and his mate who picked him up.'

Schofield sat back in his chair and pondered a moment, and then asked, 'And what of the bomber?'

'He's unknown. Which is not unusual. All terrorists use clean skins whenever possible for their Active Service Units when operating on the mainland, in order to facilitate their crossing of borders. Look how easily we recently picked one up because he'd not paid his child maintenance back in Dublin.'

'DNA?'

'It's in its infancy as you know. We have the bomber's, but it's useless unless we can compare it with a sample linked to the individual; his toothbrush or similar. And to do that, we have to have a suspect's name to begin with, which we do not. One day, they hope to be able to grow a sample and do a family tree from it.'

'That'll never happen,' Schofield said, and then added, 'the other thing which is worrying the DG, be this a known Loyalist group, or - God forbid - a new one, is that this is a major step up, tactically.'

Hastings nodded; he knew this was true. Loyalist attacks on the mainland were exceedingly rare, and usually involved attacks on Catholic Irish pubs, such as the one at Kilburn and the one in Glasgow.

'What do I tell the DG?' Schofield asked.

'Tell him, but for Romeo Troop, the attack could have been far worse, and the bomber would not be dead. And intel-wise; we were *all* caught out. But as soon as I'm back across the water, I'll speak to my source and have Romeo Troop in a state of readiness to react to any intel we get.'

'I guess that should do it for now,' Schofield said rising to his feet. The meeting was over. Hastings was relived, and never more so because Romeo Troop were still in play. For the time being.

They needed a result, and fast. He said his goodbyes to Schofield and rushed out of his office to arrange a lift to the airport. He'd already spoken to Jackson and sent them back to Ulster. He wanted them out of harm's way in case the dirt snowball headed in their direction.

WITH PREJUDICE

Chapter Twenty

Having safely made it back to Fitzrovia, Lynch and Kelly quickly parked the car in a pre-determined spot, changed into their spare set of clothes and threw the old ones into the car along with their weapons before setting fire to it. Once back at the flat they had a decision to make. Either hunker down and wait it out, or get out before the cops got organised. They had only a small window to decide through, as the police would still be up to their necks in the initial aftermath. After that, things would change quickly, Lynch knew. He had ensured that they had cleared out the flat and bleached everything before they had deployed to Grosvenor Park hours earlier, just to be ahead of the game, in case they needed to be. And as much as Murphy and Kelly had grumbled about it, he was glad that he had. It made the next decision easier. He decided that they should get the hell out of Dodge.

Kelly was an unknown, as was Murphy, and Lynch had his bent passport, which he treasured as they were a lot harder to come by than people would imagine, even for PIRA. They caught a West Coast mainline train from Euston to Liverpool Lime Street. And then boarded a ferry. He considered heading to Dublin where they could easily drive over the border, but that would mean crossing an international boundary at sea; always an added risk. Especially after such an attack where border attention would be more acute. They caught the overnight boat to Belfast and safely disembarked before 7 a.m. the following day.

Lynch put a call into Sean, his brother-in-law, to confirm their safe arrival back in the province. Sean arranged to meet him at his home as soon as he could. The Army Council would debrief Kelly the following day, so Lynch told him to take some down time and prepare himself for the inquisition.

His previous question mark over Kelly dissolved the more he got to know him. During the eight-hour crossing from Liverpool, they had chilled down, had a few beers, and got a few hours' kip. But the lengthy transit across the Irish Sea had given Lynch the opportunity to go over their spiel many times. He also levelled with Kelly as to his wider plan, adding, that if he got his way, Kelly would stay with Lynch operating in the province. He seemed incredibly pleased to be back on home soil, he said he had had enough of working away on the UK mainland. You can take the boy out of the Falls Road, but not the Falls Road out of the boy. He'd always thought that Kelly would be harder than Murphy to manage, but now suspected that the reverse was the case. He still felt a sadness at losing Murphy, and was grateful that he hadn't joined him. He nearly had when that bike wheelied up when Murphy fell off.

Also, during the crossing, he'd had time to collect his thoughts, not just about getting his script right for when he saw Sean, but as to what had actually happened. It was clear that the soldiers who engaged them had popped up from nowhere. He can't imagine they had a tip off. He'd certainly told no one and he was happy with Kelly's answers when he quizzed him. That just left Murphy, but it made no sense. He shook the thought from his head. There was no way he was a tout, or he'd still be alive. But he may have let slip to someone else, unwittingly. Lynch chastised himself once more. It could just have been bad luck. Covert patrols there as a precaution. But the speed with which they reacted to the approaching bike did shout special forces, had to be.

And something else was bugging Lynch, the soldier he almost manged to run over looked familiar, but he just didn't know why. That said, a lot of the Brit soldier boys sported the same sort of look, but these ones did look different. They certainly weren't normal army as their berets suggested, he was sure of that.

But all things considered, the operation had gone better than expected. He thought they'd just be able to blow up the two cops guarding the slip road to the front of the Embassy. He knew the motorcade would be there or there abouts, and certainly near enough, so as to appear that the whole thing was an attack on the US Foreign Secretary. But Murphy, God bless him, had even managed to get the bomb to bounce off the politician's vehicle roof before smashing into the next car. And losing three or four secret service agents, was no great loss. Just like cops really, and made the whole thing look firmly like a Loyalist hit, as planned.

Perhaps, if the soldiers hadn't got in the way, the position of the vehicles wouldn't have fallen perfectly for when Murphy launched his toy. The last though made him smile as he made his way home.

When Lynch arrived home two hours later, he walked into a row with Erin. She was rightly annoyed that he had just disappeared without a word.

'You could have at least rung me to tell me that you were OK?' she said.

'Ah come on Mot, my dear, you know how these operations are?'

'And how many times have I told you not to call me any of those daft Gaelic names.'

Lynch nearly reminded her that her birth name of Erin was in fact Irish for Irish, but chose not to.

'Where have you been gallivanting to, then?' she asked.

'Just out of the province, you know I can't say more than that.'

'And my brother is not much more help.'

'On that, is Sean coming here. Or am I expected to go to him?'

'How the hell should I know.'

Then Lynch heard a car pulling up outside and glanced through the curtains, it was Sean.

Erin, must have seen his car, too, as she said, 'I'll go and make a brew and then leave you boys to it.' She paused to peck him on the cheek as she passed towards the kitchen, and said, 'I do worry about you, you know.'

'I know you do, love, and one day when the Brits finally leaves us in peace, there'll no more worries to be had,' Lynch said and then kissed her back.

Chapter Twenty-one

Jackson and the rest of the troop had been back in their barracks within a barracks at Lisburn for twenty-four hours, and were becoming restless. They had all come down from the post-combat high and done the admin. They'd all been interviewed by Detective Superintendent John Field from Special Branch on behalf of the DIs working for the Coroner. Hastings hadn't been present like he'd promised, but there were no problems. No trick questions, Field just wanted their factual accounts of each contact. That all done and over with, they were chilling nicely, but ready to deploy at a moment's notice. Jackson hoped it wouldn't be too far off, as the longer they lounged about, the twitchier they became. It was different back at Hereford, they could go and see their loved ones, or someone else's loved ones as far as King and Harris were concerned. And when not doing that, Jackson could arrange some training for them. But here they were penned in like caged tigers.

Beyond the briefing table area was the lounge. Crompton, King, and Harris were currently sat around a small card table playing poker. Jackson had excused himself as he waited for Hastings to turn up, or call. Then the landline rang, it must be him.

Jackson answered the call with an anonymous, 'Yep.'

'May I speak to Captain Jackson, please?' an American voice asked.

'Who is this?' Jackson replied with his own question. He could see that the others had put their cards down and were watching.

'My apologises, my name is Special Agent Kurt Cichoski with the US Secret Service. You are one hard mother to track down. Your major at Here-ford, gave me this number. I don't even know where I'm ringing,' Cichoski said.

Jackson had to smile at the American pronunciation of Hereford. 'Best you don't know, Kurt. Anyway, how can I help?'

'We lost three of our guys, with one badly hurt the other day, but SOFA was unhurt, I wanted to thank your guys for that.'

WITH PREJUDICE

Jackson smiled at the acronym which he guessed meant Secretary of Foreign Affairs. He considered a joke about a sofa, but decided against it given the circumstances. 'Just doing our job, just sorry we didn't have prior knowledge, none of them would have left that park and your guys would have been OK. I'm sorry for that.'

'No need to apologise my friend. I also wanted to particularly thank the guy who got the bomber, what was your guy's name?'

Cichoski had Jackson's name which couldn't be helped, but he wasn't prepared to compromise the others' identities. 'We call him "Tone Deaf", and don't ask, it's a long story.'

Cichoski burst out laughing and added, 'You Brits love your nicknames, don't you. Though I reckon your Aussie mates are worse.'

Cichoski was probably correct on both counts. Jackson could see that Mark Harris was staring intently, now.

'Well, just pass on our thanks to Tone Deaf, please.'

'Will do, and if we come across the other two, where should we call?'

Cichoski then gave Jackson a secure number to use. And then added, 'And if there is anything your cousins across the pond can do to help, just holler. You have our number.'

Jackson thanked Cichoski and then took a punt as a thought occurred to him. 'Just one thing?'

'Shoot, buddy.'

'If we need any backdoor database checks doing Stateside?'

'Anytime, just give me a ring,' Cichoski replied before ending the call.

Jackson turned and briefed the team, and they all gave Harris a round of applause.

'I must admit, mate, that was mean shooting on the move,' King said.

Then Crompton added that to celebrate they'd let Harris play his guitar for five minutes, but only five minutes. The boys were winding themselves up for some piss taking, so Jackson left them to it. He'd just settled back at the briefing table when Hastings rushed in. He apologised for not being present earlier, and Jackson waved his comment away. It had all gone sweet. He quickly brought Hastings up to date with the phone call he'd just taken and the offer of backdoor access to the US systems.

'My God, we will make an intelligence officer out of you,' Hastings said, before congratulating him.

Jackson asked how his debrief had gone at Thames House and Hastings told him. He was impressed with the way Hastings had backed them. Few spooks would have done that. Perhaps, the closeness from him being permanently attached to Romeo Troop was working as first envisaged.

'Any intel updates?' Jackson asked.

'That's why I'm late. And you won't believe what I have to tell you all.'

Jackson called the others to order and when they were all seated at the ops table, Hastings continued.

When he had finished, they all rocked back on their stand chairs while they took it in.

'Are you absolutely sure?' Jackson asked.

'One hundred per cent. It was a Provisional IRA job and not a Loyalist one.'

'But they killed US citizens, and may even have got at the US Foreign Secretary,' Crompton said.

'I know, high risk indeed. But the team was led by an unhinged hardline Republican who is at odds with the Army Council. He thinks they know nothing of this, but the source says that some strongly suspect.'

That was the second shock. 'How come?' Jackson asked.

'Apparently, this maverick lunatic thinks the Army Council are going soft, keep talking about peace talks with us, which will never happen. But he is also angry at the lack of armed operations against the Loyalists.'

Jackson was once again amazed at the detailed information Hastings was briefing them with. It was clearly apparent now that he really must have a very well-placed source, and it was a live one, as opposed to a technical one. Though it could have still come from a telephone intercept, but Jackson was convinced now that it was a person. He'd no idea how the hell MI5 had managed to get such a well-placed informant, especially given the risks they were running. 'Any idea who the bomber was?' he asked.

'Not as yet.'

'OK, and I have to say, the whole attack smacked of opportunist activity. It wasn't well thought out, irrespective of the result. Which was odds against, to be honest. Not to mention how unreliable those pipe bombs are.'

'That also troubled me,' Crompton said. All turned to look at the sergeant as he carried on. 'It would have made more sense for the attack to be done with automatic machine guns, the chances of a pipe bomb hitting that windscreen, at the right angle, and going through it, and detonating inside was off the scale lucky for those bastards.'

All true, Jackson thought. And the others nodded their agreement.

'My thoughts are that a pipe bomb was used specifically to make it appear as a Loyalist hit, that being their usual ordinance of choice. They weren't expecting it to be effective. That was a secondary outcome. They just got lucky with that, which only enhanced the view that it must have been a Loyalist hit,' Hastings said.

'So, that means we have a hell-bent, off the scale nutter on the loose,' Jackson said.

'Looking that way,' Hastings added.

'Are you likely to get his identity?' King asked.

'Not sure,' Hastings said.

'Because if you do, sod trying to arrest him, or catch him in the act, we can just let Tone Deaf here have some more target practice,' King said.

Hastings didn't answer.

Chapter Twenty-two

After Lynch had told his version of what happened, he was confident that he had Sean onside and accepting of things. However, the Army Council wanted to hear it first hand, so he had to join Sean in a trip south of the border to a remote farmhouse on the northern outskirts of Dublin. It had been some time since he'd seen them and had never been to this location before. Sean warned him to rein himself in when he spoke to them, and he knew this was good advice.

There were seven members of the Council, normally, including Sean and his counterpart who was OC for the Southern Command which covered Eire. The Adjutant General - who was intricately linked to the leader of the political wing - Sinn Féin, would also be present. As would the Sinn Féin, leader, Geoff Gomez himself. Paddy Ryan, Commander of East Tyrone Brigade had also been a member, but his place had yet to be refilled after his recent demise. The newest member was a man called Donald James who Lynch knew of, but had never met. He'd previously been a hunger striker in the Maze prison before escaping to the south. Lynch wasn't sure what his credentials were to justify a seat at the top table, but Lynch instinctively didn't like the man as he was Lynch's replacement.

Sat in the middle of them behind a trestle table was the Chief of Staff, Shamus Walsh, a veteran who Lynch respected above all others, except Sean. But he was becoming another talking head like the rest of them in Lynch's view.

Lynch took his solitary seat in front of them, and Walsh, a forty-year-old of average build led the meeting and asked Lynch to explain what exactly had happened in London. But he first cautioned Lynch, that the Council had already had Kelly spoken to. This surprised Lynch, but he was confident the lad would have stuck to the script. He'd soon find out.

They all sat in silence while Lynch told his tale that they had been in a Loyalist-friendly Irish pub nearby, considering it as a future target, when they had picked up loose talk of the impending attack on the US Foreign Secretary's convoy.

Gomez, a skinny man in his thirties chipped in, 'That wasn't one of the three approved targets.'

'I know, we were just recceing it as a future possibility,' Lynch replied.

'We didn't know about that, or the intel you say you picked up,' Gomez pushed.

He was starting to annoy Lynch who was grateful of a moment's reprieve when Sean jumped in to support him.

'As you are aware, due to the cellular nature of our overseas Active Service Units, they have to operate with autonomy to remain secure,' Sean said.

Turning to face Sean from the opposite side of Walsh, Gomez added, 'Fair enough, but we weren't made aware of the urgent, intel.'

This politician was starting to irritate Lynch more and more. But he took a breath before answering, 'Security aside, we didn't have time. We grabbed some sidearms from the boot of the motor and deployed to the park as quickly as we could. I'm sure that any of you as an ASU Commander would have done the same.'

Lynch sat back in his chair, and enjoyed the several nods coming his way, knowing full well that Gomez had never led an ASU in his life.

'But for Lynch's quick thinking, and intervention, the attack could have easily hit the Foreign Secretary's car, Sean threw in.

God bless him.

'But would the pipe bomb have had any effect on the armoured vehicle had it been a direct hit?' Gomez pressed.

'Possibly, possibly not, but I wasn't prepared to just watch in order to find out, or was that wrong of me?' Lynch said.

'Of course it wasn't, you did well, Brendan,' Walsh said. Lynch noted that he had used his first name. Walsh then turned to face, Gomez and added, 'and none of us sat here would have just watched it unfold either.'

Then the Southern Commander, George O'Neil, a fifty-year built like a basketball player spoke for the first time. 'We lost a good man in Murphy. And the Brits are claiming he threw the bomb.'

'Political bullshit. The bike just had a rider on it. He stopped and threw the bomb. Murphy, God rest his soul, tried to stop him, and then all these Brit soldier bastards popped up from nowhere and took him out. They either mistook him as part of the attack, or have hung it on him as it suits their narrative. The man's a hero.'

'I believe they are even claiming it was them who stopped the attack,' Sean said.

'Cheeky bastards,' Lynch added.

'Murphy's a hero, right enough,' Walsh said, and then added, 'And therein lies one of the problems: we need his body back to give him a full military send off, and to do so we need to tell the Brits who he is, and that he was one of us.'

'I couldn't agree more, Lynch said, and added, 'can't we declare we were there to try and stop the Loyalist attack, and then demand the repatriation of his body?'

Walsh nodded and called for a vote. It was unanimous but Lynch noticed that Gomez was the last to say 'Aye.'

Walsh then went on to discuss the next issue. Having declared that PIRA were there to prevent the Loyalist attack, they will need to display a show of strength against the UFF or UVF of whichever faction of the UDA committed the outrage. They needed to send a message.

This was music to Lynch's ears. His grand plan was playing out perfectly. 'If I may? 'he asked Walsh, who nodded for him to continue. 'I have long thought, as this Council is aware, that we have left the Loyalists be for far too long. We have talked of reconciliation with them and the Brits, when clearly, they have not shown this Council the same respect.' Sean had warned him not to grandstand, or try and say 'I told you so' as it would backfire. He chose his words carefully. 'I fully understand now how honourable those intentions were, but I think what has happened proves that those Proddy dogs are not ready, or fit to sit at any negotiating table. I respectfully suggest that we hit them back hard. The only way to ever obtain a reconciliation with them - if that is still the wish of this Council - is to show them that they are never a match for us militarily, and that we can destroy them.'

Nods from some, and murmurs from others and then Lynch was asked to wait outside while the Council spoke in private. He'd love to be a fly on the wall, but knew that Sean would fill him later, even if he only gave him an abridged version.

A long twenty minutes later, Lynch was called back in to discover that the Council had voted five-to-one to restart armed operations against the Loyalists with immediate effect. Lynch was utterly thrilled, but guessed who the rebel voter was. Walsh added that they would release a statement and claim Murphy's body in order to give his family some solace and the chance to inter him with dignity.

Then Lynch's dreams all came true at once. Walsh said that he wanted Lynch to command a non-geographically linked ASU, staffed by whoever he wanted, irrespective of where the volunteers were currently placed. He knew that would piss some Brigade Commanders off, but so be it.

'That's brilliant. What will be my commission?' Lynch asked.

'A roving one. You will report to the OC Northern Command only.'

'Targets?'

'We will need to keep this tight, there are filthy touts everywhere. The Council gives you complete autonomy. Sean will intervene as and when he decides it appropriate, and of course he will be our link. You up for this, Brendan?'

'Of course, and I won't let you down.' Lynch couldn't believe how well the meeting had gone. The only Council member who looked less than sure was Gomez. But he could live with that.

On the drive back north Sean said, 'What have I always told you? Easy does it wins the day.'

'You're right, so you are. That couldn't have gone much better. And thanks for jumping in and supporting me.'

'My pleasure.'

'We are truly back on a proper war footing against those Loyalist parasites.'

'That we are, Brendan, that we are.'

Chapter Twenty-three

Hastings was back in the basement of the newsagents in Belfast, eagerly awaiting the routine contact call from his source. It was three days since the attack in London and he was hoping that that would have been long enough for the agent to pick up some intel. He knew he couldn't rush or push it too hard or the source might walk away. They were dicing with death, and he was still unsure as to the motivation behind it all.

The informant had approached them, which had worried Jeremy and many others at Thames House. Were they being infiltrated to vicariously obtain intel for PIRA? Just to task the source on a given subject or individual effectively gave away intel to the enemy. Letting them know that in which you were interested. He had been careful to try and reduce this exposure to a minimum, he tried not to ask too much of an individual, unless, first mentioned by the source. It was not the normal way of informant - or agent - handling. It allowed the tail to wag the dog, but this had been the decided tactic. All that said, the intelligence given so far, had pretty much validated the source and settled many nerves in MI5. But Hastings knew never to become complacent.

Then his terminal came to life interrupting his musings. He glanced at his watch, ten minutes late, not a problem, but unusual. They both went through the normal opening protocols and then spoke normally.

'Your lot are still officially claiming it was a Loyalist hit,' said the source.

'They are, but they know different.'

'It's one hundred per cent confirmed now, it was Pídàn leading a team so he could blame the Loyalists and get the war against them ramped up. He's a zealot who will never accept peace. He's told the Council he was trying to stop a Loyalist hit and they believe him.'

'What makes you think not?'

'I just don't trust him, but whichever version you accept, the outcome is the same. They've given him free reign to run amok across the north of Ireland. No one will stop him now if you don't. And forget any hope of backchannel talks of peace restarting with Pídàn on the loose.'

Hastings took a moment for the full horror to sink in, and then asked, 'What resources does he have?'

'Anything he wants, and he can draw volunteers from any Brigade he chooses. He's already identified his first target.'

'Christ, are you sure?'

'I've only got this third hand, but only a fool would ignore it.'

'Give me the details,' Hastings said, and then made notes hurriedly as the source spoke, and then the line went dead. He sat back to reread them. They had twenty-four hours' notice; he was grateful for that.

He then called Jeremy and briefly told him all that the source had said.

'So, it was a "false flag" op?'

'According to the source. But as they said, it doesn't really matter. The outcome is the same.'

Then Jeremy asked him to pause, he was being interrupted with an urgent intel update. Five minutes later he came back on the line, and confirmed that PIRA had named the deceased 'bomber' as Harry Murphy. They claimed he was not the bomber but was trying to stop it, and they want the body back.

'I've gone over this again and again with Romeo Troop, the guy they took out was on the back of the bike, and was the bomber. And the source has confirmed that the rider of the bike was Pídàn himself.'

'Then it really was a false flag op, no question, whether PIRA understand or not?'

'Yes. And now we have a further imminent attack.'

'Stay where you are I need to ring the DG and call you back,' Jeremy said and then ended the call.

Hastings made a brew and sat down sipping it as he took everything in. He had just about finished when Jeremy called back.

'I've briefed the DG who has spoken to the PM. Her instructions have the usual vagueness so as to avoid prior knowledge and grant deniability, but the subtext is crystal.'

Hastings knew what was coming, and asked what phrase she had used.

'"I don't expect there to be any further problems from Pídàn. I expect a permanent solution. Is that clear, Director General"?'

'So, she wants him dead?'

'Yep.'

'It will cause us problems going forward.'

'I'm aware of that. But when Romeo intervenes, be that covertly, or overtly, it might prove difficult to avoid.'

Hastings knew this, and also knew as far as the PM was concerned, once Pídàn was eliminated, the threat he posed would be over. But they'd lose their way in. 'What if the Provos just replace him with another hardliner, and our access dries up?'

'It's a dilemma, I know, and I did explain this to the DG, quickly, before he rang number 10.'

'I can feel a "but" coming.'

'I'm afraid so, Bert, but we have our orders. Pídàn must die.'

Hastings knew he had no option but to accept and agree what Jeremy was ordering him to do, and said, 'I understand.'

'And you can identify him to Romeo Troop, now, so there can't be any mistakes.'

'I guess that makes sense.'

'Just one more thing?'

'Yep.'

'Where did you get the codename Pídàn from?'

'It means Century Egg in Chinese. A so-called delicacy over there. They bury an egg for weeks or months and leave it to fester, then eat it. It has intense taste and is rotten from the inside out. Just like Brendan Lynch.'

They ended the call and as Hastings prepared to leave, he was still unsure how much he could or should tell Jackson. He knew there was a strain building, but he had to consider the bigger picture. Then a thought occurred, if Romeo could stop the impending attack, but make it look like an accident, it would preserve their cover for longer. Then he had another thought, and knew this one would be even trickier to pull off than the first.

WITH PREJUDICE

Chapter Twenty-four

'We still don't know the identities of this rogue team of PIRA nutters?' Jackson said, after Hastings had finished updating the whole troop.

'No, but we think that the two who got away from the park, are part of it, and the bike rider is the leader,' Hastings replied.

'Not that it matters, too much, I guess,' Jackson said.

'I take it we just need to slot them all?' Crompton asked.

'Well, on that, I was going to ask if it was possible to construct an attack plan that protected the proposed victim, but made it look like an accident of some kind rather than an elite military intervention?'

'Anything is possible. Be a bit more difficult, that's all,' Crompton replied.

'Any reason why you want a covert approach?' Jackson asked.

'It preserves you going forward.'

'But if we take them all out, job done, surely?' Harris chipped in with.

'According to my source, which I'm sure you are now only too aware is a live source; this new ASU will have a roving commission, and access to as many resources as necessary. So, if we slot two or three or however many turn up, another two or three will replace them.'

If Jackson was being honest, he'd much prefer the 'slot them when you can' approach. If they got replaced, then they would become fair game, too. But obviously, Hastings had his reasons, maybe he'd get him on his own after this job, and try to open him up fully. It was starting to eat away at the trust they had built up, and he could sense a similar feeling among the others. Not good for morale.

Anyway, down to business, they all crowded around Crompton as he opened a map out onto the table, Hastings made his excuses and said he'd link back in later, and to put him down for Zero Alpha, he'd man the base set in the office.

The target was a member of the Ulster Defence Regiment, which was part of the British Army. It was the largest Infantry Regiment within the whole of the Army and was only formed in 1970 in response to the riots which were an initial part of The Troubles. The mark was a sergeant named Gerald Smith, who lived in a side street close to the A55 in Belmont, East Belfast. A traditionally stanch Unionist area populated mainly by Protestants. According to the Provos, many of the UDR's members were secretly carrying out Loyalist terrorist actions, and rightly or wrongly - Hastings had failed to confirm which - Smith was suspected of being one of them. He'd apparently been followed along the busy A55 many times and left to run after he turned off into the residential areas. They had carried out their own form of surveillance in the estates and now knew roughly where he lived. But not exactly. They knew which junction he had to pass in order to reach the A55. They were going to ambush him on his way to work.

Sergeant Crompton was the master tactician with added insights from Harris and King. Jackson usually took a watching brief as they formulated an attack plan. The SAS regiments were not like other corps in the Army which were very rank-based and top-down led. The SAS troops were all skill based, and Jackson always forgot his rank whenever possible. Especially, when Crompton, the most tactically experienced operative among them was talking.

Finally, the plan was sorted and all were briefed and knew their roles. They would be split into four patrols: Jackson; callsign One Alpha, Crompton; Two Alpha, Harris; Three Alpha, King; Four Alpha, and Hastings would man the base set in the office as Zero Alpha.

Jackson would man an OP, on the approach to a T junction and act as trigger for the approaching friendly. Crompton would cover the left turn at the T, and Harris the right. King would be driving a 'stolen' HGV. As a big heavyweight lump, himself, Crompton said King would look more like a Yorkie-man than the rest of them. He received a grunt in reply. He had until the following morning to familiarise himself with the vehicle which Hastings was busy arranging.

WITH PREJUDICE

They would brief again at five a.m. for any intel updates and be on plot for 5.45 a.m. Fortunately, Lisburn was quite close to the plot.

The following morning, they were briefed, kitted up and on plot early. The only intel update was that the Provos had rehearsed everything and were practiced to split-second timing. It was obvious that they must have spotters out on the estate to give the Provos advance warning of Gerald Smith's approach. Because of this, Hastings had arranged though Detective Superintendent Field to have one of his Special Branch detectives plotted up near to Smith's home address, to give advance warning of his movement. He would not have access to Romeo Troop's airways, for security reasons, but he would mainline into Hastings.

The whole troop recced the scene before plotting up to aid to their familiarity of the topography of the place. Jackson noticed as they approached the side road which would form the T junction with the A55; about a hundred yards of traffic cones were evident on the run in. The A55 itself, named Parkway at this part, was an urban dual carriageway with a relief lane on its southbound stretch. On approach to the side road - Hawthornden Gardens - there was a turn left lane. It was the turn left lane, which was cordoned off by the traffic cones, effectively closing it. According to Harris, they weren't there the day before when he swept the plot, and it was too early in the day to have the local council or highways department rung to check if they were legit.

Jackson parked up on Hawthornden Gardens facing the T junction with the A55 Parkway, to give early warning of Smith's approach. Crompton - Two Alpha - was on the south side of the junction in bushes at the side of the road, close to the approach to a roundabout which wasn't far past the junction. Harris was parked on the relief carriageway several hundred yards north of the junction, on the sounthbound side, so as to give an early indication of any suspicious incoming vehicle. Not so close as to appear connected in any way to the plot, but near enough to be there quickly if it all went noisy. He was using callsign Three Alpha.

Mr Yorkie King on Four Alpha was in his HGV parked on the hard shoulder of the A55 Parkway, prior to the blocked off left turn lane, with his hazard warning lights on.

All were dressed in civies and all were armed with concealed sidearms of choice with a Heckler and Koch MP5 machine gun close to hand.

The intelligence was that the Provos knew that Smith lived on the estate, but not where exactly. Whenever he arrived home, he parked his vehicle in a garage, without exception. Jackson was conscious that if this was the case, then any spotters the Provos were using could be on Hawthornden Gardens itself. He couldn't see any stationary vehicles, so the watcher could be sat in any of the houses which lined the road in this des res area. According to intel checks Hastings had had done via Fields, nothing was known on any of the addresses on Hawthornden Gardens, but that didn't mean anything. Negatives searches just meant that the positive ones hadn't been found yet.

Jackson did a comms check to confirm that all units were on plot and that their radios were working properly. He ended this by saying, 'The visual to all units, no change, no change on the approach. Acknowledge in sequence.'

They all did. It was just a waiting game now.

WITH PREJUDICE

Chapter Twenty-five

At 7.30 a.m. two things happened in quick succession. Firstly, Crompton came over the net to say that he had a rear view of a battered old Range Rover, which had pulled over on the A55 Parkway. It was at the start of the coned off left turn lane, just before the junction with Hawthornden Gardens. It was daylight and the visibility was good. What stood out, was that the vehicle squeezed in before the first cone and parked at the very start of the left turn lane. It was not a natural manoeuvre you'd associate with someone needing to pull over in an emergency. According to Compton, it seemed a more considered action. He said he would move up the hedgerow to afford a better look. There were two men on board. All acknowledged and Jackson reminded everyone to remain vigilant. Four Alpha, Ian King confirmed that he also had a view, but would leave the eyeball with Two Alpha.

Then Hastings came over airwaves from the office base set, *'Standy, standby, standby all units. The friendly is on the move towards your location.'*

All acknowledged, and Two Alpha said that there was no change regarding the Range Rover. Jackson was thinking in his mind's eye of the set up with the left turn lane. Was the Range Rover near enough for its occupants to deploy with carbines from that distance, or would they need to be closer. His view was that any reduction in distance between the stationary motor and any vehicle held at the T junction could only serve to increase a gunman's chances. But he was looking at it through the eyes of a highly trained soldier, and not that of a terrorist. Looking at it though their eyes meant any option was possible. It was often their disorganisation or dysfunctional thinking that could outwit the professionals. He had to consider it as they might. He therefore quickly told King to start the HGV engine ready to roll, and all units be prepared to deploy from where they were.

Then the second thing happened, Smith's tiny, dark brown Morris Metro saloon approached and passed Jackson, Smith was driving alone. Jackson warned the team, and pulled his own vehicle into a loose follow seventy-five yards behind him. Not too close to scare off the bad guys, but close enough to quickly join the party.

Two Alpha reported seeing the Metro as it started to approach the junction, and quickly added that as soon as it came into view the Ranger Rover moved forward. Three Alpha reported that he was inbound at speed, and Jackson accelerated, too.

Moments later, he saw the Metro slowing to a stop.

Crompton reported that the Range Rover was accelerating hard and on a collision course towards the Metro. Jackson steered to the wrong side of the road and when alongside the Metro, hit his horn to attract Smith's attention, thumbing back behind him as he did.

But Smith had already worked that out, and as Jackson started to reverse out of harm's way, so did Smith. He had probably been momentarily caught not just by the approaching Range Rover, but by what was behind it.

At the briefing, they had all reckoned that during any attack, the Provos would always be transfixed at what was going on ahead of them and not elsewhere. It would be their mistake.

Jackson could see that the Range Rover was attempting to adjust its course, it was under heavy braking now as it tried to slow enough in order to make the left turn into Hawthornden Gardens. This of course played into their hands. Well, into Ian King's anyway, as seconds later the fast approaching, but unnoticed HGV smashed into the passenger's side of the Range Rover. It pushed the car across the mouth of the junction and into the side of a high garden fence sat on top of a three-foot brick wall fronting a corner house, trapping the driver's side against it. The vehicle was wedged between it and the front of the HGV.

Moments later, Crompton arrived at the same time Harris's motor screamed to a halt, blocking the rear of the target vehicle.

Their brief had always been to protect the life of Smith at all costs, to remove the threat. And if that could be done covertly, all the better. If not, then so be it. But if they had to declare themselves, then an arrest was the preferred option. Hastings wanted the terrorists for debrief purposes if they had to blow their cover to protect Smith. Lethal force was not to be used unless other lives were in imminent danger. Jackson was unsure how much intel hardened Provos would provide, and knew that the arrest option would be difficult if there was a full contact. He'd further briefed the troop outside of Hastings presence to add some realism.

Jackson accelerated hard and pulled in behind Smith who nearly reversed into him. He was out his vehicle in an instant with his Army ID in one hand, and his other on display to show that he was unarmed. 'PHILOS: British Army,' Jackson shouted. He could see Smith react as he slowly got out of his car, also keeping his open hands in view. Jackson had used the secret codeword known only to the Army and the RUC to confirm that he was a friend and not a foe. Philos being the Greek word for a friend, a trusted confidant.

Jackson explained that Smith needed to get to his barracks quickly where Detective Superintendent Field was waiting. He confirmed to Smith that his home address had not been compromised so his family were safe, though a house move may well be needed to ensure security going forward. But that was a discussion to be had between him and Field.

Smith thanked Jackson and got back in his car and did a U-turn before disappearing. Jackson quickly gave Zero Alpha an update.

His first response was, *'Are the Tangos injured?'*

'Not sure, I'm about to find out, but it was a heavy collision. Wait one.'

Jackson, then positioned his car so as to close the road to any approaching vehicles, and then jogged to the scene. King had reversed the HGV and Harris had the passenger door open and was leaning in. Crompton had smashed the driver's window and was also leaning into the car between a tapered gap between the fence and the front wing. Both pulled themselves out and moved away from the vehicle on Jackson's approach.

'What have we got, lads?'

'A back seat with two automatic weapons; MAC10 Machine pistols and ammo,' Crompton answered.

'Both are wearing open-ended balaclavas, pulled down under their chins ready to deploy,' Harris added.

'Ugly bastards never got the chance to cover their hideous faces,' Crompton said, smiling.

'Thanks to Yorkie's driving,' Harris added.

'Hey,' shouted King as he joined them from the wagon. 'Can I have Yorkie as my new nickname?'

'No chance, it's not offensive enough. You'll remain "Tickets Please" and be glad of it,' Crompton said.

'Anyway, children, how are our casualties? Has anyone called an ambulance? We may have to eventually,' Jackson said.

'Unfortunately, they won't need one. Both must have broken their necks in this terrible accident,' Crompton said.

'How sad. I'll get onto Hastings; he has an arrangement with Field for some of his detectives to dress up as Traffic Officers and report this "road traffic accident".'

He then gave Hastings the overview, who said everything was already in place should they have been able to keep the intervention covert. Which they had-ish.

'Not a single round fired; either way,' Jackson confirmed.

'As soon as Field's men arrive, they will take care of everything, you lot just get back here.'

'Understood,' Jackson finished with.

Five minutes later, the four 'Traffic Officers' arrived, and the sergeant in charge just cocked his head to one side at Jackson. Two minutes after that, Romeo Troop were en route back to Lisburn. Job done.

Chapter Twenty-six

Romeo were still on a high as they entered their barracks within a barracks back at Lisburn. But the mood soon flattened as they entered the main room. Hastings was pacing up and down and didn't look happy.

'I thought the plan was for a minor crash, just to stop the vehicle?' Hastings started with, aiming his remarks at all of them.

'I had to move quickly, as things unfolded faster that we could have known,' King answered, as he and the others all dropped their kit and weapons up against the wall.

'The main thing is we protected Smith. I thought that was the primary objective?' Crompton said.

Jackson could feel the irritation building.

Ignoring his remark, Hastings said, 'And the terrorists were both killed in the accident?'

'Yes,' Harris joined in with.

'You already know this. I gave you a brief update before we cleared the scene,' Jackson said.

Hastings didn't reply and looked deep in thought.

'Not sure what your problem is?' Crompton said, glancing at Jackson as he spoke. His remark clearly aimed at Hastings.

'We need to debrief this ASAP,' Hastings said.

'I'm debriefing nothing, until I've made a brew,' Crompton replied with.

The aura in the room was palpable, and Jackson would have Hastings after the debrief. He'd planned to have a word prior to this, but was livid inside now. He'd no idea what the man's problem was.

Five minutes and a boiled kettle later, they were all sat at the briefing table, and Hastings went through the limited written log he had maintained. Then Romeo Troop went through the action and made the necessary annotations to the record, which was duly signed by all.

Hastings homed in on the two terrorists. 'Did you take any photos of their faces?'

'No point, they were both smashed in by the crash,' Crompton said.

'That bad?'

'Covered in blood, I wasn't aware you wanted them cleaning up to take nice photos,' Crompton said. 'We were in a time-critical combat mission, what did you expect?'

Jackson was biding his time as Crompton exchanged with Hastings, and he thought through what any subtext might mean.

'I'm not sure what your problem is? It's clear you have one.'

'I just hoped that they had survived, so I could have debriefed them.'

'Like those two scumbags would have given you the steam off their shit,' King threw in.

'Now, I'm confused. The brief was to do a covert-accident intervention if we could, so as to preserve the fact that it was a military op. It was only in the event of it going all noisy where were supposed to try - and I repeat, try - and arrest them.'

'Well, erm, that's correct,' Hastings replied, sounding less sure of himself.

'And as, amazingly, we had managed to do things covertly, how were we to arrest them without outing ourselves. Had they survived the crash?'

'You could have kept hold of them until I got SB dressed as traffic to the scene,' Hastings replied, weakly.

'Now you are having "tin bath". How many civilians involved in an accident with armed men, obviously terrorists, would try and do a citizen's arrest?' Crompton said, getting to his feet. 'I've had enough of this BS.'

'OK, sorry, please sit down, fair point. I'm just thinking out loud.'

Crompton slowly re-took his seat.

'Any ID documents on them?'

'NO. Terrorists don't carry ID when on a job. You know that. Or are you thinking out loud again.'

'Sorry, of course. SB will fingerprint the bodies; they will no doubt be on record.'

'OK, this debrief is over. Dave, can you take the lads into the sleeping quarters and close the door,' Jackson said to Crompton, and then addressed all three troopers, 'For the record, you all did fabulous today. Job well done.'

'What's going on?' Hastings said.

'You'll find out.'

'What does that mean?' Hastings said in a haughty way, as he started to get to his feet.

'Sit back down, or I'll put you on your arse myself.'

Hastings did, and as soon as they had the room to themselves, Jackson with barely veiled anger, spat at Hastings, 'What the fuck was all that?'

Dropping his attitude, Hastings replied calmly, 'I just wanted them alive.'

'Why? And don't give me this intel debrief bull. Sounds to me that you'd be happier if they had managed to get away. And as for the troop, you've just lost them.'

Hastings paused a few moments before he answered, 'OK. I'm sorry if I've held back a bit. But sometimes it has to be "need to know" and that is dictated by "when to know".'

'Go on.'

'Don't take this the wrong way, but did they really have to die?'

'It was just a terrible accident.'

Hastings didn't reply, so Jackson pushed on, 'And just for the sake of clarity, you may be in charge overall, but once we are deployed on the ground, then it's my call.'

'I know that.'

'Well don't forget it. You have never been in a firefight. Especially one where a myriad of unexpected things can things can hit you. It's not easy. You'd do well to remember that.'

'I know that, too.'

'The easiest way of stopping today's attack, without all this "make it look like an accident" bull, would have been to hit them from the off with automatic weapons before they knew what the hell was happening, it would have been all over.' Then it hit Jackson. 'My God. You think one of the dead is your source?'

'What?' Hastings replied, sitting up straight. 'No, no that's not it.'

'You are running a source who is actually an active terrorist. And you didn't think we needed to know. Unbelievable.'

'No, you've got it all wrong.'

'That's why you wanted them alive. And we are supposed to trust you?'

'Yes of course, you can.'

'Would you sacrifice one of us just to keep your snout alive?'

'That's ridiculous.'

'Is it? Apart from the moral question of running an active killer as your tout, how can I be sure you wouldn't sacrifice any of us just to keep him alive?'

'You can trust me. We've built up a great working relationship.'

'I thought we had. And I know spooks are capable of dirty tricks, but this is off the scale. At least we have morality on our side.'

'Please calm down, I'll try and explain.'

'Save it. I'm pulling the troop out.'

'My God, you can't do that.'

'Watch me, and when my Major back in Hereford gets my update, don't think he won't back me. We are not putting the lives of anyone, let alone British troops at risk, just to keep your murdering grass alive.'

Jackson got to his feet and could see that Hastings was stunned, he turned to head towards the sleeping quarters.

'Wait,' Hastings shouted after Jackson.

Jackson paused, and without turning around, said, 'Last chance, so this had better be good.'

'The source is not one of those terrorists.'

Jackson turned to face Hastings, and said, 'How can you be so sure, the bodies have not been ID-ed, yet.'

'Because the source is not an active terrorist, as you think.'

'And how do expect me to believe that?'

'OK, truth time. The source has access to a terrorist codenamed Pídàn, who is the leader of this newly formed Active Service Unit.'

'The rider of the bike in London?'

'Yes.'

WITH PREJUDICE

'So, if Pídàn is one of those two dead terrorists from today, your intel dries up?'

'You've got it in one. I'm sorry, I probably should have levelled with you earlier.'

'That you should have. OK, but if your source had access to this Pídàn, then surely you can re-direct the source into other terrorists?'

'Technically yes. But the source has a particular dislike of Pídàn which I've not fully worked out, but I am keen to use.'

'I guess I understand that. Who is Pídàn?'

'I really can't tell you that yet, but will do when I can.'

Jackson thought for a few seconds and nodded.

'So, are we back on?'

'Yes, but you will need to level with the rest of the troop.'

Hastings nodded.

'And one last thing, before you do.'

'What?'

'What the hell does Pídàn mean?'

'That I can tell you right away.'

Chapter Twenty-seven

Lynch had dearly wanted to lead his volunteers on the hit against the UDR man, Smith. But he was forced into a decision. The next job he had in mind - of which he hadn't yet told his brother-in-law Sean about - had presented a reconnaissance opportunity that clashed, but couldn't be ignored. The two men he had commandeered from the West Belfast Brigade were seasoned veterans, who also had the network of spotters on the estate where Smith lived, so it made sense to leave them with it. They didn't need babysitting.

He had Kelly with him, who he was growing to like and trust far more than he would have expected. He'd worked with Kelly in the past, but never on a one-to-one basis, which was when you really got to know someone. He was obviously skilled, not brilliant, but more than adequate. And what he lacked in finesse he more than compensated for in loyalty. And in Lynch's book, that counted for a lot.

He'd agreed to meet the other two in the Shamrock Arms, off the Falls Road around 5 p.m. by which time they should have been clear, showered, and changed, and drinking into their alibis. This was arranged to have started several hours prior to when they actually entered the pub. The recce he and Kelly did went perfectly, in fact from what they now knew, they could act at any time of their choosing. Kelly lived close to the Shamrock and said he'd have a couple of jars with the lads and then head off. Lynch had to drive back to Armagh so only planned a short stay, too. Plus, it was good tradecraft to limit their public exposure together. Even in the relative safety of the Shamrock, a stanch Republican Catholic pub. He knew he could trust everyone who went in there, but those bastard touts could be stood on any street corner just clocking who came and went.

He hated touts with a ferocious venom. A couple of years ago, when he'd still been on the Army Council, he set up the Security Dept. to root out the touts. In total, they identified and killed eight. But not before torturing them. Six had fessed up to all their sins

WITH PREJUDICE

and their families were ostracised from the community. Two, however, held out until death. Lynch had wondered if they had got it wrong with the last two. But it troubled him, not. He hadn't liked them and it had helped send out the right message and deterrent. They hadn't died in vain. They had still given their lives to The Cause, and that was all that mattered.

Shortly before they pulled up at the Shamrock, a newsflash came over the car radio about a tragic accident in East Belfast, off the A55 involving a saloon car and a stolen wagon. Unconfirmed reports claimed that two people were believed dead, and that the police were currently hunting the lorry driver who had fled the scene. He noted the bulletin but thought nothing of it until he entered the pub. The mood was very sombre and all eyes were on them as they entered. He noted that people hurried out of their way. Trouble was brewing. The murmur of chitchat stopped as soon as they'd walked in. All Lynch could hear was the sound of their feet on the old wooden floorboards. The noise accentuated by the absence of carpets or any soft furnishings. All the tables and chairs which lined the sides, were old rickety dark wooden ones, matching the old timber bar which looked Victorian in design and age.

Lynch didn't have to wait long before his instincts were confirmed. He hadn't reached the bar when he saw, and heard, Bernie Doyle making a beeline towards him.

Doyle was a six-foot hulk of a man with jet black bushy hair, which matched a wild moustache and beard. Lynch came to a halt, and turned to face Kelly quickly and said, 'Get the ale in.'

Kelly nodded, looking relieved as he shot off to the bar.

Doyle came to a stop close to Lynch and leaned in towards his face, and said, 'What the fuck have you done?'

'Nice to see you, too Bernie.'

'Don't you fecking test me, Lynch.'

'I've no idea what you are on about, honestly. I've just walked in.'

'You haven't heard?'

'Heard what?'

'Firstly, you arrogantly commandeer two of my finest men, and then you send them to their deaths.'

'No way, how come—'

But before he could finish his sentence Doyle nodded towards the back room behind the bar. They were gaining an audience. Lynch nodded back and followed him through. They were joined a moment later by Kelly with a tray of drinks, including one for Doyle, good lad. Then Doyle hit him with the news. The two dead in the accident he'd just heard on the radio were their two. He couldn't believe it. 'How the hell did that happen?'

'You tell me. But of course, you can't because you weren't there.'

'I was on another job in the Lower Shankill. But theirs should have been a straightforward one, everything was in place, practiced and planned.'

'You didn't plan for this, though, did you?'

Lynch knew now was not the time for a fight. He gave Doyle his condolences and tried to sound as contrite as he could. Then added, 'Do we have all the facts?'

'Scant at the moment. But apparently, a stolen wagon ploughed into them at the junction. The spotter has said that the mark was on his way to them. Might even have been on them.'

'Seems like one hell of a coincidence.'

'Time will tell. If it was just an accident, then we will track down the driver and deal with him before the peelers get anywhere near him. He will pay a heavy price.'

'Anything I can do to help, just ask.'

Doyle ignored Lynch's comment, and then added, 'And if it wasn't an accident, I will hold you responsible for not being there to make a difference.'

'I can see you are rightly upset, but there is no need for threats, Bernie.'

'It's a promise not a threat. If this was no accident... And I don't care who your brother-in-law is.'

Lynch decided to not enrage the situation further. He downed his drink and stood. 'I'll let that slide Bernie as you are upset. But trust me, this is a one-time offer. Just remember who the real enemy is before you fly off on one at me again.' He then turned to Kelly and addressed him before Doyle could answer. 'Come on let's go. We have work to do.' Kelly nodded and both men left Doyle starring at them from his seat as they walked out the room.

At the doorway, Lynch turned to face Bernie once more and said, 'If all goes well, the Loyalists won't be singing in the Lower Shankill tonight. They'll pay a price for the loss of your men. Call it recompense for what your lads would have done in the future had they lived.'

Bernie nodded and then asked, 'What have you got in mind?'

'Let's just say they won't be able to cry in their beer,' Lynch replied but stopped himself saying more, aware of an audience in the bar side again. He left it there and walked out with Kelly.

Once outside, Kelly turned to head off the other way and Lynch stopped him. 'With me, we really have work to do. We need to turn this into a win as quick as we can, and before Sean gets hold of us.'

Chapter Twenty-eight

Hastings realised that he had nearly messed everything up. He'd made his peace with Jackson and then with the rest of the troop before he left Lisburn. But knew that he might not get away with such a hiccup again. He'd have to let them in more so, in order to repair trust going forward. He also knew he would have to disclose who Pídàn was soon. Though that could all be academic if he were one of the two killed in the Range Rover. He was rushing to the newsagents in order to speak to the source. If Lynch was dead, then Maggie and his bosses would be happy. But he had serious concerns how that would affect the operational effectiveness of the informant. True as Jackson had suggested, the source could be realigned into another senior Provo, but he knew it would and could never be the same. Not least due to the access the source had into Lynch, who clearly had many haters among PIRA. But mainly as Hastings was unsure if the source would be as driven. And therein lay another of his conundrums; he still hadn't worked out the source's rationale for doing what they were doing. Their true agenda. Especially given the horrendous risks they were taking if it all came tumbling down. He shuddered at the thought as he walked into the shop.

The source rang bang on time, and opening protocols over, they got straight down to business. 'Who were the two who died?'

'I only know them as Davy and Pat, both from one of the Belfast Brigades.'

'Not Pídàn, then?' Hastings asked to ensure clarity.

'A great pity, but no.'

Hastings breathed a sigh of relief. Thought for a second, and then asked, 'Where was he?'

'Elsewhere, and no one has heard from him in hours. I may know later, if I do, I've leave you a recorded message. You can pick it up whenever. But he should have been in touch by now, so something is wrong, or he's up to something. I've got to go,' the source said before ending the call.

WITH PREJUDICE

Hastings sat back in his chair and considered what had been said, and what had not. He wasn't looking forward to his next phone call. Jeremy would not be pleased and the PM would no doubt show her displeasure to the Director General. But he could turn the circumstances around to his advantage in order to take some of the pressure off. It wasn't his or the troop's fault that, for whatever reason, Lynch was not on plot at the attack. And although, he'd told Jackson that he'd wanted the terrorists alive, he could now spin it to his bosses that he ordered the troop to go in hard on the back of the PM's wishes. It was just unfortunate that Lynch was not where he should have been. That should do it. Plus, the Provisional IRA were now down by two operatives. He smiled as he picked up the secure phone, but then concern wiped it away. Why wasn't Lynch present, and what the hell was he doing that was so important to drag him away. These would be questions he was about to face. He just hoped that the source could get access to the fuller story. He'd also have to warn Derek upstairs that he'd need access to the shop later.

Five minutes later, Hastings ended the call with Jeremy. His ploy had worked, he said the DG would be satisfied he had enough to placate the PM, for now. But he expected an update later, or if it got too late, the morning would do once the source had got back to him. As he ended the call, the irony of Jeremy's words was not lost on Hastings. They wanted Lynch dead, notwithstanding how that may affect the source's motivation and their access to intel going forward. But then, they were anxious for any updates the source was able to give on where Lynch was and what he may be up to.

***

Lynch took the wheel and Kelly directed him to the lockup off The Falls Road, where Murphy kept his munitions. 'This place will need decommissioning at some stage, but hopefully we are ahead of the game.'

'Sean will know of it, surely?' Kelly asked.

'He will, but I'm going to avoid him until I have some good news to give.'

'What have you got in mind?'

'Bernie's criticism that had we been present on today's job things would have been different, are one I can hear being repeated. Especially, by that slabber Gomez who shouldn't even have a voice on the Army Council.'

Lynch glanced at Kelly who just nodded. He continued, 'The job we recced, is good to go, as you know.'

'I agree, any time.'

Lynch instinctively looked at his watch, it was early afternoon. 'And now would be as good a time as any.'

Kelly's head swivelled to look intensely at Lynch who waited until the traffic ahead eased so he could turn to face him. 'So, we do it now.'

'I guess. I thought we were just doing a run through when you said we had "work to do".'

'Normally, we would, but this'll be a piece of piss. Have you ever thrown one before?'

'No, it's usually the Proddies who use them.'

'I have, we used them a couple of times in the early days. They are actually quite effective considering our target, and as long as Murphy's garage has all we need, it won't take me long to pull one together.'

'You've obviously made one before?'

'Oh yes, nothing much to it,' Lynch lied. He then went on to explain that by doing it straight away it would justify them not being at the UDR man's assassination attempt. They could tell Sean, that it was only ever meant to be a recce and a dry run today, but they got lucky with who turned up, so went for it. It would silence any critics, and keep Bernie and other Battalion Commanders happy. After all, he was going to have to use more of their men in the future.

Kelly said he understood and was happy with Lynch's thinking.

'But if we only take out scragg ends, won't that backfire on us?'

'We can say that "so and so" was there, that's why we went for it. But they somehow survived.'

'Who should we say, just so I get my story straight.'

Lynch smiled; Kelly was a proving to be a truly loyal asset. 'Any of those top dogs from the Lower Shankill's so called Ulster Freedom Fighters. We'll name one later.'

WITH PREJUDICE

'Fair enough.'

'They are just a bunch of criminal thugs at heart. You know the stupid bastards were the first to kill a peeler back in '69. Supposed Unionists. We'll be doing their community a favour.'

'Over there,' Kelly shouted as he pointed to a narrow turn-off. 'By the phone box.'

'I can bell Sean from there afterwards.'

'In fact, can you pull up now, I'll ring the bird and tell her not to call round, I'm going to be late.'

Lynch nodded and pulled over and took in the surroundings as Kelly made his call. A Mural he'd not seen before had appeared on the gable end of a house, with the Irish Tricolour on it adorned with the figure of a hooded Provo with an assault rifle in hand. It was reassuring to see, not that he was in any doubt that they were in a safe republican area. Kelly was soon back in the motor.

'Any problems?' Lynch asked.

'No, she's good as gold. Say's she'll stay in at hers all night should I need an alibi. Not that she knows what I do. I reckon she thinks I do a bit of thieving.'

'Good enough, just keep it that way.'

Kelly nodded, and pointed at the alley entrance. Lynch drove down it to reveal a large courtyard covered on three sides with the backs of buildings and a row of garages on the remaining side. Few would know the place was here if they didn't live local. They parked by the end garage and got out. Kelly had spare keys for the several locks which Murphy had given him. Good tradecraft.

Five minutes later they were inside with the up-and-over door closed. Together they moved the huge workbench which ran across the rear of the lock-up to reveal a hatch cut into the concrete floor. That removed, it revealed a 3x2x2 foot steel-lined space. Everything Lynch needed was there to make a low explosive concussion pipe bomb.

Chapter Twenty-nine

Hastings arrived back at the barracks and continued his charm offensive with Jackson and the rest of the troop. In the short journey from the shop, he had come to a decision. Contrary to what Jeremy or indeed the Prime Minister wanted, he was going to try and keep Pídàn alive for as long as he could. Certainly, until he had ascertained the source's true motivation. He could really do with a face-to-face meeting, but that would be nearly impossible at the moment, and extremely dangerous. But he realised if he wanted to keep Pídàn, for now, he'd have to level up with the troop. At the very least, they would need to know who not to shoot.

He called in at an off-licence en route and bought a couple of bottles of Bushmills as a peace offering, which was graciously received as he called all to gather around the ops table. Firstly, to continue to dispel any rumours, he gave his word that the source was not Pídàn. He explained that the source had good links into Pídàn, which was why he needed to keep them alive, for the time being.

'At last, you are levelling with us?' Crompton said, which was backed up by murmurs from Harris and King.

'I am. But you have to understand how tricky a line I have to walk sometimes. But, if I want you to keep him alive, then I accept that you need to know who he is.'

'He obviously wasn't one of the two Range Rover occupants, then?' Jackson asked.

'No, I have that information confirmed, now.'

'Where was he?' King asked.

'I'm hopefully going to get an update on that. In fact, I'll be heading out shortly to check for any left messages.'

'Who is he?' Jackson asked.

'He's a hardline veteran Provo called Brendan Lynch.'

'He's the nutter running around with his own hell-bent agenda?' Jackson asked.

'He is,' Hastings replied, and then went on to brief them in summary all they needed to know about Lynch and his new roving

WITH PREJUDICE

agenda. When he'd finished, he leaned back into his chair and took a glug of whiskey from his coffee mug.

'Do you have an up-to-date photo of him?' Harris asked.

'I do and will pin it up on the target board in a mo, but just ask Captain Jackson what he looks like.'

'Pardon?' Jackson asked.

'He's the headbanger who clipped you at DI McDonald's house.'

'I'll not forget him in a hurry,' Jackson replied.

'Do we know the other members of Lynch's mob?' Crompton asked.

'It's fluid. But they are two less, thanks to your excellent work, but Kelly from London is probably still with him, plus, whoever he chooses to commandeer.'

All three of Romeo Troop nodded and Hastings added, 'I've got to go now and try and get an update, but as far as I know, Lynch's whereabouts are currently unknown, so be ready.'

'We'd better lay off the Bushmills, then,' Jackson added.

'Sorry lads, I hadn't thought of that. Yes, just until we can locate him.'

'Need any help?' King asked.

Hastings was glad of the offer as it showed that the relationship was back on track. 'Thanks, but I'm OK for the next thirty minutes. Hopefully, I'll have an update waiting for me, and if I don't, I'll wait until I do. Then I'll bell you either way.'

They all nodded and didn't ask any more questions. They didn't know about his set up below the newsagents, and would never need to know that. It made no difference to them, anyhow. He said his goodbyes, left the barracks and headed into the tea-time traffic back towards the shop.

Twenty minutes later, he entered the shop, to see Derek's back towards him.

'Sorry, we are closed, I'm just doing some stocktaking,' Derek said as he started to turn around, before realising it was Hastings. 'Twice in one day, you must be busy.'

'I am, and I may be here a while longer, I'm afraid.'

'No worries, I might actually do some stocktaking, see how many bars of chocolate those thieving school kids have nicked this week.'

'I'd check your magazines' top shelf, too, if I was you,' Hastings replied.

'Ah, no worries there. I keep the good stuff under the counter. Can't risk showing that off round here. This ain't Soho, you know,' Derek answered.

They both laughed, and Hastings made his way through to the back of the premises and then down into the basement. He was about to make himself a brew when he noticed a red light flashing on his terminal. He put the ear phones on and listened in horror. There was no way of knowing what time the message had been left. The caller didn't say. They had been rushed and harried. He instinctively, looked at his own watch to try and work out how long he had been away as he listened to the short missive again.

Then he picked up the secure phone to ring the barracks within a barracks. He just prayed that they weren't too, late. This could start a war of hitherto unprecedented proportions if the information were correct. Thankfully, Jackson picked up quickly and Hastings told him all he could.

'On it,' Jackson ended the call with; no time for pleasantries.

He was glad he'd told them all about Lynch now. Apart from anything else, it saved what could be vital seconds.

He then picked up the receiver to call London, he really wasn't looking forward to this. But at least he could justify being very brief in the circumstances. He'd have to cut Jeremy off if he went into one of his verbose discourses.

WITH PREJUDICE

Chapter Thirty

The Cuppa Way Peace Wall erected in 1969 was only ever intended as a temporary structure after the civil unrest and riots of the time. Initially, constructed of just corrugated iron topped with barbed wire, it had been reinforced several times, wider and higher, but was still not meant to be a permanent divide. But it did its job in helping to separate the Protestant Loyalist communities of the Shankill Road areas to the north, and the Catholic Republicans to its south. To the casual observer, both the Falls Road and The Shankill look remarkably similar. Rows of terraced houses, interspaced with commercial buildings such as clubs, bars and community centres. Many adorned with Murals pledging their sectarian allegiances with the Union Flags and the Irish Tricolour wafting in the breeze for all to see.

As far as Lynch was concerned, the Shankill looked like a shithole compared to the house-proud properties on The Falls Road, where studious housewives cleaned their front steps with donkey stones to show off their homes. As far as Lynch knew, the Proddy dogs of the Shankill cleaned their front steps with dogshit. He hated going north of the wall, it was not a place he often visited, and always felt uncomfortable when he did. It left him needing a bath afterwards, and the arrogance of the painted murals always filled him with rage.

He was driving with Kelly in the front passenger seat. They both had their windows open to increase their awareness of the surroundings. Both were wearing baseball caps pulled down low just in case any Loyalist paramilitary recognised them. They drove east from Woodvale Road which became Shankill Road. They passed the Shankill graveyard to their left. 'Not enough of these bastards are in there, yet,' he muttered, conscious that their car windows were open. Kelly just nodded. His eyes were darting everywhere.

'Be careful, don't be obvious. We will do a dry run, just so we are sure,' Lynch said.

'I'm glad about that,' Kelly said.

Lynch could see him glance down at the holdall between his feet as he spoke, and he also noticed Kelly's shoulders relax some. Good, he wanted him alert and ready, but not wound up like a clock.

Traffic was light considering it was rush-hour, though Lynch never knew when rush-hour started or ended nowadays. They were driving towards Lower Shankill when a young mother pushing her pram on a Zebra Crossing brought them to a halt in pole position. There were pavement-fronted terraced houses on both sides. He watched the woman push her pram onto the crossing, and when she was half-way across, she waved and shouted ahead of her. Lynch instinctively looked to his left and saw another young woman sat on the dirty front step of her house with a kid sat on a potty. 'Would you look at that?' he said, and Kelly glanced to his left, too. 'In plain sight on the street, no breeding.'

He then returned his gaze to the woman with the pram as she slowed in order to navigate the nearside kerb.

'How are you keeping?' the young woman with the pram addressed her mate as she rose to her feet, kid in one hand and the potty in the other.

Lynch turned to look at the woman with the potty as she shouted back at her approaching friend, 'Little 'un's just been squeezing the Pope, come on in while I get rid of it.'

'WHAT?' Lynch shouted, louder than he intended, but before he could react further, the car behind him hit his horn to hurry them on now that the crossing was clear.

Kelly put his right hand on Lynch's left arm and said, 'Leave it, we'll have our payback, we have to go.'

Lynch knew that Kelly was right, plus they were starting to draw attention with the empty crossing in front of them. He put the car in gear and drove on.

He was just starting to calm down as they approached their target. Lynch pulled over to the side of the road while they both took in their surroundings. Looking through the front windows, it appeared as though there were plenty of people already inside. 'When we come back the other way, I'll obviously pull up on the other side, right outside.'

'Yep.'

'I'll drive up at a swift pace so that it looks like I'm just dropping someone off. I'll have the sign on, too, so as to be seen, yet unnoticed.'

'OK.'

'Picture it all now, it'll be your last chance. One run through is always fine, but if someone sees us or the motor twice in the same place, that's when you risk getting noticed. So, capture it all now in your mind's eye and work out how you are going to do your bit. And don't forget, you need to follow my lead quickly.'

'I'm doing it now.'

'Then practice in your head over and over again until it is familiar and you'll find it almost second nature. As if you've had ten times to practice for real. Trust me it works.'

Kelly nodded, obviously deep in concentration. 'And if I decide to abort for any reason, we abort. Don't question me. A second's delay could cost you your life. Understood?'

'Understood. What's the abort word?'

'"Jaffa shits". It's quicker than saying "Orangemen Proddy dog bastards".'

Kelly nodded again, and smiled.

'Come on, time to go. The next run is for real,' Lynch said, as he accelerated away from the side of the road back into the early evening traffic.

Chapter Thirty-one

Within seconds of putting the phone down from Hastings, Jackson had switched to operational mode. It was a skill they all had in the SAS. No matter what one was doing when the call came, they went into a well-drilled overdrive which was almost an automation. It was one of the many things that set them apart from others. Having grabbed their weapons, ammo and kit, Jackson gave the troop the intel update from Hastings. They now had the unenvious task of creating an operational plan on the hoof, based on unsubstantiated information which had no validation by their own observations. No time to do a recce. They'd have to deal with whatever happened as it unfolded. Another skill which set them apart.

Jackson turned to his sergeant, Crompton, the master tactician, 'Thoughts?' he asked.

'We roughly know the lay out of the Shankill Road. Two in two.'

Jackson knew this meant two of them in two vehicles. 'I'll take King,' he said.

Crompton nodded, 'Me and Harris will address from the west, you and Kingy from the east.'

All nodded.

'Will we get the actual location prior to arrival?' Crompton asked.

'No idea. Hastings is arranging uniform patrols from the RUC to drive through the plot shouting a warning. It may deter the attack. We will just have to react to what we see and hear,' Jackson said.

All three nodded and they hurried from the ops room towards their vehicles. Jackson and King jumped into a MK III brown Ford Cortina 2-litre, King at the wheel. They were followed out the compound by the other two in a 1.8 Blue Morris Marina, with Harris at the wheel. They did a comms check en route and as they approached the Cuppa Way Peace Wall from opposite directions, an out of breath Hastings came over the net from their base set to say that he was in the office as Zero Alpha, and would monitor all transmissions by any of the security services and keep checking open-source news feeds, too.

Hastings said that there aren't too many bars on the Shankill Road in the area they were headed to. But he'd research working men's clubs and suchlike, too.

As Jackson and King drove from Peter's Hill onto the Shankill Road from the eastern end, a livered RUC Land Rover passed the other way with its loudspeaker hailing a warning for people to get off the streets, as a terrorist attack was believed imminent. And it seemed to be working. Pedestrians were rushing away, and cars on the usually busy road were all darting down side streets. On seeing this, Jackson was growing in confidence that what was apparent would put the Provos off. Though it would have been nice to come face-to-face with Lynch again, even if he wasn't supposed to slot him. He could certainly slot his mates. That would make him really popular with their Brigade Commanders, and hinder future recruitment for the nutter. A win-win.

Crompton using Two Alpha call-sign reported a similar scene from the west end of Shankill Road. Kingy had now dropped all the car windows to aid their hearing from the streets, it would also protect them from glass splinters if they faced any in-coming rounds. That was if the rounds themselves didn't do their intended job.

Jackson noticed that there was an absence of hysteria, no shouting or screaming, almost a resigned calm. People rushing about quickly in obeyance to the police warnings, but in an accepted way. It was almost as if they were drilled and well-practiced is such manoeuvres. A sad sight in many ways.

But as Jackson observed and mused what he was seeing, he was also scrutinising everything in a razor-sharp way. His training and skills sharpened so acutely that they allowed for full concentration at the task in hand, while also leaving room in one's mind to deal with the unexpected. It appeared like distracting meanderings. This was a further skill that set the SAS apart. It allowed for another layer of thinking if needed. In case they had to react to their environment in a milli-second of change.

They passed the Blue Marina going the other way, and soon reached Woodvale Road to the west where they did an about-turn and started to run back. 'See anything that jumped out, target-wise?' he asked Kingy.

'Couldn't see any Tangos but mark-wise, two pubs close to each other looked busy. Probably busier still, perversely, after the police warnings.'

Jackson had clocked them too and noted the macabre, but valid point King had made. He agreed with him and then shouted up Zero Alpha for Hastings to do urgent intel on both pubs.

Their run through to Peter's Hill brought no change, other than less people and cars about. As they were making a three-point turn to run west again, Crompton announced that they too had reached the end of the Shankill and were also preparing an about-turn.

That's when Hastings came over the radio, 'Zero Alpha to all Romeo units, one of those pubs - The Shankill - has just been confirmed as a stronghold and meeting point for the Ulster Freedom Fighters. This must be it.'

Jackson knew that the UFF were a violent Loyalist off-shoot of the UDA. He quickly shouted Crompton up, they would plot off around the pub and plan their next steps, quickly.

WITH PREJUDICE

Chapter Thirty-two

Lynch drove down a side street at the east end of the Shankill Road, and did a round robin so he could head back to it, do a right turn and head west. That way, they could pull up right outside The Shankill pub on the correct side. He pulled over fifty yards from the junction and turned to face Kelly. 'You ready for this?'

'Aye, that I am.'

Lynch then watched Kelly reach down into the holdall between his feet and pull out the pipe bomb which Lynch had made. Each pipe length including caps was six inches long. The three pipes were bound together in a triangle formation. He'd have preferred a pentagon, but had run out of pipe at the lock-up. Three should do the job. At one end he'd drilled a small hole on each end cap so a fuse wire could run from the three pipes into one twisted lead fuse. Lynch reckoned that the fuse length would give them ten seconds.

Kelly picked up the device and familiarised himself with its weight and feel keeping it on his lap and below the car window line. He then pulled out his cigarette lighter and held that in his left hand leaving the bomb in his right.

'Check it,' Lynch ordered.

Kelly did and the lighter lit with a large flame. He checked it several times. It repeatedly lit without fail.

'OK,' Lynch said, before reaching behind him and picking up a house brick off the rear seat and placing it between his thighs. 'Let's go.'

Lynch then drove to the T junction and watched an RUC Land Rover roll past them going east. It was travelling slowly and its loud speaker was shouting a warning of an impending terrorist attack, and to clear the street. As he was absorbing this, a second RUC patrol passed the other way, spouting the same message.

'What the hell is going on?' Lynch said, and then quickly reversed back down the side road and pulled over. He turned to face Kelly, 'Did you hear that?'

'I did.'

Lynch sat in quiet contemplation for a minute.

'It could be a coincidence?' Kelly offered.

'No way, not possible, can't be.'

'What do you think, shall we sack it?'

'I think there must be a dirty rotten tout about. I thought we had got rid of them all, but clearly not.'

'But no one knows what we are doing?' Kelly added.

Lynch fell silent once more. Another valid point he'd made. No one did know exactly what they were doing. People should have, like Sean, but they didn't. They may guess they were on a live operation, but no one knew exactly what, least of all that it featured a target on the Shankill.

'Shall we abort?' Kelly asked again.

'Like hell. We've come too far.'

'I'm not sure. What about those RUC patrols, the risks to us have just gone through the roof.'

Lynch was still trying to work out what had gone wrong. Then he recalled his conversation with Bernie in the Shamrock as they were leaving, and the attention they were attracting from the bar area. But that was a safe, staunchly Catholic Republican pub. Plus, he'd given Bernie no specifics, other than "Lower Shankill". He shared his thoughts with Kelly.

'Then it could still be all a coincidence,' Kelly said.

'How so?'

'Any ASU from any of the Belfast Brigades could be doing something, and we would never know, and rightly so.'

'But Sean as Northern Commander would know, so as to prevent crossovers.'

'And we have purposely avoided contact with Sean.'

Kelly had made a further rational point.

'That actually makes sense. But if true, it means two things.'

'What?'

'Firstly, that whatever they think is about to, or may happen, it won't be what we have planned. That's to our advantage.'

'That makes sense,' Kelly said, as he looked at the pipe bomb still in his right hand.

'What's the second thing?'

WITH PREJUDICE

'That one of the Belfast Brigades has a filthy tout among them. And when this is over, you and I are going to find out who.'

'Fair enough. But what about those RUC patrols?'

'Let's watch them for a while, we can plan our timing accordingly.'

Kelly nodded, and Lynch told him to put the device down and go and find a secluded spot on the street corner and time the patrols. Fifteen minutes later he was back. The patrols tended to pass each other roughly where their street end was, Kelly said. He added that he had found a spot on the Shankill where the two Land Rovers were at their widest points apart, before they each turned around and began a return run. He'd timed them twice to make sure.

'How long will it give us?' Lynch asked.

'At least three or four minutes.'

'That's all we need, come on.'

Lynch turned right onto the Shankill Road and headed west, and then pulled over where Kelly told him to. One RUC patrol passed them going the other way, and shortly afterwards the opposite one did the same. Lynch waited as he watched the last patrol disappear from his rear view and noted the time on the dashboard clock. 'One minute down, we are out of their view, are you ready?'

Kelly said that he was and Lynch could see that he was again cradling the device in his right hand with his lighter in his left at the ready. Lynch had put the magnetic Taxi sign on the roof while they'd been in the side street. He noted that the few people still about paid them no heed. In fact, the warnings the peelers were giving out was helping them. Fewer potential witnesses and no traffic.

He set off at a calm 25 m.p.h. Within a minute the Shankill pub came into view on their nearside. There was a recess in the road, like a parking area, outside the pub which would be perfect. It was empty thanks to the peelers.

Then Lynch's birthdays all came at once. He recognised a man on foot approaching from the opposite direction. It was none other than Billy Campbell, a senior figure in the Ulster Freedom Fighters. A case-hardened Loyalist paramilitary who had arbitrarily killed many Catholics not because they were PIRA, IRA or INLA, but just because they were Catholics. The man was a die-hard killer. A psychopath with no conscience. Lynch could shoot him as he walked past them.

'Can you see who is approaching on foot?' Lynch asked.

'My God, it's Campbell. Now, he is a bastard.'

But before Lynch could share his plan with Kelly, all his Christmases came at once, too. Campbell turned right and walked straight into the Shankill pub. His presence now totally fitted the narrative he had planned for Sean. He can say they saw him at the earlier recce and heard him saying that he would be back in a while. They can then add that they stayed put and simply waited for him to return. And now he had. It would all work out nicely.

He braked and pulled their 'taxi' over directly outside the pub. It had a normal sized doorway, with an open door to the right as you looked at it with a big square plane glass window to the left. It wasn't a traditional looking pub and struck Lynch that it had probably once been someone's terraced home.

He looked at Kelly and asked, 'You ready?'

'Ready,' came the reply.

'Now,' Lynch said, who then jumped out of the driver's side of their vehicle with his brick in hand. He could see Kelly alighting from his side, but stooped down, as per instructions. This gave Lynch a clear aim. He threw the brick as hard as he could towards the main window, and was already climbing back in the driver's seat as he heard the sound of the glass breaking. He looked to his side and saw Kelly straighten up with the bomb in his right hand. He'd lit the fuse whilst crouched and once stood back straight, he lobbed it through the broken window. He was back in the car as Lynch counted to four seconds since Kelly lit the fuse.

As if reading his mind, Kelly shouted, 'Five seconds.'

Lynch accelerated hard away from the pub westwards as Kelly continued shouting. He reckoning that they had taken three minutes, start to finish since the RUC patrols had jointly passed them.

Lynch nodded as he continued to count the seconds. When he reached nine, he heard an almighty explosion behind them and could see a wall of flame in his rear-view mirrors erupt from the front of the Shankill pub.

Then as he returned his gaze to the front, their windscreen shattered.

Chapter Thirty-three

Jackson and King pulled over and reported that they had a long-distance visual of the Shankill pub. The were on the west side of it, facing east. Crompton reported that he and Harris were similarly placed on the opposite side. Then the ante went up, big time. A known UFF leader named Billy Campbell walked past them towards the pub. Jackson pressed the hidden radio transmit button under the dashboard to update the team. Then Crompton reported a taxi pulling up outside the boozer, two on board. He passed the registration to Hastings at Zero Alpha for checks. Then Jackson saw Campbell turn right and enter the pub.

'That taxi's fare hasn't got out yet. Prepare weapons,' Jackson said to King, and then he spat over the net, *'Consider the taxi hostile.'*

Jackson told Crompton that he and King would approach on foot and that they should remain mobile but close in. Crompton acknowledged. Jackson and King were wearing casual clothes, as were the others. He was wearing a baggy Puffa-style jacket covering a Heckler and Koch MP5 machine gun slung across his chest. King had a Parka style jacket on for the same reasons. They were now thirty yards away from the taxi and neither the driver nor passenger had moved. Jackson gave King a hand signal and he nodded before quickly crossing to the opposite side of the road. They were now approaching with a wide vector in front of them.

At twenty yards both driver and passenger alighted. This was it. The driver lobbed a brick through the pub's front window and Jackson drew his weapon and dropped to one knee in a firing stance. He concentrated on the crouched down passenger. His finger was on the trigger, taking up the slack. But if this was just a brick-throwing exercise they couldn't open fire. He was concentrating on the passenger who was stooped double. He knew what that could mean.

As soon as the man stood back up, he could accurately assess any threat, and respond in a millisecond; as would Kingy.

WITH PREJUDICE

Then the worst possible luck happened. Directly in front Jackson was a side road, and a large HGV suddenly blocked his view as it turned right onto the Shankill towards the pub. One of the many obstacles that urban warfare presented. He only hoped that Kingy would still have a view from the opposite side, though that would soon be blocked, too. On the plus, there was no traffic about, so the wagon didn't have to stop, and made its turn in a continuous movement.

But as it did, he could hear a car engine revving towards him. He steadied his aim as he looked through the weapon's sights waiting for the wagon to complete its turn.

A moment later it did, and the taxi came into view at the same time a huge explosion happened. Jackson could see in his peripheral vison that huge flames had shot out from the front of the pub, but he kept his main focus on the fast-approaching vehicle. He pulled the trigger having aimed at the driver's side of the windscreen. He knew the first round could be easily knocked off line by the tempered safety glass, so in a practiced move, he waited a millisecond before releasing a burst of gunfire aimed at the large hole he had just created in the windscreen. The rest of the windshield was intact but shattered, held together by the Laminex membrane between the two sheets of glass.

But as he fired his salvo, he could see that the driver was no longer on view. He must have ducked down the instant the windscreen had shattered. That was an amazingly fast reaction, it told Jackson a lot about his prey.

As all this flashed through his mind, he heard further rounds fired from Kingy's position.

The motor was now screeching from side- to-side, at an increasing speed, and Jackson had to leap out of the way as it mounted the pavement in an attempt to hit him. He heard further rounds from Kingy's position chase after it. Several people had foolishly come out of their homes to look at the commotion, which made further contact by Jackson or Kingy hopeless. Plus, the car was now too far away, and continuing to accelerate. Jackson then heard the screaming engine of Crompton's Blue Marina before he saw it. It flew past them at great speed in pursuit of the taxi. A moment later as he looked on, he heard one of the Marina's tyres blow. They had driven through all sorts of debris as they powered past the pub after the attackers. These were surveillance cars and not armoured military vehicles, another unavoidable hazard thrown up by urban warfare.

What a major cock-up this had turned into. Jackson had to switch off from attack-mode now. The bombers had gone. He turned his attention to the pub, to go and see what help they could give the injured. He ran to their vehicle to grab the Medi-kit bag as Kingy updated Hastings and requested the emergency services.

Jackson has seen a lot of death and mutilation during his time, and it never got any easier. The front window frame was gone, and the front door had been blown out and was lying on the pavement on fire. The air was thick with a cloud of dust and the place was in a stunned silence. But the abeyance of sound paused out of shock did not last long. Those who could get to their feet inside the pub soon became fully aware of the horror around them. Several ran screaming onto the street with blood-stained faces and bodies, few had any clothes on above the waist. Ripped from them in the blast.

As horrible as some of those injuries will have been to the walking wounded, Jackson knew he had to prioritise his efforts to those still prone. Some were clearly beyond help, and some were no longer recognisable as bodies, let alone as people.

Behind the small bar, were three people trying to untangle themselves from each other. One had a bar person's apron on and two did not. Probably punters blown over what was left of the counter. He put a field dressing on one woman's leg and a tourniquet to stem the flow of blood. Her pulse was weak and her complexion, ashen. He could only hope he had stopped the blood loss in time.

He was joined by the other three, and as they went to work in similar fashion, Crompton whispered in Jackson's ear.

'We shouldn't be here, boss.'

'I know, Geordie. But we've no choice. As soon as the first of the ambulances arrive, we'll do one. We'll all be out of Medi-kit by then. We'll just say we were passing off-duty soldiers. They'll never trace us.'

WITH PREJUDICE

'Fair enough. I've said as much to the two RUC outside. They are busy with the vertical wounded.'

'As long as we are away before the detectives arrive.'

Crompton nodded and returned his attention to an injured man in his sixties.

Jackson then heard a grunted breathing coming from past the bar where a narrow way led to a rear saloon. It was empty. He guessed the walking injured had fled from there. He approached the noise to see a man in his forties laid up against the side wall. His face covered in blood, as was his left trouser leg. Jackson immediately assessed that the man's blood flow was not rapid. No arterial damage.

The dust in the room was continuing to clear, being sucked out by the gaping holes that were once a window and a door. The man was conscious, and as he asked him if he was alright, he recognised him once more. Billy Campbell.

'I am, but those Fenian bastards won't be when I catch up with them,' Campbell said.

He could hear Harris and King in the background announcing that they had run out of kit.

'It'll be a while before you are running after anyone,' Jackson answered. 'But lay still and you'll be alright.'

'You Army or RUC?'

'RUC; passing off-duty.'

'So that'll be army then.'

'Doesn't matter. Just lucky we were passing.'

'Aye that it was. Thank you soldier boy.'

'Don't thank me yet, and I'm only doing my job. And before you start to think about revenge, just remember that when you throw a stone, one surely comes flying back at you.'

'They threw the first stone, here.'

'It only takes one to stop.'

Lynch could hear many emergency vehicles approaching and they sounded close. It was time to go.

'Can you give me anything for the pain?' Campbell said as he held his left arm up displaying the stump that had once been his hand.

'Sure, I've got one Morphine jab left,' Jackson said and quickly injected Campbell through his good thigh. Almost immediately Campbell's head lolled to one side and his eyes glazed over in an unfocused way.

Jackson quickly got to his feet and followed Crompton and King outside as Harris quickly gave the arriving ambulancemen an update.

They hastily made their way to Jackson's parked vehicle and left the scene. They'd get Hastings to recover the Marina via his SB mate, later.

WITH PREJUDICE

Chapter Thirty-four

Lynch saw the chasing Marina grind to a halt, so quickly took the next left turn and slowed down in an attempt to limit the attention they were drawing to themselves. The shattered windscreen was bad enough. He then turned to look at Kelly for the first time and could see that something was wrong. He was breathing heavily and his complexion looked ashen. He was also holding his left side.

'You OK, Stuart?'

'I'm hit, but I don't think it's too bad, but I need help,' Kelly answered in a laboured voice.

'Where?'

'Through my waist. In and out, I think. Must have come through the back of the seat.'

'Keep applying pressure, we'll soon be south of the wall. I know a friendly nurse not far from here.'

'I hope she's in.'

Lynch did too, but didn't answer.

Five minutes later, they were south of the wall and in friendly territory. The nurse, Jane, lived at an end terraced house so Lynch parked a little way past her rear alleyway and then helped Kelly to walk to her back door. Jane answered it. She was dressed in her nurse's uniform and said she was just about to leave for work, so they'd better be quick. Lynch thanked her and she helped him get Kelly onto a kitchen chair. She grabbed a first aid bag she always kept at home for such eventualities and attended to Kelly. He was relieved to hear that the wound had indeed been a 'through and through' as Kelly had thought. The round had passed through his waist missing anything important, according to Jane.

'You could do with losing a few pounds from around your middle, Stuart, but this is an extreme way of doing it,' Lynch said.

Kelly just rolled his eyes, and then winced as Jane started to suture the wound.

'Keep still, you big baby,' Jane said.

'You must have failed your "bedside manner module",' Kelly replied.

'Do you want this stitching or not?'

'Only messing, I'm very grateful to you.'

Lynch asked if he could borrow her phone while she finished off with Kelly and she told him to help himself. He walked into the hall where it was positioned on a small table with a seat built into it. He sat down and dialled Sean's number. He just hoped he was in. Sean answered on the first ring. Lynch took a deep breath and then launched into his prepared script about all that had happened. After he finished his speel the line went quiet for what seemed like ages before Sean replied.

'I'll ring the Army Council right away before the news breaks. I'll tell them I knew in advance. It'll take the heat off you. But the fact that we went ahead knowing that Campbell was there will upset one or two, that's for sure.'

Lynch knew that there was an unofficial agreement between paramilitaries on both sides of the divide that they wouldn't target each other's chiefs.

'You mean Gomez?'

'For sure, he'll be one.'

'Campbell is not the top dog, though he lauds himself about as if he is.'

'True enough.'

'And in any event, the agreement was only ever meant to cover the political leaders in the main.'

'Also, true.'

'So, Campbell is a legitimate target,' Lynch said, but stopped short of adding, 'they should be thanking me'. He didn't want to make Sean's job any harder that it was.

'Do you know if Campbell survived or not? Could make a difference.'

'I've no idea, we had to leg it double quick, as you know. And therein lies another problem.'

'What do you mean?'

'I don't know who attacked us but it wasn't the patrolling RUC. And in any event, why were the RUC there shouting a warning?'

WITH PREJUDICE

'I was going to dig into that when we met later, but what are your thoughts before I ring the Council?'

'The RUC warnings were non-specific. They suspected something, but didn't know exactly what.'

'Meaning?'

'Meaning one of the Belfast Brigades may have a leak.'

'I was afraid you'd say that. But could any leak be closer than you would wish? I have to ask, Brendan?'

'No, because we told no one, not even you - although you'll officially say you did know. Sorry about that, again.'

'Were your attackers just SB backing up the RUC patrols?'

'They could have been, and that would make sense, but it felt like army, and not normal soldiers. If I hadn't reacted as quickly as I did, they'd have done me. It was but for the grace of God that the first round through the windscreen missed me.'

'Thank the Lord you reacted like you did. We'll chat more later. I need to get off and ring Shamus. You drop Kelly off and I'm meet you at yours in an hour or so where we can talk properly.'

Lynch said his goodbyes and let Sean go. He hoped the Chief of Staff didn't give Sean too much grief. He walked back into the kitchen to see Kelly on his feet.

'All done, he'll be fine. I've given him some antibiotics in case the wound becomes infected, but it should be OK. Now get out of my house, will you, I'm going to be late for work,' Jane said.

Lynch thanked her and then left with Kelly.

***

As Jackson and the rest of Romeo Troop put their kit away at their barracks, the mood was sombre. They hadn't been able to stop the attack as they hadn't known exactly what and where it would take place. They had guessed correctly that it would be the Shankill pub, but hadn't known for sure. And but for that damn HGV blocking their line of fire, they would have stopped it. They weren't invincible.

On the journey back in, Jackson had told the rest of them that irrespective of Hastings's wishes, he had had to try to stop the driver, for obvious reasons. All had agreed that that was the correct thing to do. The fact that the driver was Lynch was not their fault.

In fact, he only recognised him when he'd got out to throw the brick.

'Anyway, boss the jammy bastard got away,' Crompton said.

'We can say we couldn't tell it was Lynch, if that helps,' King offered.

'That'll do it for now,' Jackson replied.

'I have to say, boss, it's not going to be easy to keep missing Lynch. Hastings isn't SAS, he should realise that we have a way of doing things which must take precedent, or else we risk putting ourselves and others in increased danger,' Crompton said,

Jackson knew this was true.

'And if we slot Lynch, surely the tout will have access to others in the know. Or be able to put themselves there?' Harris said.

Jackson thought for a moment before he answered. He'd love to know who the source was, but knew Hastings would never tell him. He'd be happy if Hastings would at least share with them more about the source and how they had access to Lynch. But for now, they could get round things as suggested. Hastings didn't need to know everything that happened on the ground. Then he made another decision and decided to put it to the vote.

'OK lads, listen in. For me, if we get a chance to slot Lynch from hereon in, I reckon we take it. If the intel dries up, then that's Hastings's problem. It may not. He may be worrying about nothing, and meanwhile Lynch carries on murdering and maiming people. I say we do him if we can, but only if all agree?'

The vote backing Jackson was unanimous.

Back to the briefing room in the barracks and after everyone had put their stuff away, they went through everything. Hastings agreed that they had done all they could do, but kept pushing to know if Lynch could have been one of the two. They all told him they didn't get chance to get a decent view. It was all over in a minute start to finish. Crompton and Harris were behind the action, and Jackson explained to the non-soldier, that once one is looking through a weapon's sights, it is an extremely focused view. Plus, the targets were in a car which was accelerating fast.

Hastings accepted this and then asked Jackson to go over his conversation with Campbell again, which he did.

'This is the bit that will worry London when I ring them.'

'How do you mean?' Harris asked.

'The unwritten rule that neither side targets their top brass. Campbell was close to the top of the UFF. We think he is the deputy and in reality, calls the shots. The Loyalist paramilitaries have been quiet of late.'

'I think that's about to change, judging by Campbell's reaction,' Jackson said.

'Yep. The whole thing could escalate exponentially in a flash.'

'If it wasn't for that bleeding wagon,' King threw in.

The debrief over, Hastings went to the secure phone to brief London, and the rest of the troop started to clean and check their weapons and replace ammunition so that they were ready to re-deploy in an instant. Hastings finished his call and told Jackson that there were no problems coming their way re their after-action report, in the circumstances. He added, 'However, I've just had the insipid Jeremy chew my nuts for not having the exact intel to give you. This coming from a man whom I doubt has ever handled an agent in his life. Nevertheless, I've been tasked find out what is going on, and what the potential fallout might be. I'd better get on it.' We can do the admin a bit later. He then hurried out of the room.

Jackson watched him rush off, and then came to a further decision. One he would keep to himself for now.

Chapter Thirty-five

Jackson hurried out the briefing room on a false premise leaving the rest of the troop cleaning their weapons and preparing some food. He had to rush to get to a different motor from The Det's pool, and was relieved not be stopped as he did so. They would be getting pissed off by the number of different cars Jackson's mob were using, and he was relieved to see that the blue Marina had yet to be recovered. 14 Field Security and Intel Company - to give The Det their full title - would not be amused.

Thankfully, there was no queue at the gate and he was soon through it. He turned right and accelerated hard towards a major T junction ahead. He saw brake lights on the saloon he was now following suggest a left turn, he did the same. He accelerated again, and then had to brake hard as he neared the vehicle. There was one other car between them, which was enough cover.

A short time later he was in the centre of Belfast, and the car he was tailing was driven in a practiced way. The driver was following a familiar route. Then suddenly, the motor pulled over into a side road and Jackson had to drive past. A quick glimpse saw the vehicle's only occupant get out and head back towards the main road. Jackson pulled over and used his rear-view mirrors to track the driver as he walked in the same direction as Jackson. If he got too near, then Jackson would have to get out of the way. But he need not have worried. The man entered a newsagent's premises in a row of shops. They all appeared closed. Jackson quickly alighted and walked past the row once. The shop appeared shut; it was in darkness, bar a security light left on to highlight the till area. The view through to the rear was blocked by a curtain.

Jackson looked around for cover, and noticed a phone box opposite. It would do for starters, but his shelf life in there would be limited. He entered, picked up the receiver and kept a firm gaze on the shop frontage.

Fifteen minutes later and Jackson was starting to feel exposed. On a normal surveillance operation, he would have flit from the box before now. It was only the darkness and the quietness on the street that had extended his use of the kiosk. But that aside, the itch to move was becoming too much. He put the receiver down and opened to door to find somewhere else to hide. He could always go back to his car, but one man sat alone in a stationary motor was never a good look. Then he noticed the privacy curtain in the shop twitch.

Hastings walked through it followed by another man. The man stayed by the curtain as Hastings made his way to the door. Jackson shot across the road at a forty-five-degree angle and down the side street where Hastings's car was parked.

A moment later, Hastings walked around the corner slap bang into Jackson.

'Christ, Vernon, you nearly gave me a heart attack. What the hell are you doing here?'

'I could ask you the same thing?'

'Hang on a minute, you've followed me.'

'Sorry, Bert, I have.'

'And you've been waiting by my car?'

'I saw you come and go from the newsagents, so don't worry about that.'

Hastings groaned, and then asked why?

'It's time you and I had a proper chat. Remember your promise to be more open?'

'Sure, when I can.'

'I can't keep promising to keep Lynch alive. Is he the source?' he asked. It still made no sense to him that Lynch could be. How could he report on attacks he was doing only to have them compromised each time by Romeo Troop. His bosses would soon smell a rat. But what had happened today had deeply bothered Jackson, which was why he had made the decision he had. The fact that they didn't have all the intel to stop the attack on The Shankill - though they nearly managed it anyway - really troubled him. He knew that they were fighting a dirty war, but was Hastings, and whoever, really prepared to allow Lynch's mob to commit an atrocity causing serious harm and loss of life, just to protect his cover. He quickly outlined his worries to Hastings, who he noticed looked shocked at his hypotheses.

'Oh my God. No of course not. London wants him dead. He's not what you are suggesting.'

Jackson had a quick glance about to ensure that they were still alone. They were. The street was dead. 'If you had to let one get through, then today's would be the perfect one. It didn't involve RUC or SB or Army as targets. Not the general public either, though you can't know that all those in The Shankill were Loyalist paramilitaries. In fact, I dressed one man's wounds who was in his seventies. He may have been a sympathiser, but not a terrorist.'

'Believe me, Vernon, you've got this all wrong.'

'You need to convince me. I'm not prepared to allow my men to risk their lives when innocent people are being allowed to be killed just to keep a source's cover. It's an obscene thought and we have standards, though many don't think we do.'

'What can I say to convince you?'

'You can tell me what you were doing in the shop for starters, and before you answer, remember that we are on the same side.'

Hastings paused in thought and then said, 'OK, but we better be quick before Derek locks up.'

'Who is Derek?'

'That's classified, come on be quick,' Hastings said, and then turned and hurried back around the corner. Jackson had to trot to keep up. They reached the front of the shop, just as Derek was locking the front door.

'Sorry, Derek we need access again,' Hastings said.

The man called Derek, sighed, and then looked at Jackson and said, 'Who's this?'

'Sorry, that's classified, but he's with me.'

Derek then spat out a stupid rhyme which Hastings completed. He then turned back to unlock the door.

Hastings whispered to Jackson, 'He's just checking that you are a friendly and I'm not acting under duress.'

Jackson nodded his understanding, but thought "Bloody spooks".

Once inside, Derek locked the front door and led the way past the privacy curtain before turning to face them. 'I'll be in the back when you are ready, I'll do some stocktaking.'

Hastings thanked him and Jackson watched Derek disappear behind a further privacy curtain. They were left standing in what was little more than a passageway between the front and rear of the premises with only a rug for company. Then Hastings pulled the rug back, and Jackson received his next surprise as Hastings operated a hidden trapdoor.

Chapter Thirty-six

Jackson followed Hastings down the steep staircase into the hidden cellar and was amazed at what he saw. Several computer terminals around an oblong desk, all with headsets attached. A kitchenette area with a hammock and a sleeping bag.

'I'm putting you properly on trust now,' Hastings said.

'I appreciate that you are. It means a lot.'

'And it stays between you and I; agreed?'

'Agreed. What is this place anyway?'

'It's a secure field communications and operations centre. Exclusively for use by MI5 and no one else. As far as you are concerned, this place doesn't exist. And for the record, had you not seen me enter and leave it, you still wouldn't know about it. I want you to trust me, but the risk of you nosing around here without my knowledge is too great. That's why you are here.'

'Understood.'

'I'm going to play you a voice recording of a conversation I have just had with the source. The voice is distorted so as to add further protection to the agent. But it will prove to you that the informant is not Lynch. It is important that we put that one to bed, once and for all.'

Jackson nodded and then took a seat at a terminal as directed. He was mightily impressed with Hastings, and the revelations here showed him in an added light. The guy may not be SAS, but he clearly had his own bunch of pressure going on. The intel world was always dirtier than many could imagine. What he was seeing here just served to reinforce that.

Hastings sat next to him and put on a set of headphones and instructed Jackson to do the same. He explained that he had arrived just in time to receive the contact so was in a position to have a two-way conversation, which was not always possible.

'Do you ever meet in person?' Jackson asked.

'Only at recruitment. Since then, never. It's too dangerous. If the agent sees me again, then something terrible will have happened.'

'Are they doing it for money, or for another reason?'

WITH PREJUDICE

'They all want money, and I use a dead drop to "pay expenses". But this one is different.'

'How do you mean?'

'I haven't quite worked it all out yet. Usually, they want money, or are in the shit, or both. Occasionally, it's ideology, but that is more usually the case with the Soviets.'

Jackson raised his eyebrows, and asked, 'Have you ever worked in the Cold War arena?'

'Whether I have ever worked from the Soviet Desk is classified. But that is usually the prerogative of our sister outfit at Six.'

Jackson nodded again, and decided not to pry too much.

'You ready?' Hastings asked.

Jackson said that he was and Hastings manipulated the mouse control to his computer and Jackson heard a crackle through his headset followed by a ringing tone and then the conversation which started off with some two-way banter, which Jackson knew would just be security protocols.

Then he heard Hastings's voice continue: *'What the hell happened?'*

'Pídàn has gone mad. Went AWOL this morning and pulled off one hell of a stunt this afternoon.'

'Yeah, I heard!'

'All hell is breaking loose here.'

'Why? Wasn't it authorised?'

'The OC is saying it was, but others have their doubts.'

'And you didn't know the specifics.'

'I'm not the bloody oracle, so I'm not. You've no idea what it's like here.'

'Sorry, no offence meant. I know you are doing your best. I really meant no offence. I am incredibly grateful.'

'Aye, that might as well be, but the lunatic is still causing mayhem.'

'What's the fallout from today?'

'Campbell from the UFF is maimed. Injured leg, and has lost most of one hand. Not that he doesn't deserve it, the way he randomly attacks innocent Catholics. At least we only go after legitimate military targets.'

'Oh, I fully except that.'

Jackson glanced at Hastings who paused the play back.

'Just tradecraft, Vernon, keeps them onside. In my line of work, we have to smile and agree with all kinds of unpalatable things.'

Jackson was glad he wasn't a spook. Hastings then resumed the replay.

'Anyhow, some on the Council think he has crossed a line that will bring about a fierce backlash, which is probably what the nutter wants. The armed struggle should only ever be a means to an end. For Pídàn the armed struggle is everything.'

'I understand.'

'You need to finish what we have started. What we agreed.'

'Oh, I intend to.'

Jackson glanced at Hastings again, only too aware of the hypocrisy in his last comment. This time he failed to engage with Jackson, who turned back towards his screen and continued to listen in.

'I have to go,' the source's mechanical sounding voice said.

'Just before you do. One last question.'

'Go on, but be quick.'

'If we finally achieve our joint objective. Will you, A) be able to get close to others similar to Pídàn? And B) is that something we can do so as to carry forward your excellent work?'

'I don't know. Let's get this done first.'

'If it continues and leads to peace and agreement, isn't that what we all want?'

'Yes, but we'll see. You keep your end of the agreement re Pídàn and we can think about that afterwards.'

The line then went dead.

'That was very illuminating. Especially, the last bit,' Jackson said.

'You have to be so careful with agents, you can turn them off in an instant. They can take offence so easily. It's a question I've been wanting to ask for a while.'

'And it wasn't a no.'

'Nor was it a confident, yes. So just for now, we keep to the plan. Lynch is allowed to live, even if we have to cover our tracks in how we do it, to keep the agent, and London happy.'

WITH PREJUDICE

Jackson nodded for the sake of peace, but wasn't sure if he could stick to that. He was in some ways even less sure why Hastings was so hell bent on keeping Lynch alive. The subtext in the agent's answer to Hastings last question was enough for Jackson. Even if it wasn't a resounding yes. As far as he could tell, the agent was desperate for Lynch's removal. Surely, that would curry much favour with the agent going forward. He was about to raise this point with Hastings, but decided to save it for a future conversation. The man had gone the extra mile with him today, and he didn't want to spoil things now by pushing too hard. Plus, it was clearly time to leave as Hastings had started closing down the terminals. They still had the formal debrief of the log to write up before the day was done.

Chapter Thirty-seven

Lynch arrived home before Sean got there, and had just finished a cup of tea with Erin when he saw Sean's car pull up outside. Erin let her brother in, and greetings over made him a brew and poured Lynch a second cup, before leaving them in the front room to talk business. As soon as they were alone, he spoke first. 'How did you get on with the Council? I sincerely hope I've not caused you too much drama.'

'Gomez won't be happy, but feck 'im. Shamus is pleased, especially as he's had Bernie Doyle on whinging about you.'

'Has he now!'

'Ignore him, you know how Bernie blows hot and cold.'

Lynch did, but wasn't sure he could ignore him, for different reasons. He let Sean continue.

'But as pleased as Shamus is, he is very aware of potential fallout as Campbell was scooped up in it. To limit any fallout on you, I told them that Campell was not the target. Irrespective of what you told me on the phone about overhearing that he was going back to the pub.'

Lynch was irked that Sean had watered it down, and was about to remonstrate with him when Sean raised his hand to silence him. Lynch bit his tongue, just.

'I said that he just turned up as the attack was going down, and before you whine at me, remember that I'm the diplomat between the two of us.'

Lynch had to smile at that, and his anger eased.

'It had allowed Shamus to speak to the UFF via backchannels and explain that Campbell was collateral damage, so if they are thinking of breaking the unwritten rule knowingly, they can expect a severe backlash.'

'Do you think they will believe Shamus?'

'Maybe, maybe not. But it has allowed for a second benefit.'

'How do you mean?'

'Well, if they suspect for one second that Campbell was the target, it'll leave them with an unconscionable truth to wrestle with.'

'And what's that?'

'That if you knew that Campbell was to visit the Shamrock when he did, then they may have a tout on their side. It will unnerve them and set rumours running.'

'A good thing, surely, but there is a but.'

'Indeed, there is, and it's ironic, is it not.'

Lynch knew they were thinking the same thing. The fact that the RUC and Army were there could mean the same problem existed on their side. Not that the Loyalists would know that. Sean then checked with Lynch that he had told no one of their plans prior to the attack. He initially said no, but then recalled his conversation with Bernie and his promise to make them pay as he left. How he had said no specifics in case anyone on the public side of the bar overheard him. Even though The Shamrock was one of the safest Republican bars in all of Ulster. Sean pushed Lynch to see if he had come out with any specifics. He said he had not, but then remembered his final words to Bernie.

'Christ, I may have been a bit slack in my haste to placate Bernie.'

'How do you mean?'

'As I was leaving through the bar I turned back to Bernie and said, "*Let's just say they won't be able to cry in their beer*". Sorry, Sean.'

'Don't be. This could work in our favour.'

'How?'

'Think about it. You comment was non-specific, as you no doubt intended.'

'That it was.'

'But nevertheless, it potentially alluded to a bar, or somewhere where you drink ale.'

Lynch nodded.

'Which fits in with your thoughts that the Army didn't know exactly where you were going to hit, or they would have taken you out before you got chance to throw the bomb.'

Lynch had to agree it all fit, but was unsure how it could work in their favour, so he asked Sean what he meant.

'It means, that if we have a tout among one of the Belfast brigades, or in The Shamrock; we weren't aware of it before today. Your loose promise of retribution to Bernie may have just outed a rat we didn't know, and may never have known about.'

My God Sean was right. No wonder he was the OC Northern Command, he always saw things from a wider perspective than Lynch did.

'What do we do?' Lynch asked.

'We suspend all ops until we out this filthy rat, and I'm putting you in charge of catching it.'

'Be a pleasure.'

'First thoughts, Brendan?'

'As you say, it has to be one of Bernie's men at The Shamrock.'

'Go and speak to Bernie first thing. I'll call ahead and tell him I'm sending you and to play nice.'

'Cheers, Sean, I'll grab some food and then head back to Belfast. Are there any updates on the accident which foiled out attempt on the UDR man's life?'

'It appears to be as it seems; an accident. One which cost us dearly. But we are keeping an open mind. But it's hard to imagine it could have been a planned event. The timings required would have to be too precise. Not even the Sass are that good.'

'Do you want me to hunt down the driver and deal with him?'

'No need, I've already got someone on that. I'll let you know how that goes.'

'Fair enough,' Lynch said as Sean rose to his feet. He shouted a goodbye to his sister and received a muffle reply from the back of the house. At the door, Sean turned to face Lynch and paused. 'One thing you must promise me, Brendan.'

'Sure, anything.'

'No more of this Lone Ranger stuff. I covered for you today, but it won't work twice. Plus, I need to be able to trust you, and before you kick off, I do. But I need to know everything you have got planned, and if I veto anything, I don't want a bleeding debate about it.'

Lynch knew he was not in a position to argue, he enjoyed autonomy, but accepted that there was a chain of command. Plus, if he lost Sean's support, he knew that the many wolves waiting in the wings would be on him in a flash. 'You've got it, Sean. I'm grateful for your backing today, and I know I can be an impulsive, arsey bastard sometimes.'

'Only sometimes?' Sean said with a smile.

'Aye, maybe most of the time. And I don't want to make your job any harder than it already is with some of those wimps on the Council.'

Sean ignored his last comment, but did say, 'And I expect there to be a bottle of Bushmills on the table when I next call.' He then turned and headed towards his car and Lynch closed the front door and headed towards the kitchen.

Chapter Thirty-eight

Two hours later and Lynch was sat in the backroom at The Shamrock with Bernie Doyle. As he entered the pub, he noted that there were two men stood guard outside, just in case the Loyalists decided a tit-for-tat on the place after what had happened at The Shankill. Good thinking, Lynch had mused. His initial exchange with Bernie had been almost pleasant, well, as pleasant as Doyle was capable of. Obviously, Sean's call in advance of Lynch's arrival had supressed his usual foul temper. Lynch could be a pain, but Bernie Doyle was in a league of his own. That was until Lynch questioned whether any of his men could be the tout. After scrapping Bernie off the ceiling, he convinced Lynch that he hadn't told any of his men that Lynch had something imminently planned. Lynch had no option but to accept this unless he learnt to the contrary.

Once calm again Bernie said, 'Fair play to you, Brendan, you did promise that they wouldn't even be able to cry in their beer. I get that now.'

Rich praise indeed coming from one so gruff. Lynch thanked him, and then added, 'Then it can only be someone stood at the bar who overheard me. The barman was away collecting glasses, that I remember. But there were three men leaning on the bar top.'

Bernie asked him to describe them, so he did.

'The first one is Hiram, a plumber, the second is Paddy O, can't recall their full names, and the last one is John Shaughnessy. All sympathisers, all regulars, all I would normally bet my life on. What do you suggest?'

'We need to keep this between you and me and one of them at a time. They don't know me, so put me near one and I'll ring you and let slip some disinformation. You and I can cover it and see what happens. Then we'll know.'

'And if nothing happens?'

'Then we do it again with number two and then number three if we have to.'

Bernie nodded.

WITH PREJUDICE

'You choose who to go first.'

'That's easy, there is a darts match due to start soon and John Shaughnessy should be in any minute as he's on the team.'

'How do you propose to put me in close?'

'Simple. You and I can be having a drink near the dart board as I'm also on the team. And just before it starts, I can be called away, I'll introduce you as my stand-in. You can bell me in a while when it suits you and lay the trap.'

'Fair enough, now tell me what I need to know about the man.'

Bernie did. Shaughnessy was a staunch Catholic as was his mother, but interestingly, his father, who had now passed was a Protestant. This was an irritation that Shaughnessy had always carried, and it had put a bit of a chip on his shoulder. He was always the most vocal and it was as if he were constantly trying to prove his republican credentials to anyone who'd listen. He was married, in his mid-thirties, and worked as a cab driver. Something else which Lynch found interesting. His job gave him free movement all over Belfast with perfect cover.

When he entered the pub Bernie pointed him out. He was six feet tall but skinny with dank long brown hair. He said hello to Bernie as he passed them to get to the bar.

Thirty minutes later the away team of four arrived, and they were all preparing to play. Then Bernie took his pretend call from the landline behind the bar, and spoke in an almost over-the-top way. He'd balls this up before they got going if he didn't calm it down. Thankfully, he put the receiver down after a minute and then approached the team. Lynch was leant on the side of the bar which led to the rear saloon, as if he was preparing to watch the match. Bernie went through the script in front of the four-man team and introduced Lynch as his mate and replacement. He was accepted straight away. It was a while since he'd thrown an arrow, and to be honest he was looking forward to a game. He'd played a lot in his younger days and reckoned he could still hold his own.

He spent the next thirty minutes cosying up to Shaughnessy and bought him a drink. And then as they approached the hour - as agreed with Bernie - he quickly emptied his glass and announced that it was Shaughnessy's round.

'So, it is. What will it be?' Shaughnessy asked.

'Another pint of the black stuff will do me just fine, so it will,' Lynch replied. He then loosely wandered towards the bar after Shaughnessy, and hung back on his shoulder as he ordered the drinks. Lynch glanced at the wall clock as the minute hand clicked over the hour.

The bar phone started ringing, and the bar man had to interrupt pouring the second drink and apologised to Shaughnessy as he took the call. A pause followed and then the bar man shouting out Lynch's name.

He took the receiver and was as close to Shaughnessy as he could be. There was some chatter around the bar but it was relatively quiet. He then 'repeated' what he had agreed with Bernie, who was on the other end of the line, as if he had just been told it. He glanced at Shaughnessy and saw his eyes widen briefly before he made a point of purposefully looking the other way. Lynch reached over the bar top to replace the receiver and turned to look at Shaughnessy squarely. He seemed a little nervous, or surprised, or a mixture of the two. He offered Lynch his pint, which he took with thanks. They then headed back towards the dart board.

The trap was laid, and Lynch was as sure as he could be, that Shaughnessy had clearly overheard what he was intended to.

Lynch noticed that through the remainder of the match, Shaughnessy's mien became a little stiffer. Not unfriendly, but slightly more reserved than it had been. The rest of team, who obviously knew him well also picked up on it. He was asked why he was being quiet. Why he wasn't being his usual 'gobshite self'. He just laughed it off with return banter, and blamed his poor performance with the darts for his lowered mood. Lynch was even more convinced by the end of the game that Shaughnessy had picked up every word. Whether he was the man, remained to be seen, but they'd find out soon enough.

After the match was over it just so happened that it was Shaughnessy's round again. He looked mightily relieved when Lynch politely declined. He told him that he had to get going as he had an early start in the morning.

That much was true. Five minutes after leaving the pub he spotted a phone box and pulled over. He'd give Sean a quick update and keep his brother-in-law onside. Then he'd put a quick visit into Kelly to see how he was, and find out when he would be fit to resume.

Chapter Thirty-nine

It was towards midnight and Jackson and the rest of the Romeo Troop were preparing to get their heads down at the barracks within a barracks. It had been one hell of a day with two deployments, which was rare and tiring. Writing everything up afterwards while the events were still fresh in everyone's memories was probably the worst bit. It was certainly the most boring bit at the wrong end of the day. Hastings had shot off about an hour ago after all the post action stuff was done, and Jackson and the others had sunk a couple of drinks to warm down mentally.

Jackson took the opportunity to allay the others' fears about Hastings. He told them about his earlier following of him and what transpired, though he kept back some of the specifics including the description of the newsagent's premises. They didn't need to know that.

'I wondered where you shot off to,' Geordie Crompton said.

'I was acting on impulse, and I'm glad I did. Though I'm not totally persuaded in the reason for his over-protection of Lynch.'

'Me neither,' Crompton said, which was followed by murmured agreement from Harris and King.

'But I am reassured that whatever it is, he is acting honourably.'

'Perhaps it is like he says; he's bothered that once Lynch is removed, the source will either not be able to get close to any other senior Provos, or won't be minded to,' Crompton added.

'Sounds to me that this tout is working their own agenda, and that is fuelled by a hatred of Lynch,' Harris threw in.

'They all work to their own agendas, that's why they are all so slippery,' King added.

Jackson agreed. And from what he had heard and learnt in the newsagent's cellar; it did fit. It would explain why Hastings was worried the relationship would come to an end once the informant's objectives were met.

'What are your instructions re Lynch? Do we slot him at the first opportunity, or not?' Crompton asked.

WITH PREJUDICE

Lynch didn't answer straight away, in the light of what they now knew and perceived, he was in two minds. 'Let me think about that. I don't want to upset Hastings too much now we have him opening up to us, yet it is clear from what he has said that his bosses and the PM herself, want Lynch gone.'

'Sounds like they aren't too worried about losing this particular source, then,' Crompton said.

'Apparently not. Though Hastings does comment that his boss, this Jeremy, has never handled an agent, and probably couldn't find his arse without a valet to point him in the right direction.'

The other three laughed and then the desk phone started to ring.

Jackson took the call. It was Hastings, he'd called in at the newsagents on his way home, wherever home was, he never had explained exactly where he spent his evenings and nights. He certainly didn't rough it in the barracks with the rest of them, even though he had his own bunk here. Anyway, he was excited and out of breath. He'd apparently just listened to a message left a little earlier from the source. They now had a job on in the morning and it was an early start, he said he'd fill them in properly then. He just wanted to halt any more drinking tonight. Jackson said that they were just turning in anyway, and bid him goodnight. He quickly told the others what little he knew and then headed for his pit.

***

Four hours later, they were all up, showered, dressed, and chewing slices of toast when Hastings landed. He quickly briefed them with what he knew. The intel was that the Provos had an arms dump hidden in the Lagan Valley, an official Area of Outstanding Beauty, south of Belfast, a few miles due east of their Lisburn Barracks, on the east side of the M1 motorway. The dump was hidden under a yellow grit bin somewhere on the Ballyskeagh Road, the B103, close to its junction with the Quarterlands Road. It would be light around six and at some stage this morning, someone would access the hide. They were unsure whether the person would be taking from it, adding to it, or simply checking it.

Crompton was the first to comment, 'This won't be easy tactically, as there are houses about and it can be a busy little minor road according to my maps.'

Jackson knew that their tactical maps prepared by Military Intelligence had all sorts of information on to assist operationally.

'Ideally, I would suggest that we enter the hide and put a tracker on the weapons, and then track them when moved. However, that might not be possible. Surmising that the grit bin is full of grit, that sort of intervention will take time and can only be done in the middle of the night. Even if we use some sort of cover, the chance of compromise will be too great,' Crompton added.

'I take it we have no idea when the Provo is supposed to make the approach,' Harris asked.

'Just sometime this morning after daylight. I'll head back to my comms place and monitor from there in case of any intel updates, but I don't expect we will get any,' Hastings answered.

'Then we either go overt, and have the hide searched by the RUC, or we watch and if any one attends it, we deal with what we see,' Crompton added.

'What do you mean exactly?' Hastings asked.

'If someone attends the hide and puts something in, we take them and the hide. If the Provo attends and takes something out, we can keep one eye on the hide and then follow the Tango with whatever they have removed, and observe where they take it, and to whom,' Crompton said.

'And if someone attends and neither puts something in, nor takes anything out?' Hastings asked.

'Like before, keep one eye on the dump and follow the Tango and see what happens next.'

'Obviously, option one - going overt is discounted. So is option two. We can empty the hide later if that is required. Let's just see who turns up, and regardless of whether they put anything in or take something out, follow them and house them. We can approach the hide properly during the hours of darkness and deal with it appropriately then,' Jackson said, followed by, 'Any questions?'

The others all shook their heads. It was going to be a long day and possibly a long night, too.

As they all started to gather up their kit, Crompton shouted, 'Forty-eight-hour food packs everyone.'

WITH PREJUDICE

Chapter Forty

By 4.45 a.m. all of Romeo Troop were on plot. The yellow bin was located on the north side of Ballyskeagh Road opposite houses. A privet separated it from open fields, but thankfully, nearby, a dividing border hedge ran due north from the road splitting the open grassland and farm buildings. Harris and King were dug into the border hedge with a good view of the rear of the bin and all approaches to it. They were using the call sign 'visual' as there was no target to 'eyeball', yet. Crompton and Jackson were both in the back of a local council livered observation van parked nearby with a good view of both approaches. They were dressed as Highway employees and had among other things, a workman's canvas hut which they could throw over the bin, as and when they needed to access it. They were using Jackson's callsign One Alpha whilst they were together. Hastings was in the newsagent's cellar on Zero Alpha. Jackson did a comms check, and all units replied. He then handed control over to the observations team.

They were all trained in the art of Covert Rural Observations Post surveillance, and CROPs operatives could find themselves dug in for days on end in extreme circumstances, but he'd already agreed with Crompton that they would take their turn and relive the other two if needed. Depending on how long the job ran to.

'It's been a while since I've shat in a plastic bag,' Crompton said.

'I did that much CROPs work in Kenya on one deployment, that when we were returned to base I couldn't shit on the bog unless there was a carrier bag in there to catch it,' Jackson replied, and both men laughed.

'Visual to the team, there is no change, no change,' Harris's voice spoke inside Jackson's head via his covert earpiece. It was going to be a long day.

An hour later, Hastings gave them an intel update, not from the source, but from database checks, there were several known Republican sympathisers living in a couple of the houses opposite the plot, so to be extra vigilant. The enemy may well have a spotter keeping tabs on the bin, just to further complicate things.

By midday, several people had walked past the bin, but no one had given it any attention, apart from a dog who clearly considered the bin his, as he cocked a leg and marked it.

***

Lynch was grateful that Bernie had managed to secure an upstairs bedroom in a sympathiser's house on Ballyskeagh Road. The room had net curtains at the window and afforded a direct view across the road from the yellow grit bin. They had filled it with extra grit just to make the task that bit harder. But he had been surprised when Bernie had said that he wouldn't be able to man the OP with him, said he had urgent business to attend to. Something sent down from Sean himself, so he couldn't get out of it. Thankfully, Kelly was itching to get back to work, he was glad he'd paid him a late visit the previous evening. He said the wound was healing nicely, but pulled a bit as it was becoming tight. Lynch knew that was a good sign.

'He's probably just a lazy sod who doesn't fancy sitting here all day to God knows when,' Kelly had said to Lynch, when he raised the issue of Bernie letting him down.

'Plus, as a Battalion Commander, he probably sees it as beneath him.'

'I used to be on the Army Council, but I'm here,' Lynch replied.

'Well, I'm glad he swerved it,' Kelly said, and then added that he was grateful to get out and about on operations again. Though that had been several hours ago and Lynch was now starting to wonder if Bernie hadn't made the right choice dodging this OP. He glanced at his watch and noted that it was now approaching three in the afternoon, and the road was getting busy.

'Look,' Kelly shouted, and pointed at the window.

Lynch had to wait a few seconds for a school bus to pass, but once it had, he saw what Kelly was on about. A council van had mounted the kerb and parked just before the bin. Two municipal workers, with their backs to them were busy erecting a red and white stripped canvas workman's hut. Once done, they lifted it and placed it over the bin. The bin itself was about three feet by two feet and roughly three feet high. The canvas hut was at least twice that size. Both men without turning around then disappeared into it.

Lynch and Kelly stared avidly at the entrance to the hut as traffic multiplied, but it became increasingly difficult to get a view for long. By three-thirty, there was a long line of standing traffic edging forward, affording only brief glimpses of the hut, which appeared unchanged.

'Do you want me to go for a walk in the fields see if I can't get a vantage point from the other side?' Kelly asked.

'Too risky,' Lynch replied.

Then there was a sudden break in the traffic, but only because a lorry had stopped to let the council van out. They had missed the hut being taken down, but clearly it had, and now the van was away.

'What do you reckon?' Kelly asked.

'Too much of a coincidence. But there's a way to be sure, hang on a sec,' Lynch said, before making his way downstairs where the householders, a couple in their sixties were watching TV. 'Nearly done, he said, but can I just use your phone?'

'Help yourself, it's in the hall. I'll shut the lounge door to give you some privacy,' the man said rising to his feet.

Lynch waited until the door was closed then grabbed the phone directory and rang a number once he'd found it.

'Good afternoon, Lisburn and Castlereagh Borough Council, how can I help,' the receptionist at the other end started with.

Lynch asked to be put through to the Highways Department and after several moments the line was answered. He put on his best aged voice and said, 'I live on Ballyskeagh Road and some workmen have just left, near to where the grit bin is, opposite Quarterlands Road.'

'Oh, I know where you mean, sir, my uncle Dougie lives near there. How can I help?'

'Well, it's my wife who saw it, but she's no good on these things. Says it was either a council van or Telecom van.'

'OK, sir, what was?'

'Oh, there's nothing wrong,' Lynch said responding to the obvious caution creeping into the receptionist's voice. 'It's just that one of the men has left his flask, so he had, I have it here in front of me. He'll be having no coffee with his butties tomorrow without it. They can pick it up if you could tell them where it is.'

'OK sir, just let me check something,' the lady said, and then the line went quite for a minute. She then came back on the line. 'Thank you so much for your call, sir, very public spirited of you.'

'Aye well, I remember what it's like to have no brew come baggin time, especially, when you have worked up a thirst grafting,' Lynch said, just about maintaining his fake voice.

'Quite sir, but I've just checked and we have had no one working in your street today. It must have been the Telecoms lot, can I suggest you give them a call, I'm sure they will be grateful to you.'

Lynch thanked her for her time and told her that he'd ring the telephone people straight away. He then put the receiver down and then went back up to the front bedroom where Kelly was waiting. 'Come on, Stuart. We've confirmed our rat.'

WITH PREJUDICE

Chapter Forty-one

Jackson and Crompton had made an executive decision to do a covert approach of the yellow grit bin. Jackson informed Hastings on Zero Alpha what they were going to do. Hastings panicked a bit in case there were spotters about, but Jackson reassured him that they knew what they were doing. He explained that a fully covert approach during the hours of darkness was always going to be problematic given the additional intelligence with regard to potential sympathisers or spotters opposite. Far better to 'go overt to be covert' and approach the hide in plain sight but with cover. They had all agreed that by 3 p.m. no one was likely to attend it now. Especially given the increase in traffic and footfall going on.

What they had learnt, was this was indeed a hide. The bin was just a container full of road grit, but when they moved it, they discovered a manhole cover underneath it. Hastings had some urgent enquires done with the Council via Special Branch and discovered that the cover was an inspection hatch, which led to a disused sewer which had long been bricked up. All that remained was a shaft down from the cover to a small area now blocked off.

Crompton quickly confirmed this by going down the metal ladder which was cemented into the wall of the shaft. Rank still had its privileges, even in the SAS. Once back up and out, Crompton said that there was a steel crate at the base which was unlocked and empty.

'It's definitely been a *sealed* hide,' Crompton added.

Jackson knew this meant that it was not one to be used often, but more for storage of weapons and explosives for emergency situations.

'We'll debrief it properly back at the barracks, time to get out of here before anyone catches us,' Jackson said, and Crompton agreed.

Jackson gave the 'standdown' command and he and Crompton cleared up and cleared out as quickly as they could.

Thirty minutes later they were in their briefing room with a brew on waiting for Hastings who joined them five minutes later. They first went through the log, got that agreed and signed for what it was worth, and then got down to discussing what had happened.

'Do you think we missed them?' Hastings started with.

'Not a chance. We'd have seen them,' King jumped back at Hastings with.

'Sorry, I didn't mean that. I meant that if the intel was not wholly accurate, could they have gone to the hide before you arrived?'

'They could have, what do you reckon, Geordie?' Jackson asked.

'I'd say not. From what I could tell from dust and shit disturbance, or the lack of it, my best guess is that the steel box has not been opened for quite a while.'

'Well, that's a relief. I'd hate to think that they had emptied it before we got there, and were planning an attack,' Hastings said.

'What of the intel? Any updates?' Jackson asked.

'The original information was as vague as I gave it you. They didn't know why the hide was to be visited, it could have just been a routine check, rather than anything more nefarious. But because of that lack of clarity, we had to cover it,' Hastings replied.

'Totally understood,' Jackson said.

'And at least we now know of a very cleverly placed hide, I'm guessing we didn't know about it before,' Harris joined in with.

'Absolutely, I checked with SB and Military Intelligence and it's a new one on both of them,' Hastings said.

'Anything further from your source?' Jackson asked.

'No, it all started by a chance overheard snippet, and they have not heard any further reference to it since.'

'Well, we can monitor it going forward,' Crompton said.

'That was my next question whether you managed to put any toys in there?'

'Yep. I've put a pressure pad under the steel box hidden in shite with a twenty-eight-day battery in it. And a magnetic trip under on the underside of the manhole cover which will only trigger if the cover is lifted. Also, with a twenty-eight-day battery. Both patched by microwave to the console in the corner here.'

'You did well there, Geordie,' Jackson said.

'I'll get it patched through to The Det next door, they have a 24/7 monitoring capability, and they will be chuffed to have a potentially active hide no one knew about. They can service the batteries, too,' Hastings said.

'It might sweeten them up a bit after we keep nicking - and scrapping - their motors,' Harris said.

'All in all, a good deployment. The intel was good, which helps me when dealing with Jeremy in London, and we now have a hide we didn't know about.'

What if whoever was supposed to attend it this morning rocks up later, or tomorrow, now?' King asked.

'It's ten minutes away from here, I'm sure The Det can respond to it. They are better set up to deal with it than us,' Hastings added.

'OK, what next?' Crompton asked.

'We may as well grab some downtime while we can,' Jackson said.

'Agreed,' Hastings said and then turned to face Jackson and added, 'I'll ring London from my comms centre and hang on there a while in case the source gets back in touch.'

Jackson walked Hastings to the door, and as he opened it, Jackson asked where he was off to later.

Hastings paused and said, 'I'll just watch some telly and bed down. My comms landline is routed to wherever I am, as you know.'

'You never stay in your bunk here.'

'I don't want to intrude on your lads' downtime. Me being a spook and all that.'

Jackson had suspected as much. He turned and could see that the others were busy out of earshot. He closed the steel door and told Hastings that they were all one team. That he should spend some time with them. Apart from the obvious bonding side of things, it wasn't good for him to be alone all of his downtime. 'Or are you not alone?' Jackson ended his comments with, together with a raised eyebrow and a smile.

'Ha, ha, I wish.'

'You never did say where you were staying?'

'Don't worry, I'm not living it up in the Europa Hotel, if that's what you are thinking.'

'Where then?' Jackson pushed.

Hastings paused and then sighed, and then said, 'OK, if it dispels any rumours and puts your mind at rest, too, I'll tell you.'

'Go on. Between you and me.'

'I've been kipping down in the comms room below the newsagents. I have a set of keys that Derek doesn't know about. I'm not supposed to be there unless he is. Protocol. I just make sure that I'm out before he arrives, and then I head straight back in.'

Jackson was shocked. 'My God, man that's no way to live.'

'It's not so bad. Behind the kitchenette there is a loo and a shower, so it's not too grim.'

'But why?'

'In case the source calls urgently.'

'But the calls are recorded, and can be redirected.'

'I'm acutely aware that the risks the source are taking is off the scale. If you knew who or what the source is, you'd understand. Unlike Jeremy and his ilk. I have a solid responsibility to keep the agent safe. And not just for intelligence reasons; I have a moral duty.'

'You really do care, don't you?'

'Yes, I do. If they were compromised, you can only imagine what PIRA would do to them before eventually killing them. This informant is so well placed, it would be PIRA's greatest ever breach of security. And their greatest embarrassment, too.'

Jackson was starting to understand why Hastings was so protective of Lynch if his removal meant losing the source.

And as if reading his mind, Hastings said, 'It's far more than the thought of losing the source and therefore the access to the higher echelons of the Provos. And notwithstanding that I haven't yet worked out what is driving the agent, if you only knew what they were, you'd get it.'

Jackson nodded.

'But, if they feel that they are under threat, I've told them to get to a phone while everyone else is asleep and ring, and I'll come and extricate them. I can't cover things during the day, but from what we know, they only "arrest" people during the hours of darkness when they know where people are, and that they are at their most vulnerable.'

Jackson was mightily impressed with Hastings once more, and told him so. He again saw him a new and brighter light.

'Being there at night is the least I can do.'

'Couldn't you route any source calls to here?'

'I only wish I could. I lied when I said the comms landline can be routed to any landline where I am. That is true re the intel line as both end users are MI5 and can therefore use tradecraft during the call, if needed. But sources can't be relied on; so for security reasons, all agent contact calls can only be made and received in the secure comms room. I shouldn't tell you this, but a couple of years ago The Det discovered that the Provos had managed to bug some of the landlines here at Lisburn.'

'My God, how the hell did they manage that?'

'Good question, even I don't know the answer to that one. Look, anyway I'd better get back there.'

'Just a sec,' Jackson said, and then he turned back to face the room. 'I'm nipping out for a few or more hours, catch you all later,' he shouted.

'OK, Boss,' Crompton replied.

Jackson turned back to face Hastings and said, 'Tonight Bert, you will have some company. I'll grab a pack of cards and hope you are shit at poker.'

Hastings's face broke into a wide smile. 'Thanks, Vernon, I appreciate this.'

Chapter Forty-two

At 6 a.m. seventy miles away from Lisburn down a rural track off the Goshenden Road, situated near the A6 close to Ballynamore, is one of Northern Ireland's most beautiful areas. The Dungeon Waterfall is there, and nearby in Ness Wood is the even more impressive Ness Waterfall. The latter attracted a lot of tourists and visitors, so the barn buildings the Provos used were ones close to the quieter Dungeon Waterfall. The Internal Affairs of the Derry Brigade of PIRA maintained the premises. They were only a few miles south of Derry.

Sean had told Lynch to crack on. He said that he was aware that the Internal Affairs Department of the Belfast Brigade might feel slightly aggrieved, but he'd deal with that. And in any event, the subject was not actually a member of the Provisional IRA, just a sympathiser.

When Lynch walked into the disused cowshed, Bernie Doyle and Stuart Kelly, both greeted him.

'Any problems on the lift?' Lynch asked.

'None,' Bernie answered, 'although he has shat himself, literally.'

In the centre of the room sat on an old wooden chair, and with his hands tied behind its back, was John Shaughnessy with a rough canvas hood, fashioned from a potato sack, over his head. His head was hanging down and his breathing was laboured.

'What has he said?' Lynch asked.

'Nothing yet, other than swearing on anything and everyone that he has done nothing wrong,' Bernie answered.

'Has he had a slap yet?'

'No, but I've told him that is next if he doesn't wise up.'

Lynch nodded, and then walked up to the front of Shaughnessy and yanked the hood off. The man looked up and blinked at the light coming from two poacher's lamps that were positioned at forty-five degrees to each other in front of him. They were aimed directly at him.

WITH PREJUDICE

'We know it's you, so just fess up and you'll just get a slap, or two. We've lost a hide, but no other harm has been done by your treachery.'

'Honestly, I have no idea what you are on about,' Shaughnessy answered.

Lynch could tell that he was squinting and trying to see the face behind Lynch's voice. 'If you were a member, you'd have been Courts Martialled and I'd be reading from the Green Book before ordering your killing. But be under no illusion that because I am not impelled to carry out that fate upon you, it doesn't mean I can't. A rat is a rat.'

'My God it's you. We played darts together, we became friends, this is some huge misunderstanding.'

Lynch then iterated the phone call he had taken and how it had been engineered to be in Shaughnessy's earshot. Shaughnessy didn't reply.

'And do you know who I was talking to?'

'No,' he then said.

'Me,' Bernie boomed.

'So, you can see the corroboration I have to exactly what was said in your presence. No debate.'

'I'm not disagreeing with you, sir, I did hear what you said, but ignored it. It was not my business.'

'We told you, and only you, and guess what happened?'

'I'm guessing something bad.'

'You could say that. We watched the hide yesterday, and the fecking SAS turned up dressed as Council workers.'

'That has nothing to do with me, how would I pass on anything I heard. I wouldn't have the foggiest idea how to do that. Not that I would anyway. I'm a Republican Catholic. I hate the Brits.'

'Then you must have told someone else who did know how to pass it on.' This possibility particularly worried Lynch, the thought that they could have a further rat out there still unidentified. Perhaps the real rat. Also, Lynch was unsure how much Shaughnessy could pick up in idle chatter. Though The Shamrock would no doubt have its fair share of PIRA members as customers. And a false or elevated sense of security mixed with copious amounts of alcohol were never a good mix.

Shaughnessy then spent several minutes pleading with Lynch that he had not told anyone. How he had gone straight home to bed after the darts match, and had been at work all day today, and had spent the evening on his own watching television. He even went into detail as to which programmes he had watched, and what they had been about.

When he had finished, Lynch turned to Bernie and Kelly and nodded. They needed to satisfy themselves that Shaughnessy had told no one else other than the authorities. Kelly stepped forward and started with slaps to the face, left and then right. This was followed by punches until he stood back to catch his breath.

'Head up,' Lynch said to Kelly, who then walked behind Shaughnessy, grabbed the man's hair, and pulled his head backwards.

'Be grateful that you are not a volunteer, or else it would be Internal Affairs here and not us: and they are brutal. The last time I watched them interrogate a rat, even I had to look away. And that's not to say we can't call them in. We can, they are always looking for an opportunity to hone their skills.

Shaughnessy's face was bloodied, and his nose looked broken and his left eye was starting to swell. He pleaded with Lynch that he had not passed on what he had heard to anyone. Lynch was starting to believe him. This worried Lynch. The rat they were after had been grassing over a period of time and not a one-off. He'd always found a subtle difference between someone denying something they had done, in order to protect themselves, and someone who had actually not done what they were being accused of. A nuanced distinction, but it was there. A truthful denial often still gave an element of hope in the voice. They knew they were telling the truth so still hoped that they would be able to convince their interrogators of it. A liar's hope was built on weak foundations and therefore carried less authority. It wasn't an exact science, but Lynch thought he could feel the difference here on this point.

'OK, just so we are clear. If you are lying, then irrespective of whatever happens to you, your immediate family will pay the ultimate price, too. And believe me, if we let you live, you'll probably wish we hadn't once we have finished with your kin. No man should carry that amount of guilt.'

Shaughnessy iterated his earlier pleas of innocence on this point. Lynch now believed him. When he fell silent, he glanced at Bernie and then Kelly, both shrugged as if to suggest that they too believed him, or at least were not convinced of his guilt.

At least they may not be dealing with a further compromise. Now to move things on to who he told among the Security Forces.

'OK, as you are not a member, here is the deal. You tell us exactly who and how you passed on the information, and why, together with anything else you have ratted us out on, and you will live. You will have life changing injuries, but will live. And before you claim this is a one-off, we know different. So, choose your words carefully.'

Again, Shaughnessy pleaded sincerely that he had not told anyone, anything, ever. Lynch stopped him with a slap, and then said, 'Purposefully, the only person to know about the test we gave you, are stood in this room, apart from the Officer Commanding the Northern Area of Ireland. No one else.

Again, Shaughnessy pleaded with valour, his innocence.

Lynch again stopped him with a slap. He was losing his patience, though he had to admit that Shaughnessy's pleas were nearly as convincing as they had been on the first issue. Nearly, but not quite the same.

'Here's the thing that stumps you, no matter how much you plead your innocence, we know you are guilty. We have proof. We just want to hear it from you.'

'What? Please tell me, I beg you; I'll be able to explain, or at least convince you, it's not come from me.'

Lynch had to admit, the last plea did appear to have that undertone of truth-based hope in it. This confused him. But the irrefutable proof told a different story. He moved back to the current issue and in some ways the most important bit. 'You say that you did not pass the information on to someone within the Security Services.'

'Absolutely, even if I was of a mind to do such a terrible thing, I wouldn't know how.'

'What about simply ringing the RUC confidential tout-line? God only knows that the bastards are constantly advertising it.'

Lynch stared intently into Shaughnessy's eyes to try and read his reaction. The man paused before he spoke his next denial. Was that a telltale sign?

'You see the problem I have is this: the OC and the lad here who slapped you knew of the plan, but they did not know the specifics, such as the exact location. Only Bernie here and I knew that little nugget. The proof therefore is undeniable, unless of course you think Bernie or I am the tout?'

Shaughnessy looked gobsmacked at hearing this. He paused once more, interestingly, and then spoke.

'Honestly, I can't understand it then. Of course, you and Bernie are not touts, but neither am I. Maybe someone else overheard you in the pub?'

Lynch knew that no one had. He had made sure of it. This eejit was now questioning Lynch's tradecraft in his desperate attempt to clear himself. He called the other two over to the far side of the barn and asked them what they thought.

Both Kelly and Bernie agreed with Lynch that he had not told anyone else, but they would no doubt find out for sure soon enough if problems persisted.

'I'm as happy as I can be that he told truth on that part. I'm also minded that he probably just rang the hotline.'

Both Kelly and Bernie agreed again. Lynch was deeply troubled. If this man had done a one-off following a chance opportunity, then they still had a deep cover tout among them.

'Any thoughts as to why he did it?' Lynch asked them.

'Perhaps it was a money thing. I've heard that they are experimenting with a new anonymous hotline that pays money. Comes from America, called Crimestoppers or something like that. God help us if that catches on,' Bernie said.

'Yes, I agree. When we lifted him, I had a rummage around and found his bank statements. He's in a lot of debt. I also saw several letters headed "Final Demand",' Kelly added.

'Are you saying that if he was a long-term rat, he'd not be in any debt?' Lynch asked.

'It makes sense. But he could be a gambler and poor with money generally. Maybe he is our long-term tout, maybe he has picked up various tit bits from loose-lipped volunteers,' Bernie said.

Lynch wasn't sure all that had gone wrong could be linked to The Shamrock. Certainly, he and Kelly hadn't been in there for months. And he couldn't exactly ask the dead volunteers from Bernie's unit.

'Are we all of one voice then, that he told no one else, and we can't establish that he is behind other failures, though we suspect not.'

Both men nodded.

'In that case you may have to get brutal with him to make sure.'

Both nodded again.

'And when you're done, do him the usual way.'

'And an unmarked grave?' Kelly asked.

'Yes, then spread the word without naming him. We need to send a message, but to save face, too. It'll also unnerve the other rat if we have one. May cause them to make a mistake.'

Kelly and Bernie then got to work on Shaughnessy. Lynch was a hard man, but he didn't take pleasure in watching the last twenty minutes of Shaughnessy's life. But touts were touts and they knew the risks they run. In Lynch's eyes they were the author of their own misfortune, whatever their motivation was.

After ten minutes, he decided to grab some air and when the screaming stopped, Kelly and Bernie joined him outside, both were breathing heavily and covered in blood splatters.

'He's passed out,' Bernie started with.

'And if he is our long-term rat, he has more guts than I have ever witnessed. He continued his denials until he fainted,' Kelly said.

'Conclusions?' Lynch asked.

'He's either, the bravest rat that ever lived, or he was just an opportunist rat in a shit load of debt. But he can't even admit the latter for fear it makes him look guilty for the lot,' Bernie added.

'Either way, he's suffered enough. We are not sadists. Put him out of his misery and let's just hope he was the bravest rat that ever lived.'

Chapter Forty-three

Hastings had really enjoyed Jackson's company the previous evening, even though he had lost a small fortune at poker. It had also given them both a chance to further cement their blossoming relationship on a more personal level, which a one-on-one situation allowed. Jackson left at midnight and Hastings had slept well until his alarm went off at 5.30 a.m. He wished the firm had chosen a different retailer to front their comms room, Derek would be in soon to sort the morning papers. Hastings showered and got himself out and to a near-by all-night café he often used. Suitably fed and watered, he made his way back to the shop. It was now 7 a.m. and he knew that the paperboys and girls would be long gone.

'You keep putting in early shifts,' Derek commented.

'Tell me about it,' he replied, as he was shown through to the rear of the shop.

As soon as he was in the cellar he checked to see if the agent had left a message while he'd been out over the last hour. Nothing. As Romeo Troop were stood down today, he decided to stay in case a call came in. It also gave him a chance to catch up on the mountain of admin he needed to do. First up he had to file his written versions of all the verbal intelligence reports he had passed to London. This took him to dinnertime when he grabbed a sandwich from the shop.

By mid-afternoon he was starting to suffer the cabin-fever of the cellar, so went for a walk before returning. Still no messages. Midday was the usual time that the agent rang in, though it wasn't a hard and fast rule, and only when they had something to say. Though he had been a little perturbed by the original message re the hide. He replayed it. It was hushed and rushed and he started to worry that the agent had taken a risk making the call when they did. Or was he worrying too much. It was just that usually after action was taken a result of the intelligence supplied, the source was quick to give a post-action update. This was important, as it reassured Hastings that no suspicion had fallen on the informant afterwards. Always nice to know. It was this and the panicked mode in which the call had been made that was troubling him. But

WITH PREJUDICE

was he being paranoid. According to Jackson, the way they had approached the hide was done properly. Even if they had been spotted from one of the houses, it would not have looked suspicious.

He had to admit that the way Jackson had described it at the debrief sounded very covert and clever. He was probably panicking about nothing. He had too much time on his hands today. But as the afternoon dragged on, he couldn't shake the feeling of unease. In fact, it was growing. Probably exaggerated by his inertia. He knew the best way to deal with it was to do something positive. He hadn't visited the dead drop in quite a while for safety reasons. It was situated in Crossmaglen, South Armagh close to the Irish border. He only ever went there for specific reasons, or if there was information he would need to urgently pass to the source. Or if they had been incommunicado for a while and needed to pass a message but couldn't use the agreed phone box.

There was a public phone box on the outskirts of Crossmaglen specifically earmarked by the source for use. MI5 tech guys had fitted equipment to it to ensure that it was secure from interception, and that there were no radio bugs or mikes in the box itself. He put a quick call into the Technical Support Unit at Thames House in London to check that there were no reported problems, and there were not.

For operational ease for the agent, the dead drop was not far from the phone box. Then a thought hit him: he'd ask Jackson to join him. He was the expert at making covert approaches. Just on the off chance that something was wrong and the area was receiving more than normal scrutiny. Plus, it would help further enrich their relationship, and although Hastings suspected he was worrying too early, he and Jackson were at a loose end today so it was a perfect time to do it. The fact that he had decided to do something had him feeling better already. He put a quick call into the barracks and was pleased when Jackson jumped at the chance to join him.

***

An hour later, after a detour via The Det - again - Jackson and Hastings were dressed as British Telecom workers in a British

Telecom livered van. The sergeant in charge of The Det's fleet of covert vehicles threatened blue murder if they didn't bring the vehicle back in one piece. Jackson assured him they would, pointing out that they brought the Council van back the previous day with no issues. He just grunted his acceptance as he handed over the keys. Once mobile, with Hastings driving, Jackson made the comment that all sergeants in the British Army, were grumpy, irrespective of regiment.

'Were you grumpy when you were a sergeant?' Hastings asked.

'Oh yes, but I grew out of it when I received my commission.'

An hour later they arrived in Crossmaglen. Deep in bandit country. They found the phone box on Newry Road, and having received instructions from the tech guys in London, Hastings entered it to ring a dedicated number and double check that all was well. As he did this, Jackson stayed in the van and kept discrete observations. Thankfully, Hastings was back in the van after only a few minutes.

'According to the tech guy, all is good on the line and the safety devices are working correctly.'

'Good,' Jackson said, as Hastings fired up the engine. He was relieved to get away from the phone kiosk. Although, he'd seen no sign of anyone paying them any attention, the Provos were not idiots and would soon find anything unusual suspicious.

A hundred and fifty yards away, Hastings pulled over next to a BT roadside box. It was an old GPO green junction box. He gave Jackson a key and asked him to open the front doors of the unit and pretend to do something while he attended the dead drop around the back of it.

Jackson opened the double doors to reveal a mass array of wires of all colours. Hastings had said that the dead drop was in a hole under a rock a couple of feet away from the back of the steel unit, hidden deep under a hedge. He disappeared around the rear and out of sight. A couple of minutes later Jackson was suddenly aware of someone approaching from his left on foot. He shouted a "shhhush" for Hastings's benefit and then glanced up at the advancing man. He was in his thirties, heavily built, thick busy unkempt black hair, and a thick black moustache which covered his top lip. He had a steely visage about him and alarm bells were ringing in Jackson's head.

He used his left elbow to feel the reassuring presence of his shoulder holster under his jacket and more importantly, what was in it. A Beretta .22 handgun. Small and light but highly effective at close range. An ideal concealed weapon.

Moustache Man was walking with purpose. Jackson glimpsed him using his peripheral vison so as not to appear interested in him. He was glad that Hastings was currently out of view at the rear.

'You'll not be messing up with our phone lines now, will you?' Moustache Man said without a smile as he neared.

'Sorted,' Jackson said, with his best Belfast accent. He actually felt nervous, more than conscious that a native may distinguish the smallest of accentual differences in his diction. 'A small fault,' he finished with, trying to use the least number of words.

Moustache Man slipped his right hand inside his outer pocket and kept it there. Jackson tensed. He had now turned to face the man talking to him, and let his right hand drop to his waist. He was sat in a squat position which allowed him to rest his dropped right hand on his lap. His jacket was short, cut just above his waist. Any movement whatsoever from Moustache Man's right pocket and Jackson would draw. He'd slot the man before he could fumble any weapon out of his jacket.

The next few moments were only a second or two in time, but felt like an eon. Jackson broke the impasse, if indeed that was what it was. This way he kept control of the situation. His thighs were now screaming at him, so as he spoke - which is a distraction - he slowly dropped his left knee to the pavement. He now had a rock steady firing stance. 'All done,' he said.

No response.

Further moments passed, and nothing more was said.

Jackson slowly got to his feet and approached the van keeping Moustache Man in view. 'I'll be away, now,' Jackson said, as he closed the two steel doors, and put the key in to lock it. He used his non-dominant hand, while keeping one eye on the man who was now stood a yard in front of him.

'You're not from these parts, are you?' Moustache Man asked.

'That I'm not. Had to come from Belfast. Your man's off sick.'

'Well, thanks for coming out of your way.'

'No bother,' Jackson said as he climbed into the driver's seat and started the engine. As he pulled away, he saw that Moustache Man was stood watching for several seconds before continuing on his way.

As soon as Jackson was out of sight, he turned off the main road and pulled over in a spot out of view from the main road. He waited several minutes before turning the van round and heading back up Newry Road. There was no sign of Moustache Man, but he soon saw a frantic looking Hastings reappear from the hedgerow.

He stopped and Hastings jumped in, before he accelerated away.

'Let's get the hell out of here.'

'I nearly shat myself,' Hastings said, who looked decidedly flushed.

'You did the right thing staying out of sight. He'd have sussed you in an instant. No offence.'

'None taken. I was only glad to see you return.'

'They can check the box if they are suspicious, they'll find no devices or tampering, which is what they would be concerned about. It's a good place to have your dead drop, it allows for a good misdirection.'

'You think he was a Provo?'

'Hundred percent.'

'Can't wait to get back to Belfast.'

'How secure is the dead drop?'

'If you didn't know it was there, you'd never find it. It's deep in the hedge and underground. I've left a cryptic note that only the source will understand. Even if discovered under the rock, it will just look like a scrap of paper that has got trapped there.'

Jackson turned to face Hastings as they left Crossmaglen behind them, and said, 'You worried?'

'There will be a reason which could be anything innocent. But if I've not heard from them by this time tomorrow, I will start to worry properly then.'

'OK, do you fancy some more company tonight?'

'Dead right, I need to try and win my money back.'

WITH PREJUDICE

Chapter Forty-four

Twenty-four hours later and Jackson told the troop that he'd just spoken to Hastings and that he had heard nothing more from the source and was starting to panic for real. Also, London have told Hastings that all the usual chatter that they pick up on has stopped. Is it a lull before a shitstorm?

'Let's go proactive then,' Crompton suggested, and added, 'I can't abide much more of Tone-Deaf Harris's guitar playing.'

'That's gratitude for you. Keeping you lummoxes entertained.'

'Yeah, boss let's get out and about. I'm going stir-crazy in here,' Kingy added.

'OK, teams of two. Kingy with me and Harris with you, Geordie.'

All three men nod.

'Me and Kingy will check all known Belfast haunts, you and Harris, Sarge, cover Antrim and Londonderry. We'll stay away from South Armagh for now after the other day. I certainly got the impression that a state of higher alert was in process.'

'Target objectives?' Crompton asked.

'Find any hint of Lynch.'

'And if we do, are we cleared to slot him? Crompton asked.

'Not sure yet. If something has happened to the source then, probably yes. I'll double-check with Hastings as and when, and in what circumstances we find him.'

'Keep all normal channels monitored, and stay covert at all costs.'

More nods and then everyone got busy kitting up. Jackson put a quick call into Hastings at the newsagents where he knew he would be and briefed him.

Thirty minutes later, Jackson and Kingy were patrolling around the Falls Road area in a battered old Transit van complete with ladders on the roof. They were patched into the RUC's overall channel, but if they pulled the cigarette lighter out of it housing, they would receive the Army's General Channel. Their earpieces were connected via a wire loop system hidden in the van's roof lining to keep the onboard speakers silent. They also had their Racal Cougar radio body sets on. Hastings was operating Zero Alpha from his Comms Room.

Jackson offered to drive as Kingy had a list of all known addresses and haunts on a clip board courtesy of Hastings's Special Branch contacts.

After two hours, they were drawing blanks wherever they went, and when they checked with Crompton, they reported the same from Antrim and were en route to Londonderry.

Then the RUC overall channel - coded as White Channel - went noisy. A pipe bomb had hit an RUC patrol Land Rover but had failed to explode. The two Constables had engaged the two suspects and had and come under heavy fire. They were currently pinned down in a side street in Lower Shankill.

'UDA/UFF?' Kingy asked.

'Could be, or it could be our Provos. It's not far from where the Lynch Mob last struck. Come on let's join the posse heading there. Give Geordie an update via Zero.'

'Will do.'

Jackson drove the van as swiftly as he could, but without going too fast so as not to draw attention. They were not the primary response.

They were probably half-way to the location when the RUC radio operator announced that back up had arrived on scene and as a result, the two terrorist attackers had broken cover and legged into one of the estates. Then it all went quiet.

A few minutes passed and Jackson slowed the van down and tried to imagine where he would park a getaway vehicle if he was a terrorist. He could see that Kingy was doing the same as he already had a street map of Belfast opened across his clip board.

They passed numerous police patrols floating around in all directions. Then it hit him. What if the RUC were working on the assumption that as the attack had involved a pipe bomb, they were looking for Loyalist terrorists. A fair assumption. And as they were in Loyalist land, the attackers could have disappeared into any number of friendly addresses. So, leave the RUC to cover that. If it was Lynch, then he was exposed in an unfriendly place, with

WITH PREJUDICE

no back up. His getaway car must be in a non-residential place, not overlooked, but close by. He shared his thoughts with Kingy who vehemently agreed and studied his map in light of their hypothesis.

A minute later Kingy shouted, 'Got it. Shankill Graveyard. It's surrounded by trees, not overlooked, minutes away from where the attack took place and in the general direction the Tangos were last seen legging it in.'

Jackson did a quick U-turn and was soon approaching the graveyard. Jackson could see two stone pillars by a non-vehicle entrance. It had two wrought iron gates, which were pegged open. According to Kingy it led to a monument. But it was wide enough for a small car. They were twenty yards away when a battered old Morris Mini drove out of the graveyard and headed west along the Shankill Road. Two men on board. This had to be it. Jackson allowed a car out from a side street to keep themselves one vehicle back from the Mini.

'Did you get a good look at the men?' Jackson asked.

'No. But they fit the profile and the passenger has a general similarity to Lynch.'

'That's what I thought.'

'Ambush?' Kingy asked.

'Not until we are a hundred percent sure. And if we can follow them unseen, we might uncover a base, a hide or whatever as well.'

'OK, I'll prep weapons, then.'

Jackson nodded as he raised Hastings on his body set by resting his left wrist onto the steering wheel which depressed the transmit button hidden up his sleeve.

Hastings concurred the plan, and said he'd get Crompton and Harris to join them ASAP. He'd also have urgent intel checks done on the Mini. Five minutes later, as they headed onto the A55, the West Circular Road, Hastings came back on to say that the Mini had been stolen at gunpoint this morning by two men in balaclavas and the owner was ordered not to report it stolen until tea-time, but had done so anyway. The RUC patrol that was attacked had ironically been looking for it as they suspected an attack was imminent. This was it, game on. They decided not to share with the RUC that they'd found it, even though it was their men who had been engaged. Fortunately, they were unharmed.

'If they make us and get spooked, bearing in mind we are a one vehicle surveillance and in an old, battered van at that, we'll have no choice but to engage,' Jackson said into the transponder under his coat lapel.

'The fact that we received no prior notice of this via the source, gravelly concerns me now. They could be dead already. Or being held. Lynch, if it is him in the Mini, could lead us to them,' Hastings replied.

'Granted.'

'It appears to have been a random attack on any RUC patrol.'

'Agreed, so not overly preplanned.'

'Try and see where they lead you. They could have the source in custody. In my experience they don't kill them for days. God only knows what terrors they might be enduring. But if there is half a chance of locating the source then we must take it.'

'Also agreed. But if we get burnt, then it will have to go noisy.'

'Also agreed,' Hastings said and then cut the connection.

Jackson quickly updated Kingy and then concentrated on driving covertly. They were now passing Andersonstown and headed south towards the M1 motorway. If the Mini took the M1 the follow would get easier. For now, they had two cars for cover, which was good. Plus, in their favour was that an old, battered van was not the most likely of a mobile surveillance vehicle. And also, the Mini would be nearly as underpowered as they were.

WITH PREJUDICE

Chapter Forty-five

Lynch and Kelly travelled south on the M1, Kelly at the wheel, and Lynch continually checked his door mirror.

'Something bothering you, Brendan?'

'Not sure yet,' Lynch replied. 'Just keep us at the speed limit, I tell you when I want you to slow down a bit. Then we'll see.'

Kelly nodded.

Lynch had noticed an old, battered van with ladders on the roof earlier, and again before they had joined the M1, but it could be nothing. It was currently between them and an HGV, so it kept disappearing from view. 'What speed do you reckon the wagon behind is doing?'

'Fifty, tops. Since we increased to sixty, we are leaving him behind.'

'There is an old van behind it, which you'd think would overtake. Especially now as we have created a gap.'

'I saw that before, it's an old knacker, it might be struggling.'

'True enough, but it does no harm to be sure. Slow down to the wagon's speed, and keep as close to it as you can without inviting it to try and pass us.'

Kelly did as he was instructed. Lynch glanced out the side window at the countryside and knew they were approaching Moira a couple of miles up ahead. He'd see how things developed. Kelly might be right; it was easy to become over-paranoid in this game.

***

Jackson didn't need to tell Kingy what to do as they travelled south on the M1. He was an expert surveillance operative. They had good cover behind a laden HGV which was trundling along at a steady fifty. Fortunately, the Mini was either in no rush, or was struggling, too. It looked like its best days were behind it. Kingy was rightly keeping close cover behind the wagon, which did mean that they lost eyeball on the Mini for most of the time. Occasionally, he would pull back to grab a glimpse of the car, before resuming cover. Jackson was leaning on the passenger window so if the Mini suddenly hit the hard shoulder, he would see it appear on the nearside. Likewise, if it left the motorway. He had noticed the signs informing them that junction nine at Moira was approaching. He'd pay extra attention when they reached it. As he had with the previous exits.

Then Hastings came blasting in his ear, he hoped that meant Crompton and Harris were not far away.

'Go ahead, Zero Alpha,' he said into his transceiver hidden under the collar of his jacket.

'Good news, at last,' Hastings said.

'The others joining the party?'

'Not just yet, but they are making ground fast. But I've just heard from the source in a live conversation.'

Jackson was doubly pleased, not only because that meant the source was safe, but hopefully, they were now clear to engage the Tangos, as and when. He was sick and tired of fannying about with Lynch. It was time to slot him. He voiced his thoughts to Hastings.

'Let's stay covert for the moment, I know the risks are now reduced but he could still lead us to a hide or hideout, or whatever.'

Jackson didn't reply.

'But we still have trouble. The source is considering going dark as they are becoming terrified. Lynch has already lifted, tortured, and killed one poor sod he'd fingered as a tout. But according to the source he's not done. He thinks there is another one. So, the source is rightly concerned that the threat is not over.'

'It'll be over with three rounds through his head.'

'Let's keep it fluid for the mo. If we play this right, we'll get him, and protect the source and therefore convince the source to carry on.'

'If the source wants to? As you have always said, it seems very personal to them.'

'I know, it'll be my job to keep them onside. I've got a couple of ideas in mind that might work.'

'OK, status quo - for now.'

Hastings agreed and then cut the connection.

'Frigging spooks,' Jackson said.

WITH PREJUDICE

'I thought you liked him?' Kingy said.

'I do; but once a spook always a spook.'

Jackson returned his attention to the view of the nearside up ahead through the passenger window. They were passing junction nine. Then he saw it and shouted, 'Shit, shit, shit.'

***

'It's carried straight on,' Lynch said, now risking a look through the Mini's rear window as they left the M1 at junction nine and headed southwest on the A3 towards Lurgan.

'Any reaction to us leaving?' Kelly asked.

'The van is tucked up behind the wagon,' Lynch replied, he was impressed with Kelly. He'd left it until they had almost passed the exit before shouting at him to make the turn. He'd skidded across the end of the chevrons kicking up loads of dust and debris in the process. They had only just made it onto the exit road in front of a Cortina which had to brake to let them in. Followed by a long horn blast, but that didn't matter. What mattered was that the van couldn't come with them. But the bad news was the reaction.

'Didn't you see it?' he asked Kelly.

'See what.'

Lynch explained. As Kelly had made the late turn as instructed, Lynch had spun around to scrutinise things. The van on realising what they had done jumped on its brakes in a vain attempt to also make the exit, but it was too late. It would have rolled onto the hard shoulder had it tried. It was trapped behind the lorry. But it confirmed Lynch's worst fears. Sass had been there, and that meant only one thing. But on the plus side, no other vehicles followed them off the M1. Not that he had expected any to. Had the van had backup, the frontmost following vehicle would have swopped about many times, he knew.

They were approaching the centre of Moira and there was a roundabout up ahead. He told Kelly to get off the main road and find a phone box. They'd have to dump the Mini now and find another way to Crossmaglen.

***

'I'm sorry boss,' Kingy said, but Jackson knew it wasn't his fault. They were a one- man surveillance team in a van doing their best. If anything, it was Jackson's fault for not being able to give King advanced warning, even if the Mini had done its manoeuvre at the last possible second. Had he been concentrating on his view up ahead through the passenger window, he might have been able to give King a split-second heads-up, but even that might not have been enough. He voiced this to ease Kingy's guilt as who had the van flat out towards the next exit, where they would head back to junction nine and take the A3 southwest. Geordie Crompton came over the body set to announce their arrival so Jackson brought them up-to-date and asked them to do the A3 northeast from junction nine.

Then he had the unpleasant task of telling Hastings, who said he'd warn the source as soon as they rang in next. He'd asked the source to do an hourly contact, if possible, while things were fluid.

WITH PREJUDICE

Chapter Forty-six

Lynch picked up the phone and dialled a number from memory. Sean answered after the second ring, 'How did it go?'

Lynch quickly told him all that had happened. Starting with the fact that the pipe bomb had failed, though that was the least of their worries now.

'Jesus,' Sean exclaimed as Lynch finished his report.

'And you are sure you managed to lose them?'

'Hundred precent.'

'Who were they? SB? RUC? SAS?'

'I'm sure they were Sass. The same Sass who have been sticking their noses in everywhere. We need to revisit that lorry accident, too.'

'You think that was them, as well?'

'I do now, Sean.'

Sean groaned down the phone, and then added, 'They do seem to be well-informed.'

'It can only mean the unthinkable.'

'But I thought you'd sorted that?'

'It's like I said, Sean. I thought he had just been an opportunist tout, and not the main leak. There was just something honest about his denials. And this morning proves it.'

Sean sighed again, so Lynch filled the pause, 'It's not an exact science, you know?'

'I know, Brendan, and I trust your instincts above many. But this morning changes everything. It's clearly not Shaughnessy.'

'I know. And it proves the unthinkable.'

'Tell me again, the exact words you used?'

'I kept it vague on purpose. I just said that we'd attack, "Any Proddy dog RUC on the Shankill. And if they turned out to be one of the few Catholic RUC, even better, disloyal bastards".'

'You didn't say exactly where, or when?'

'Just the Shankill this morning.'

'OK.'

'And apart from you, I only told the one person. Only the one. And I'm as upset as you will be. I'm stunned if I'm being honest. But you know what this means?'

'Are you absolutely certain?'

'Sean, they nearly rolled the van trying to get across to the exit lane. And I kept the next bit to myself.'

'Go on?'

'It was the same van I initially saw as we left the cemetery on the Shankill. No mistake.'

After a long pause, Sean said, 'In that case, Brendan you must do what you have to do. I won't tell anyone, not even the Chief of Staff until they are lifted. Stay where you are and I'll get a motor dropped off by your phone box.'

'OK,' Lynch said, sighed and then replaced the receiver.

***

After two hours searching for the Mini, Jackson was about to call a 'Stand-down' when Hastings told him that the stolen car had been found abandoned in Moira. It was shoved behind a scrap yard which is why they hadn't seen it on their many recces through the place. The RUC were on their way to recover it, and Hastings said he had fed in Lynch's details as a possible suspect through his Special Branch contact. He was duty bound to do so now. Jackson said he understood but hoped Romeo Troop found him first. On the plus side, there were now thousands of eyes looking for Lynch. Hastings added that he had an analyst in London monitoring the RUC radio with a 'Keyword search' scan so that they would be alerted every time Lynch's name was mentioned. Jackson was impressed, it just might give them the heads-up to get there first. Or at the very least, give Jackson an area where they could concentrate their searches.

Until then, they were going to resume the search plan that each pair were doing prior to this morning's attack, and Hastings promised to update them on possible haunts as soon as he had them.

Hastings added that the source had gone quiet again, missing the last two hourly contact calls. Jackson said that could mean anything. They'd said they were thinking of going dark. Hastings said he'd considered having a drive around the phone box and the dead drop, but Jackson talked him out of it. He'd be at risk of standing out.

***

Hastings didn't know where the source lived, but suspected that they probably lived miles away from the phone box and the dead drop. He would consider that good tradecraft.

'You know, if your concern grows again, we can covertly watch the source's home for you, while we are looking for Lynch. If the source is in danger of compromise, that might be a perfect place to put under obs,' Jackson said.

'Thanks, but there are difficulties with that,' Hastings replied. He didn't want to admit to Jackson that he didn't know where the source lived. They had always refused to say where, and he had accepted the reason why. 'Anyway, at the moment, I don't want to miss a live call from them.'

'I think the address needs covering and one of my lads will do it better than you. But we'd need to know the address, and therefore the source's identity. Is it that time yet?'

'Maybe, but as I say, there are difficulties with doing that. I'll give it a bit longer, and get back to you, thanks,' Hastings said, rushing to end the conversation.

Chapter Forty-seven

It was going dark as Lynch drove past Ballynamore headed towards the barn near Dungeon Waterfall. He didn't relish the task in hand, and took a moment to take on the beauty of the countryside in this part of the north of Ireland. The midges were out in force tonight and would have plenty to feed off soon.

He parked his car outside the barn and could see lights inside starting to show through the cracks around the two huge swing doors as the outside light faded. As he alighted his motor the cracks of light momentarily grew brighter before dulling again. Kelly opened the doors slightly and slid through the gap. He met Lynch by the side of his car.

'Any problems with the lift?' Lynch asked.

'None. But as you were aware, we just missed him the other day. Had to await his return from Dublin. I used the Nutting Squad who had to hear it from Sean first before they believed the order,' Kelly answered.

Lynch knew that the 'Nutting Squad' or Internal Security Unit, to give them their official title, answered only to the Army Council themselves.

'They were desperate to know the charge, and were put out that they were not to do the interrogation,' Kelly added.

'I'll square it with them later, in fact, we may need them, probably will.'

'That's what I told them. I also explained why Sean had sanctioned you to start off proceedings, because you had the first-hand evidence. Sean must have told them the same.'

'We are in unprecedented times. No one of such senior position has ever been accused before.'

'I still can't understand why?'

'That's what we are here to find out. Come on, let's get on with it,' Lynch said and started towards the barn doors, followed by Kelly.

Inside tied to a chair, with gaffer tape over his mouth, and two poacher's spot lamps on tripods facing him, was Bernie Doyle, the

WITH PREJUDICE

Officer Commanding the 1st Belfast Battalion of the Provisional IRA.

The chair was secured to the floor and didn't move as Doyle became agitated and started to rock violently against his restraints on seeing Lynch.

Lynch stood in front of Doyle, and Kelly took up a position behind him. Lynch waited until Doyle had finished his tantrum and then he ripped off the gaffer tape, and stood back.

Doyle yelped and then said, 'This is outrageous. I can't believe you have managed to get Sean's approval for such ill-informed action. I will eat your liver when I'm free from this kangaroo court.'

Lynch allowed a short pause before he spoke. 'You know that the first principle of any volunteer is to show total allegiance to the organisation.'

'How dare you quote the Green Book at me, you tosser.'

'What, this Green Book?' Lynch countered as he pulled his personal copy of the IRA's 1977 edition of the Green Book out of his pocket. It was the operating manual with procedural instructions that every member of the IRA and PIRA was given, and expected to learn on joining the organisation. It also contained instructions on any Courts Martial that were required. He put the book away.

'I've known you many years, and for most of that time I have respected you. I didn't always like you, but believed in your honour. Until now,' Lynch said.

'You've always been an arrogant shit. Deluded by your exalted rank when on the Army Council. And embittered when they fired you off. I now outrank you. This is contemptable.'

'And you are the deep-rooted tout that has been causing all the problems. All the leaks. All the failed or compromised operations. All down to you. I just want to know why?'

'Christ, man, we interrogated and killed the tout as well you know. What the hell is this?'

Lynch ignored the question and pressed on. 'Did they finally get enough dirt on you to blackmail you? Or was it money? You've never been good with cash. Or are you just bitter at the direction the Provisional IRA is headed? I can understand the latter. I too have my reservations about some of the current policy. Is it that?'

'Enough of this rubbish. Show me your evidence.'

Lynch stepped forward and punched Doyle in the face as hard as he could, causing his nose to explode like an overripe tomato. Blood sprayed out and ran into his mouth.

'I'll eat your heart, too, for that.'

'When I rang you from the Shamrock in the presence of Shaughnessy, no one else was near enough to hear what I said to you.'

'So you kept telling Shaughnessy.'

'Do you accept that?'

'If it'll get this charade over with quicker, yes, I accept that.'

Lynch nodded at Kelly behind him, who then took pen and paper from his pocket and wrote down the admission.

Lynch nodded again, and then continued, 'So only you, I, and Shaughnessy knew.'

'Yes, yes, don't labour it.'

Lynch nodded at Kelly once more, who again wrote a short note on the paper.

'We initially thought that Shaughnessy was an opportunist tout, and that the real one still existed.'

'Yes, yes.'

Kelly noted this.

'But what if you have always been the tout, the only tout? Using Shaughnessy this way gave you the perfect opportunity to protect yourself and blame Shaughnessy.'

'What nonsense,' Doyle said, before spitting bloodied phlegm onto the floor.

'You had knowledge of the other operations. The alleged accident with the lorry, for one.'

'You told me that was just an accident.'

'But what if it wasn't? What if it was Sass?'

'You really think I would send two of my best men to their deaths?

Lynch ignored the question and carried on, 'You knew about the attack on McDonald, the RUC killer-excuser.'

'Of course I did, have you forgotten who I am?'

'I nearly killed that SAS bastard at McDonald's home address but couldn't get at his family. Why was that? How did they get there so fast?'

'All speculation by a deranged fool.'

'But you didn't know the specifics of the Shankill pub, and guess what, that went through but only just. You did know we were on our way to do something in the Lower Shankill, didn't you? And that was nearly enough to stop it.'

'Evidence, show me some evidence, or I'm not answering any more of your stupid questions.'

Lynch took a deep breath and then said, 'What about the other morning's pipe bomb attack?'

'You mean the one you fucked up. You couldn't even get that right.'

'Yep, that one.'

'What about it?'

'The Sass turned up.'

'Feck off.'

'Tell him, Stuart.'

Kelly then spoke from behind Doyle to confirm what had happened at Moira.

'And what does that prove?'

'Proves you are the tout.'

'Proves you gobbed off about it, more like.'

'I only told you, no one else. Not even Stuart.'

'That's correct,' Kelly confirmed.

'You said, Sean had authorised it,' Doyle said, suddenly starting to look less bullish.

'I gave Sean no details of the attack or the location, just that there would be one. On purpose. We had jointly agreed this in order to test *you*.'

'What horseshit is this?'

'Only you and I knew. And again, you did not know the specifics. Just that a random RUC patrol would be attacked. And guess what? The fecking SAS turned up. They followed us and very nearly compromised us. They would have done so but for

Kelly's quick reactions. If it's any consolation, I actually didn't think it could be you, though it all makes sense now. I was as shocked as Kelly when that van started following us. Not some RUC patrol who guessed lucky, but a covert vehicle with covert operatives in it. They can only have been there ahead of the attack. A preplanned deployment by them. They would need advance knowledge for that.'

'Then you must have been sloppy and someone picked up on it.'

'You know, Sean wasn't totally convinced that someone else in the Shamrock couldn't have overheard our conversation in front of Shaughnessy. About the hide. That's why we have done this. We had to be sure. And now we are.'

'I want to speak to Sean.'

'Don't worry, I'll be doing that shortly. And if he concurs, then you will be Court Martialled and punished accordingly. If you fess up before I get back, then your body will be returned to your family courtesy of the nearest gutter, at least you'll get a proper funeral that way. But don't expect a twenty-one-gun salute. But if not, then you will be buried in an unmarked grave never to be found. Plus, you'll also save yourself a lot of pain.'

Lynch then pointed to the bolt cutters on the floor and for the first time saw genuine horror in Doyle's face, mixed with a veneer of shock, disbelief even. Lynch turned to face Kelly and said, 'Start with the left-hand fingers.'

Kelly nodded and moved from behind Doyle.

Lynch turned and headed towards the barn doors as Doyle screamed his innocence. Nothing said by Doyle, or any expressions Lynch had noted, had that edge of true innocence underpinning them. He was convinced they had found their super-rat. He'd use the landline in the small farm cottage across from the barn. He knew exactly what he would tell Sean and he could guess what his response would be.

WITH PREJUDICE

Chapter Forty-eight

Two days had passed since the failed pipe bomb attack and Hastings still had had no contact from the source, and was starting to become concerned again. He was going stir-crazy waiting for a call in the comms room under the newsagents, so had borrowed the BT van from the Det again and paid a couple of visits to the dead drop. He considered asking Jackson to join him but decided against it. If the man who had challenged Jackson last time saw him again, it might raise suspicions. Plus, he wanted him and the rest of Romeo Troop to concentrate on trying to locate where Lynch was or is likely to be. Not that they were having any luck.

At the first visit to the dead drop, Hastings had taken a prepared scrap of paper with him. It was a bottom corner piece and had two lines on it which would appear to be part of a shopping list which had become entangled by the rock covering the dead drop hole. The first line said, '5 lbs of potatoes' which both he and the source knew meant to contact Hastings urgently. The second line said, 'Apples'. This meant that the note was from Hastings. The clever bit was that should he ever place a second note, it would be signed off with an item beginning with the letter b, such as bananas, and so forth through the alphabet. That way, even if compromised, the Provos would use 'apple' again, not knowing the protocol. Hastings had even put the note in an oven for a few seconds, which yellowed the paper and bleaching the ink to give it an aged effect.

When he found the note undisturbed on his second visit, he knew that the source had not attended the dead drop. That could be a good thing, or a bad thing. He decided not to risk a third visit. He also had the tec support team at Thames House pay attention to all calls from the telephone kiosk, and nothing of note had come from that.

Jackson had offered, again, to deploy one of his team to be properly dug in in a rural observation post, but he declined without explanation. He didn't want Jackson to realise why, until it was time to ID the source to him. This was the way the source had insisted things were from the beginning. Even Jeremy in London didn't realise this.

As he sat in the comms room mulling everything over, a scheduled call came in from Jeremy.

'Still no change,' Hastings started with as he answered the call.

'Look, the source has done brilliantly, as have you, but if they have gone fully dark, or have been compromised, then it's time to move on.'

Hastings knew that Jeremy had never run an agent, and indeed had little experience in the field, so tried to stifle his irritation as he responded. 'We still have a duty of care to them, and in any event, we are not sure, yet, whether or not they can be further deployed, post-Lynch?'

'You raise two issues here: firstly, I understand why you have elongated Lynch's reign, in order to learn more and take out other Provos we might not have previously known about. But are you forgetting the PM's prime instruction in all this?'

Hastings shook his head at the irony of the situation. On the one hand Thatcher had sanctioned a shoot to kill order against Lynch, while at the same time ordering a shoot to kill investigation into the security forces in Ulster by Deputy Chief Constable John Stalker from Manchester. He simply replied, 'Of course not.'

'And the second point is this "duty of care" poppycock. I worry that you are getting too close to the source?'

Hastings could not hold back anymore, 'How dare you. Of course one has to show due consideration to an agent's welfare, or we wouldn't have any agents. And part of forming a false relationship has to involve empathy. Creating a shared understanding. Anyone who has actually handled a source, especially, a deep-rooted one, would know this.'

'Now steady, here, Bertie. Remember to whom you are talking. Forget about the source unless they get back in touch. Just find Lynch.'

'But the two are inextricably linked: we find the source, we locate Lynch.'

'Stop wasting your time trying to find the source, concentrate on locating Lynch. You know why the PM is so driven. Lynch was

the architect of the Brighton bombing. You have your orders.'
Then the line went dead.

Sod Jeremy. Then the phone rang an incoming call and it made him jump. He recognised the number's tag; it was one of Detective Superintendent John Field's Special Branch analysts. He took the call, listened, and then thanked the caller. There was no time to waste, he quickly contacted Jackson over the radio, and asked, 'Where are you, now?'

'On the outskirts of Londonderry, why?'

'Excellent; get yourself headed towards Ballynamore. Close to a place called Dungeon Waterfall. A hillwalker heard screams coming from the direction of an abandoned barn. About an hour ago. It's taken them until now to find a phone box.'

'RUC in attendance?'

'No: SB overruled them, said they'd have a look first, but have passed it onto us. How far away are you?'

'Be there in ten, Zero Alpha.'

'You going in overt?'

'Loud and proud if it's Lynch, or any of the provos; they won't know what hit them.'

'Mind the hostage,' Hastings said, immediately regretting the comment.

'Hostage rescue is one of our core skills. It's why we practice with live rounds in the Killing House at Hereford. You may have heard of it.'

'Sorry, I know that. Just, you know…'

'I know mate, but we are the world's best at this. Got to go, out.'

Hastings had a terrified feeling as to what was going on in that barn. Just the sort of place that the Provos used for interrogation. And he could feel it in his blood that it was the source who was screaming. He just hoped and prayed that Jackson would get there in time.

Chapter Forty-nine

Earlier on, Jackson and Crompton had changed areas, so as not to over-expose themselves in Londonderry and Belfast. And because of that, when the radio call came in from Hastings at Zero, they were only ten minutes away from the Dungeon Waterfall area. Albeit playing catch up of at least an hour since the witness heard the screams. In an effort to calm Hastings, he'd commented that it could simply be an animal. Not that he believed that for a minute. Crompton and Harris were making ground from west Belfast as quickly as they could, but would be some time away, yet.

Jackson and Kingy were in an old-looking Morris Maxi and approached slowly along Goshenden Road. They had a cover story ready in case they were challenged, and Jackson told Harris that he would do all the talking. It took a further fifteen minutes before they happened upon what looked favourite to be the place. Down a small lane, which was a cul-de-sac, was a raised area of land, surrounded by a high fence and barbed wire complete with 'Private' and 'Keep Out' notices, including one which declared that 'Poachers would be shot' which Jackson thought was a nice touch.

They abandoned their motor and approached on foot. There was a small, detached farmhouse and a nearby barn building. From the outside, both appeared abandoned and were in a poor state of repair. Jackson signalled for Kingy to approach the rear aspect as he did the front. The farmhouse was in darkness with curtains drawn back. The front door was locked, but Kingy said the rear door wasn't, or wasn't now. Jackson had not heard a noise, Kingy's forced entry had been done well. A minute later, he let Jackson in, and they quickly and quietly cleared the property. It didn't look as if anyone had lived there for some time.

Next, they approached the barn, and quickly did a circular recce. There were no lights on and no noises from inside. It was obvious that the two huge doors at the front were unlocked and had been designed to let large animals through. They stood either side of the doors. Kingy drew his Glock sidearm and Jackson donned his infra-red goggles. Peering through the cracks around the doors he could see that the barn was empty, except for a chair in the middle which had two tripods facing it with extinguished lamps on top.

They entered and soon realised what they had chanced across.

The chair had Gaffer tape across the arms and legs which had clearly been used as restraints. There was blood on the floor around the chair, some congealing and some that still looked very fresh. Whoever had been here had not been gone long. Damn.

Then Kingy made a gruesome discovery, several bloodied digits on the floor around the sides of the chair. He was tempted to use a flashlight as the view through the infra-red goggles was limited, and very green, but knew that would be too much of a risk.

'Seven fingers and two thumbs,' Kingy announced. Then corrected himself before Jackson could respond. 'No, sorry, just found another finger.'

'Not good at counting, Ian, are you?' Jackson quipped.

'Better than this poor sod will be, now. You think it's Hastings's source?'

'Must be.'

'Obviously an interrogation centre.'

'And one we didn't know about, so let's leave everything as we found it. We can tell SB that we found nothing but a worried sheep. That should close down any interest.'

'What about the source? Where do you reckon they have taken them?'

'I don't think it matters, now, look,' Jackson said pointing at the floor between the tripods. In close formation were three discarded bullet casings. Jackson bent down to have a closer look and said, 'They look like 9mm, probably from a Beretta pistol.'

Kingy stooped for a closer look and then stood up and said, 'Agreed. What do you think they will do with the body?'

'It'll be dumped in a back street, or buried in an unmarked grave in the countryside.'

'I don't fancy your job having to give Hastings the good news, boss.'

'Me neither. Plus, you know what this now means?'

'We are flying blind.'

'Yep. No idea where Lynch is, or what the bastard is planning.'

Kingy nodded, and Jackson added, 'Come on, let's get out of here before we push our luck.'

WITH PREJUDICE

Chapter Fifty

Hastings pulled the headphones off after finishing his radio call from Jackson. 'Shit, shit, shit,' he shouted as he threw them down on the desk. He quickly left the newsagents without speaking to Derek, who was fortunately serving a customer, and headed to the 24-hour fast-food restaurant around the corner. Once seated with a coffee he mused over what Jackson had told him. Then the guilt kicked in. Could he have done more, sooner? Should he have kept pushing for more from the source. Should he have had Lynch taken out sooner, as Jeremy had wanted? He'd delayed things for his own selfish reasons; wanting as much intel as he could get, so they could take out as many Provos as possible, while trying to cajole the source to carry on after Lynch was gone. Done for honourable reasons, but at what cost. God, this intelligence game he was in was a dirty business. Neither side fought a clean fight. He was getting sick of it. Especially, when he had to deal with the likes of Jeremy spouting from the safety of London. He'd never last a day out here, yet he was the one trying to call all the shots.

Then his mind wandered as to how Lynch had made the source. Their cover was as near perfect as you could imagine. He was only too aware that a witch hunt had been taking place, but he ensured that all intel was only ever acted upon when he knew that more than the source had advanced knowledge of it. It was a question he always asked the source, so much so, that even when he had to rely on left messages, the source would always state that more than they knew. He'd always accepted the source's judgment on this. Perhaps, that's were complacency had crept in. Even if the agent believed more than they and Lynch knew something, it didn't mean that that was correct. These are the sort of questions that Jeremy would be asking, as if *he* knew better. Hastings would have to give this some thought before he rang London with the update.

He pondered things through again, and decided to keep quiet for now. Even though the source was clearly dead from the description of the scene that Jackson had described. No body had been found. And he knew that the chances of that were very slim.

Then a thought hit him, he should have asked Jackson to recover one of the severed digits. As macabre a request it was, they could check the fingerprints they had on a secret file of the source. The Provos on their return would not notice one missing, surely. And if they did, they'd assume a rat had taken it, or suchlike. In his heart of hearts, he knew it was a pointless exercise. And it came with risks, asking Jackson to return to the barn when the Provos could turn up at any minute. That said, it would be a good place to watch just in case Lynch did return. Though that could be today, tomorrow or in a week's time. But at least it was one place they could watch; and the recovery of the finger would justify his delay in telling Jeremy. He'd better get back to the comms room quickly and speak to Jackson.

Hastings left his coffee and rushed back to the newsagents and was soon below ground once more. He picked up the headphones and was about to call Jackson over the covert radio when he noticed a red flashing light on his monitor. A recorded message. Probably bloody Jeremy. He logged on and pressed play. His jaw fell open as he listened to the soft Dublin accent.

It was from the source.

The diction was hurried and quick. He could tell that they were under pressure. Then he got a grip, he realised that the message must have been left before Lynch had got to them. But why hadn't he noticed it? He ignored his self-recrimination as he listened.

Protocols over, the source said, 'This will probably be the last contact you receive from me, unless you stop Pídàn this time. No more extensions, he's out of control. Tomorrow morning, he aims to commit an obscene act of vindictiveness which will put The Cause back, and serve only to create a war with the Loyalists that will make everything hitherto seem like a playground tiff. It's what he wants. It's what he's always wanted.'

The source then went on to explain how some young mother on the Shankill had made a crude comment about 'squeezing the Pope' whilst her youngster had been sat on a potty. And as foul as that was, they knew the Republicans could be just as cutting with their comments.

WITH PREJUDICE

The source said that he made his intentions truly clear, 'He intends to publicly kill that poor young mother and her wee bairn. You have to stop him. For the obvious reason, and for one other.'

The source then explained that as tight-lipped as Pídàn had become, there was always one other person he often spoke to. The source. And for the obvious reasons. But on this occasion, the source was absolutely sure he had only told them.

Notwithstanding, that Pídàn was now sure he had killed the real tout - he'd said that their own side would try to stop him if the news of his plans leaked out.

So only the two of them knew; guaranteed. Hastings would have to stop Pídàn - not just for the apparent reasons - but if he escaped any intervention, he would know for sure, this time, with absolute certainty, who the real deep-rooted tout was.

Hastings slammed his fist down on the table, if only he could speak with the source, he could tell them to flee to a safe location, now realising that whoever had been in that barn was not them. But he knew that was a non-starter. He quickly replayed the message to make sure that he hadn't missed anything.

He noted the time and date of the call.

It had been left while he was out drinking coffee feeling sorry for himself. He blinked at the details on the screen in front of him. He'd not misread it. Nor had he missed any other calls, well, not prior to his coffee break, that's for sure.

But the source was definitely alive. For now.

God only knows who had been in that barn, but it wasn't the source.

They had a chance to end this right, and ensure the source's safety.

Hastings replayed the recording once more to absorb all the details of the proposed attack that they were able to give. Then he picked up the headset and called Jackson to arrange an urgent meeting at the barracks.

He was about to rush off when he noticed that the red flashing light had not cleared. He quickly put his headphones back on and navigated the controls on his terminal.

The source had left a second message.

He listened and made a note as he did so. For safety reasons, the source had always refused to disclose their home address. In fact, it was the source who suggested where - location-wise - the phone box and dead drop should be. Hastings had always thought that this was actually nowhere near where the source lived. He was wrong.

He was then stunned at what was now revealed. The why.

The last comment in the message was, 'I'm disclosing where I live to you now, on trust. Because, if you miss Pídàn and he realises you were there, then he'll be coming straight here for me. I've got nowhere else I can go to, and if I leave now, they'll know. Plus, I won't even know if he's spotted you before he comes flying through the door. You must not fail.'

WITH PREJUDICE

Chapter Fifty-one

Jackson and Kingy were the last to arrive back at their barracks within a barracks at Lisburn. Crompton and Harris were already there and were making a brew. Minutes later, Hastings came rushing in. They all listened in silence as he described the calls he had received from the source.

Crompton was the first to chip in while Hastings took a sip of tea, 'And you are sure about the time of the calls?'

'Absolutely. Whoever that poor sod in the barn was, it wasn't the source,' Hastings replied.

'Probably just another mad guess by the mad man that Lynch is.' Harris threw in.

'Can I ask what sex the source is?' King asked.

Hastings hesitated, before he answered, 'Why?'

'It's just that we all assumed that the source was male,' King added.

It was a reasonable assumption, which Jackson mirrored.

'But why do you ask, now?' Hastings asked.

'Well, the poor sod in the barn was definitely male judging by the stubby fingers left behind,' King added.

Hastings ignored the comment and changed the subject asking what sort of attack plan they would work up.

'It'll have to be fluid. At the moment, all we know is that the young woman lives on the Shankill Road close to The Shankill pub,' Jackson said.

'I can help narrow it down. Apparently, they only heard the "squeeze the Pope" comment as they were held at a pedestrian crossing. The woman was talking to a friend who was using the crossing. She was sat outside her house, a few doors away from the crossing,' Hastings added.

'That should help a lot,' Jackson said, and Harris immediately went to a computer terminal and started tapping on the keys.

Then Hastings went on to highlight the danger the source was in, and added that they had only just released their home address to him.

'Ah. Ok well, it'll need covering, now,' Jackson said.

'I know, I thought I'd take a car and sit off near-by to provide a safe passage out for the source if it all goes to rat shit,' Hastings answered.

'No offence, but you are not equipped to do that. You will need us for that. Ideally, I'd suggest a minimum of two, depending on the layout. But on this occasion, it may have to be just one with you as driver. We will need at least three, for the Shankill,' Jackson said, and glanced over at Crompton as he did so. He was the master tactician.

'Agreed,' Crompton said.

'I was afraid you would say that,' Hastings said.

'We need the address to do our prep, and we need to know what the source looks like and their name. It's that time, Bertram,' Jackson said.

'I know. It's "need to know" and now you need to know.'

All eyes were on Hastings, apart from Harris who was studying the data terminal, but was no doubt all ears.

'OK, the source is Erin. Lynch's long-suffering wife, and sister to Sean Delany, the Officer Commanding the North of Ireland area of the Provisional IRA.'

There was silence in the room, and even Harris stopped what he was doing. Jackson couldn't believe it. He'd no idea how Hastings had managed to recruit someone with such high access to all things PIRA. Her treachery in the Provos eyes would be off the scale. But there she was. Hidden in plain sight right amongst them. Eventually finding his voice, he spoke, 'I won't ask how, as you'd no doubt not tell me.'

'Don't and I won't, though I have only just found out why.'

'So, all your intel was basically pillow-talk?' Crompton asked.

'Partly, and partly because Sean would often pop around and discuss stuff face-to-face with Lynch, and the wee woman was never far from earshot. She is the perfect agent. Perfectly placed, and above suspicion.'

'I understand now why you were so intent on keeping her going, post-Lynch,' Jackson said.

WITH PREJUDICE

'I was, but now I know why, I'm not so sure that the motivation will still be there.'

'About the "why"?' Jackson asked.

'She explained it in her last message. She has suffered at Lynch's hands for years. He regularly raped her whenever he saw fit, and had forced her into having two abortions over the years. Which shows the man's brutality, and breathtaking hypocrisy, given his religion. Divorce was not an option for her as a staunch Catholic, and she had been forced into further sins apart from the abortions, for which she also hates him for.'

'What was that?' King asked.

'After the second abortion she secretly had a contraceptive coil fitted to save her from any further heartache, but she is fundamentally opposed to contraception and detests Lynch for it.'

'Her motivations are personal rather than political?' Jackson asked.

'Mainly yes. But what has put her over the edge, is Lynch's demented desire to heighten the conflict with the Loyalists. She probably agrees that we are legitimate targets - though I've never gone there with her - but he is fervently opposed to any talk of peace. It's why he was thrown off the Army Council for being too hardline. He wants all-out war with the Loyalists. He thinks if they can destroy the UDA, and its affiliates such as the UVF and UFF, they can drive all Loyalists out of Ulster and reclaim the six counties.'

'He's demented,' Crompton threw in.

'But if she had given you her address, we could have lifted Lynch, long ago,' Jackson said.

'I know, but she wanted to do it her way. Said it was her home and she didn't want cops raiding it or me putting bugs in there. She said if things became too bad, she reserved the right to give me the address.'

'A hard one for you to swallow,' Crompton said.

'It was, but I suspect she was protecting her brother. She didn't want him caught up, she just wanted rid of Lynch,' Hastings said. 'But this plot against a young mother, and in particular, a young child, has deep resonance with Erin considering what she has suffered herself. It is too much for her to bare.'

Jackson nodded his understanding, but could not in any way appreciate how Erin must feel inside, and the continuing nightmare she was having to live through.

'All along, she knew exactly who and how many knew what. Lynch never considered her, even when he had openly told her stuff, he never counted her in his reckoning. If he told Sean and her something, then in his mind, he'd told only one. His arrogance towards her is his undoing.

'She was truly hidden, but ignored, right under his nose. This is why what she is doing now is so brave, because she knows without reservation that Lynch has told no one else. Not even his sidekick, who he plans to take with him tomorrow.'

'What about, Sean?' Crompton asked.

'Not even him. He said he'd kept it from Sean, and everyone else, as he knew they would try to stop him. He knows he is crossing a line.'

'OK,' Crompton said, we have two plans to do with limited resources. We'd better get started.

'Got it,' Harris shouted, before he rejoined the others at the table. 'Jenny Jones, she is a widow, her husband was a Loyalist paramilitary, killed in action a year ago. A big mate of Billy Campbell injured in the attack on The Shankill. She lives close to a Zebra crossing and it's the only one anywhere nearby. She has a two-year old toddler. This has to be it.

'Right, to work. Everyone gather around,' Crompton said.

WITH PREJUDICE

Chapter Fifty-two

The briefing the following morning was at four a.m. Crompton was to partner up with Hastings at Erin's home address. This was on the outskirts of Crossmaglen, South Armagh. Right in the middle of 'Bandit Country' and surprisingly close to the phone box and dead drop. The plan was for them to quickly check the dead drop on the run in, and thereafter, covertly cover the approach to the address. They had one main objective, stop Lynch. But according to Hastings, when Erin rang in, she said that Lynch was not there. He often stayed closer to his target the night before a job. She guessed he was with his sidekick Kelly, but she didn't know where he lived, other than Belfast.

But things change sometimes, so they were going early in case Lynch showed up for whatever reason prior. And to take him out if he escaped One Alpha on The Shankill, and turned up afterwards. If the latter were the case, they would have to move fast and decisively as by then, he would probably know Erin was the tout. And he wasn't known for his forgiving nature. Not to mention the embarrassment it would cause him when it got out, which would no doubt drive his mania to new depths.

According to the maps, there was a hedgerow opposite the entrance to the farmhouse where the Lynches lived. Crompton would cover that and keep Hastings out of view nearby with the motor. Jackson issued Hastings a sidearm, and Harris talked him through how to use it, just in case. By the look of horror on Hastings's face, you'd have thought Jackson had placed a turd in his hand.

Jackson, King, and Harris were to take up covert positions on the Shankill. Jackson would keep the OP on the front aspect of Jenny Jones's house, King would do the same at the rear, and Harris, the ace shot, would have a roving commission.

By five a.m., Jackson had parked his Highways van, courtesy of The Det, in a side street opposite the address, and at an opportune moment had climbed in the back. He had a good view albeit occasionally interrupted by passing traffic. The target address was a pavement-fronted terraced house. The intel was that Lynch would strike in the morning. Why the morning in particular, no one knew. Jackson was operating as One Alpha with the front visual.

Ian King was using callsign Four Alpha with the rear visual. He had parked his observation van with a view down the back alley between the target's terraced row, and the one from the street behind. It was just like Coronation Street but without the cat wandering about.

By six a.m., Crompton on Two Alpha confirmed that he and Hastings were in position, and that there had been no update from the dead drop. In fact, things were undisturbed since Hasting's last visit.

Harris on Three Alpha had confirmed he was on comms with nothing to report. It was now a waiting game.

At 7.30 a.m. Harris came over the radio. *'Three Alpha to the team, a Post Office van is parked in a nearby side street, which wasn't there ten minutes ago. No one in it and no approaches.'*

Two Alpha, acknowledged, and Jackson added, *'Received, and there have been no sightings of a postman from the front aspect.'*

'Four Alpha acknowledged and ditto from the rear aspect,' King said.

Jackson knew that this could mean nothing, or everything. It was the art of sensing something rather than computing what your senses were telling you that often made the difference.

Ten minutes later at 7.40 am Harris was back on. *'There is a postie on Shankill Road heading east on the target side; wait.'*

Three minutes passed, then Harris was back on, *'Three Alpha to the team, close recce shows that the postie is carrying a shoulder bag and is posting only flyers through letterboxes, and not at everyone's. He's got no envelopes in his hand and has not addressed the bag.'*

Both Jackson and King acknowledged the last, and Jackson confirmed that Harris was the eyeball and had control. This could be it, or not.

'Three Alpha with the eyeball, Tango is a hundred yards away, One Alpha can you deploy,' Harris said.

WITH PREJUDICE

'Yes, yes,' was Jackson's answer. He quickly got out of the van and using gable ends for cover slowly made his way towards the junction with Shankill Road. Directly opposite the target address.

Harris then issued a description of the postman and confirmed that it was not Lynch. This could be a red herring.

Harris then asked if Jackson was in a position to take up the eyeball as he was nearing the junction where the Post Office van was and wanted to check something. Jackson peered around the corner and could see the postman seventy yards away and confirmed he had the eyeball.

Two minutes later, the postman was thirty yards away and Harris came back over the airwaves asking for permission to speak, which Jackson granted.

'Just checked the back of the van and can hear muffled noises. Someone is bound and gagged in there. Said I'd be back shorty to free whoever and asked for three bangs to confirm that they had heard. Which I received. This has to be it. I'll take up a position.'

Jackson knew that Harris's last comment meant a firing position. King confirmed that he was leaving his van and was en route. And Jackson confirmed that the postman was now knocking on the target address.

The door was opened by Jenny Jones who had a youngster under her arm. The postman took a small parcel, probably nine inches square in size, out of his bag and was trying to pass it to Jones. She was shaking her head, as if to say it was not for her. She wasn't expecting a parcel. Jackson quickly relayed all this and then had to make a split-second decision. Get it right and they were heroes, get it wrong and they would face trial for murder. *'Strike, strike, strike,'* he shouted as he started to run across the Shankill Road.

The postman started to turn around towards Jackson who screamed for Jones to get in and close the door. Which she immediately did.

In the next second, Jackson saw the postman's head explode into pink mist. Followed shortly after by the report from Harris's rifle. He glanced towards Harris and saw him with smoke coming from the end of his weapon.

As the postman's body started to tumble, Jackson snatched the parcel from his lifeless hands as he started to drop it. Jackson turned to use his back as a brake as he collided full pelt into the brickwork next to the door. He caught his breath in the millisecond that passed and waited for the explosion.

A second later he was still stood there with the parcel in his hands. It hadn't gone off. In his reckoning as he dived for the parcel, he assumed that the bomb would be on a timer. It made sense, it gave the postman time for a safe retreat. A motion switch made no sense. But as clear as that thinking was, you never know, and in the heat of the moment, you just react and hope for the best.

That second up against the wall was the longest second of his life. He breathed out.

A man popped his head out of a nearby house and Jackson screamed at him to get a bucket of water. The man needed no explanation and soon reappeared with one. Harris took it from him and ran up to Jackson. He gently placed the parcel in the bucket.

He just hoped and prayed that it was actually a bomb, or else they were in deep shit. And surrounded by an ever-growing crowd of witnesses.

WITH PREJUDICE

Chapter Fifty-three

Jackson stood guard over the bucket while shouting at people to keep their distance. People are naturally inquisitive until you shout the word 'BOMB' and then they seem to quickly lose interest. Harris herded them backwards, and then ran to free the guy in the back of the Post Office van.

Kingy ran in from the east side and said he would stop traffic from that direction. Harris said he will do the same from the west. Jackson glanced at Kingy who was approaching from about a hundred yards. Then he heard him scream over the radio.

'Incoming from my position. Green Avenger. Tango One.'

Jackson then saw what King has seen. A Green Hillman Avenger had appeared from nowhere, must have been parked up in a side street. It was driving fast, westbound, one on board - the driver - who was definitely Lynch. The driver's window was down, and Lynch braked hard to a crawl.

Jackson drew his Beretta only to see the barrel of a sub machine gun rest through the open driver's window pointed his way. Jackson recognises it as a Yugoslavian Zastava M56 sub machine gun. He's trapped. In the instance he had to react, all he could do was stand, take aim, and fire. As he zoned in and fired a couple of rounds, he was aware of rifle fire coming from Harris's position, and small arms fire coming from behind the vehicle. Kingy.

None of Lynch's bullets hit Jackson. Then the front door behind him opened and he felt hands on his shoulder. He was dragged back into the house and the door slammed shut. He turned to see Jenny Jones, this time without child, thankfully.

'The Fenian bastard will not get past that door. It's made of steel. My husband insisted on it as a matter of security before those Provo scum killed him.'

'He's a shit shot, he should have done me, but thanks, anyway.'

'Don't mention it. I owed you one.'

Jackson thanked her again, before springing to his feet and back into action-mode. He opened the door to discover that Lynch had driven off west along the Shankill. His motor had taken several rounds according to Harris and King who joined him on the pavement, but he had still manged to get away, nonetheless.

Then Jackson examined the scene, and realised that Lynch hadn't been such as shit shot as he'd thought, well, not that good either as it turned out. The wall behind the bucket was peppered with bullet holes, and one had clipped the top of the bucket. He'd been shooting at the parcel. Any device in it shouldn't still be viable, as in, the water should have prevented electronic detonation, but if it contained dynamite for example, as its explosive element, a bullet could have easily set it off.

The bastard was trying to finish what his partner had started. He looked at his watch, which had a stopwatch function. He set it for forty-five minutes on countdown. As determined by Phase Two of the operation, which they had hoped not to need.

Jackson told Harris to remain on scene until SB and the RUC arrived. There was no other way. They couldn't leave the bucket unattended and needed him to keep the public at a safe distance. They'd soon start emerging to have a nosy again as the dust settled. But as soon as the SB landed, he could give them a quick update, hand over control of the scene, and play catch up.

He then called Hastings and Crompton on the radio to give them the update and to prepare them. Hastings came back on after only a few seconds to confirm that SB were on their way. Also, the Logistic Corp's Explosive Ordinance Team were en route to sort out the IED. Jackson could hear approaching air horns and guessed a member of the public must have rung the RUC, which was a blessing.

Then Jackson told Hastings to call Lisburn and activate Phase Two. He acknowledged and Jackson turned to Kingy and said, 'St. Michael's is only a couple of minutes away, off Malvern Street, let's make lively.'

They each rushed back to their vans and drove the short distance to St. Michael's and abandoned their vehicles near the church side wall, leaving plenty of space to keep the grounds empty. They each grabbed their bergens and weapons and stood by waiting. Jackson glanced at his watch as its stopwatch function continued its countdown. It was now T-minus twenty-five. As he did this, he could hear the sound of the approaching helicopter.

Part of Phase Two was to have a helicopter ready to go at Lisburn barracks which was only about seven or eight miles from their present position. Five minutes away, once airborne.

Crompton and Hastings knew what they had to do once Phase Two was live, and hopefully, Jackson and Kingy would be with them in time. As part of their planning, they reckoned that it would take Lynch fifty minutes to traverse the fifty-eight miles from Belfast to his home in Crossmaglen, even considering the speed he would be driving at. Jackson had knocked off five minutes as a buffer and started his stopwatch as soon as he was aware that Lynch had escaped. He'd been reliably informed that the helicopter could do it in fifteen minutes; give or a take.

The noise of the approaching aircraft soon became almost deafening as it swooped into view overhead. The force of the downwash from its rotor blades never ceased to register with Jackson, though he'd crouched under them hundreds of times. The door had been slid open before the craft touched down and Jackson and King were aboard in an instant, it lifted off as the co-pilot closed the doors.

Jackson glanced at his watch; T-minus nineteen.

They spent a couple of minutes trying to pick up the green Avenger on the basis that it should stand out as it would be driving fast. It was a calculated risk. If they could see it, there might be an opportunity to take it out before it reached its destination. But they didn't see it and Jackson just hoped the futile search hadn't wasted too much time. He ordered the pilot to go direct cross country. Then he asked for an updated ETA. The answer he got was 'Eleven minutes.'

He glanced at his watch; T-minus eleven.

Chapter Fifty-four

Hastings parked the car as close to the back of the plot as he could. There was a rough track off one of the lanes which ran besides a privet which adjoined the rear garden to the Lynch property. There was an open field on the other side. He turned the car around which took a ten-point turn, and then found a hole in the hedge. It was small but the best entry and egress point he could see. He was glad it was daylight. *'Zero Alpha, in position. Permission to go,'* he asked Crompton over the radio.

'No change, no change from the visual. Permission granted, Zero.'

Hastings was aware that when they first arrived, Crompton had done a close target recce and said that he was confident that Erin was the only one in the house. And he had seen nothing since to change that opinion. Hastings's heart rate was pounding, he just hoped the sergeant was correct. This sort of field work was way outside his comfort zone. He crawled through the hedge hole and made his way across the rear lawn to the back door. A quick peek through the kitchen window was negative. He tapped on the back door and waited.

A couple of minutes later the door was opened a crack and he saw Erin peering through the gap. He'd only ever met her once, at the very beginning of it all, but recognised her right away.

'Mary, mother of God, you nearly gave me a heart attack,' she said, as she opened the door fully.

'You alone?'

'I am that, but my brother Sean will be calling at some stage as it's my birthday. Another anniversary Brendan has forgotten about. Not that that bothers me now.'

'Come on, we've got to go. Lynch is on his way.'

'What about that young mother and her wee bairn?'

'Safe and sound, but we missed him. Come on, I'll tell more once I have you safely away from here.'

'OK, I'll just grab my things.'

WITH PREJUDICE

'For God's sake be quick, we don't have much time,' Hastings said, as Erin shot back into the house.

***

'ETA?' Jackson shouted above the noise of the rotors.

'Five minutes,' the copilot shouted back. He then added that they had identified a field on the east side of a rough track at the rear of the target premises where they intended to put down.

'Roger,' he replied. And then spoke into his radio. *One Alpha to The Visual. Five minutes from your position; sit rep?'*

'Acknowledged. No change, and Zero has deployed to remove the friendly,' Crompton replied with his soft Tyneside lilt.

Then.

'Contact, contact, contact. Tango One approaching. Zero, update?' Crompton shouted.

'She's just grabbing her things,' Hastings's voice replied in Jackson's ear.

'Get her out, now. I'm going to engage,' Crompton shouted.

'Quick as you can gents, it's about to go noisy,' Jackson shouted at the pilots, and then he and King started to check their weapons.

***

Lynch had made it home in record time, but his demeanour hadn't eased any on the journey. Not only had that bitch on the Shankill survived along with her brat. But poor old Kelly had lost his life, too. And he had also come close. The dashboard and passenger seat were ripped to shreds from the incoming fire he'd sustained. But he just couldn't believe what it all meant. He couldn't get his head around the depth of the betrayal. Let alone, why?

He'd not told anyone of his plans except Erin, not for some security reason, but he knew that even Sean would have ordered him not to do it. And try to stop him had he refused. But Lynch knew that they had to get real about the true threat the Loyalist paramilitaries posed. All the Army Council wanted to talk about was peace talks in the future. Concessions and other sellouts. The only way to win the war with the Brits, was to win the war against the Loyalists paramilitaries first. And that meant annihilation of them. Only then could they drive the Proddy dog population out of Ireland.

Then his mind returned to Erin. The level of her duplicity was in unknown territory. The embarrassment was stratospheric. He couldn't face that. It would be too much once others knew. He made his mind up.

He ideally wanted to torture her to find out why, and then kill her as slowly as he could, but he knew he didn't have time for that. She may have given the Sass their home address details, but Lynch reckoned not. As they'd have tried to bug the place at the very least, and Sean was insistent that all senior members' homes were swept for radio bugs weekly. Plus, in reality, if they knew where he lived, why hadn't they come for him ages ago. It made no sense, but he wouldn't take any chances. He'd kill Erin and blame the Brits. The Provisional IRA need never know the truth. Plus, the outrage that Sean would feel in his grief should open the way for some of Lynch's more extreme plans.

He slowed as he approached the entrance to his driveway. Then realised he'd reckoned it up all wrong.

A salvo of bullets ripped through the windscreen from the direction of a hedge opposite the drive. Those damn Sass bastards. He grabbed his weapon and aimed his car at the hedge. That should buy him a few seconds. Next, he bailed out of the car and hit the ground hard before rolling into a kind of parachutist's landing roll. He lost the grip of his weapon, but as he rose to his feet, it was in front of him.

The incoming fire had ceased. The shooter was obviously trying to get around the obstruction which had now rolled into the hedge and stopped. In the momentary impasse, Lynch ran towards the house whilst firing over his left shoulder behind him. Wild and inaccurate, he knew, but it may be off putting enough to get him to safety.

Seconds later, he crashed through the front door as more rounds peppered the front of his house. No sign of Erin. But his first concern was to get the shooter to back off, and so ran to the hidden stash of armament he kept under the stairs. He grabbed a hand grenade and rushed into the front room. The bay window was gone, and he sighted the shooter running towards the house. Lynch pulled the pin and threw the grenade through the smashed window at him.

***

As the helicopter was landing in the field, Jackson heard the explosion coming from the front of the premises. He shouted over the radio, *'Two Alpha, report?'*

Silence.

'Zero report?'

'Zero in my vehicle with the friendly. Did you hear that explosion?'

Jackson ignored the question but told Hastings to stay put for the moment. He and Kingy alighted and started to run towards the rear of the property, and Jackson shouted over the radio, again, *'Two Alpha, report. Geordie, you OK?'*

Silence. Shit.

Then Jackson heard the sound of automatic fire coming from the front. For a second, his heart lifted, but as he listened to the report, it sank. He glanced at Kingy who was running besides him, and by his grim visage, he saw that he understood, too.

Jackson would recognise any of his Troop's trained, drilled and finely tuned weapons use. This was ill-disciplined. Lynch.

'I'll go to the front to support, Geordie and help draw the fire,' Kingy shouted. Jackson nodded as they both tore across the rough track and leaped over the pivot like a couple of Grand National jockeys but without the horses. Jackson caught a glimpse of Hastings in his car with a woman as he did.

***

After the grenade exploded, Lynch quickly ran through the small cottage screaming for Erin, but she was not there. She could have been hidden, but he didn't have the time to search thoroughly. From the front bedroom window, he used the butt of his weapon to smash the glass and let loose with several rounds until his magazine clicked empty, it would buy him some more time. But he couldn't see his attacker.

He ran down the stairs and then noticed the open back door. Damn. He quickly fitted a new magazine and grabbed some spares from his stash. Time to go. But first he'd lob his second grenade out the front to make sure the soldier was dead. He'd not heard any incoming fire since the first explosion but wanted to make sure before he fled. The shooter at the front was the only potential threat, though his mates would no doubt be joining him very soon.

He pulled the pin and turned his attention to the front door. He'd surprise him if he weren't already dead by attacking from a slightly different position. He opened the door and threw the grenade before he slammed it shut. He heard the explosion two seconds later.

WITH PREJUDICE

Chapter Fifty-five

Jackson heard the second explosion as he neared the back door. Then he heard controlled return fire. Kingy or Crompton, he didn't know which. It could be either. And now was not the time to ask. But he suspected it was Kingy; Crompton was usually exceptionally tight with his bursts of fire. This didn't bode well.

He slowed to a stop as he reached the doorway. He slipped in as he heard a burst of random fire from within coming from the lounge. He peered around the door jam and saw the rear of the man who had shot him at McDonald's house. The lunatic who had attacked the US Foreign Secretary and much more. He'd just finished firing the same looking weapon he'd seen an hour ago on the Shankill Road.

As Lynch started to turn, probably sensing Jackson's presence, Jackson, whose Heckler and Koch MP5 sub machine gun was set to selective fire, let loose with a three round burst aimed at Lynch's weapon. It flew out of his hand with sparks flying and landed smashed on the floor.

Lynch looked startled. Then gathered his senses and said, 'I never heard you come in.'

'You were making a noise.'

'Don't you know it's rude not to knock.'

'How do you I didn't?'

Lynch didn't respond and a deadlock ensued. Jackson was paying particular attention to his arms which were currently hanging down by his side. He broke the pause by saying, 'Hands on your head, fingers interlocked, now.'

Lynch didn't move. He was clearly weighing up his options.

'You've caused me a lot of problems,' Lynch said.

Jackson knew that any frivolous conversation was just an attempt to cause a distraction. He let loose a further selective burst of three rounds in front of Lynch's feet and shouted, Hands, now.'

Lynch complied, and said, 'You can't shoot me soldier boy, I'm unarmed now.'

'How do I know that?'

Lynch then turned around keeping his interlocked fingers on top of his head and said, 'Search me.'

Jackson placed the barrel of his weapon into the back of Lynch's head and searched him with his free hand. He took two loaded magazines from his pocket and threw them to one side. He then told Lynch to turn back around, which he did. He then pressed the transmit button of his radio and said, *'All callsigns, I have Tango One under control. Zero Two report?'*

King replied, *'Four Alpha, here. I'm with Two Alpha now, he's unconsciousness and injured. Need medivac now.'*

The helicopter responded and said they would be with them in two.

'Just tell me how you turned her before you take me in?'

'I don't know what you mean?'

Lynch smiled and said, 'I know you won't tell me, but I'm impressed.'

'I'm not here to impress you.'

'OK, let's get the cuffs on, so we can both relax.'

'How do you know I'm going to cuff you?'

'Because you know I'm an ocean of potential intelligence. Not that I'll tell you anything, but your masters will want to try.'

Jackson was starting to become irritated with Lynch now, especially as he seemed to be regaining his arrogance.

'You know we are not that different, soldier boy.'

'Yes, we are.'

'No, we are both psychopaths.'

'Maybe. But I'm on the side of the good guys.'

'Depends on your point of view. Anyhow, as entertaining as this has been, I'm getting bored,' Lynch said as he then thrust his arms out together in front of him.

Just as he did that, Jackson's earpiece burst into life. It was Hastings.

'Zero to One Alpha, as we have control of Lynch. London now wants him alive to debrief. Received, One Alpha?'

As he was listening to Hastings, Lynch said, 'I hope your soldier boy out the front is OK?' and then he grinned.

'Maybe we are similar in some ways,' Jackson said, and then put three rounds through Lynch's face and watched his cadaver fall to the floor.

He then pressed his radio transmit button and said, *'Sorry, Zero. He went for a hidden weapon. Tango One is dead.'*

THE END.

Printed in Great Britain
by Amazon